BATTLEBORN

"The most captivating voice to come out of the West since Annie Proulx—though it's to early Joan Didion that [Watkins] bears comparison for her arid humor and cut-to-the-chase knowingness." —*Vogue*

"Readers will share in the environs of the author and her characters, be taken into the hardship of a pitiless place and emerge on the other side—wiser, warier, and weathered like the landscape." —*The New York Times Book Review*

"[*Battleborn*'s] true setting is a Faulknerian desert of the heart, where the soil is cursed by its precious metals and one's personal history can be just as toxic... Clear-eyed and nimble in parsing the lives of her Westerners, one of Watkins's strengths is not dodging the simple fact that love can be tragic, involving, as it does, humans so flawed, so often tender and yet incapable." —*The Boston Globe*

"As grounded as they are in real places, the stories are fictions, crafted with the skill of an artisan, working from the starting points of Mary Gaitskill and Aimee Bender." —*Los Angeles Times*

"Vibrant and assured ... The settings of Watkins's home state—evoked with craft that echoes Cormac McCarthy or Richard Ford—were the perfect settings for heartbreak." —*Time Out New York*

Additional praise for *Battleborn*

"[A] breathtaking debut . . . [Watkins's] stories . . . carry the weight and devastation of entire novels."
—*Flavorpill*

"The book feels like a portrait of the human heart, famished for beauty and love, but finally and almost always wrecked by its own hungers."
—Paul Harding, author of the Pulitzer Prize–winning *Tinkers*

"[An] assured debut . . . Here's hoping Watkins will continue to delve into Nevada's unsound caverns and emerge with such worthy plunder."
—*The Dallas Morning News*

"A fresh, fierce, fabulous collection. Watkins writes like the divine Didion—cool and clean with not a word wasted. Where'd she come from? I'm glad she's here."
—Joy Williams, author of *The Quick and the Dead*

"What distinguishes Watkins's work . . . is her command of time. Nearly all the stories are set in the present, but her characters constantly live with aftereffects of the past. They're not simply 'scarred' by history; they're irradiated by it, queasily lit from within."
—*Minneapolis Star Tribune*

"In these stories, you have the authentic voice of the American desert—hard, dry, brutal, and tender. Claire Vaye Watkins emerges as one of the most exciting young voices in American fiction."
—Hari Kunzru, author of *Gods Without Men* and *The Impressionist*

"A powerful new voice that deserves recognition . . . [Watkins maps] a regional portrait while pausing for detailed sketches, with a strong perspective that blends the romanticized past of Larry McMurtry, heartbreaking characters of Annie Proulx, and bleak timeless landscapes of Cormac McCarthy."
—*The Onion AV Club*

"Watkins digs and sifts . . . finding the bright flecks hidden in her characters' darkest moments, until each story shimmers and shines."
—Hannah Tinti, author of *The Good Thief*

"Exceptional . . . A writer of great precision and greater restraint, Watkins is a natural storyteller whose material enriches that gift rather than engulfing it. . . . One doesn't have to be from the Battleborn state to recognize and appreciate literature that resonates like this."

—*The Rumpus*

"Watkins marries character to landscape as well as anyone I have read in years. These stories are gritty and brilliant, and foretell an auspicious literary future for their author."

—*Largehearted Boy*

"As blistering hot and wondrously expansive as the gritty, wide-open Nevada desert."

—Donald Ray Pollock, author of
The Devil All the Time and *Knockemstiff*

"The people in *Battleborn* . . . aren't characters in stories, but human beings perpetually yearning for warmth. . . . Entering the varied lives is akin to watching a tightrope walker high overhead, moving with steady confidence without a net. . . . Watkins writes with precision and care, the sentences themselves as surprising as the events, the dialogue, and the spare description. . . . There is a purity to the prose that is a constant pleasure to read. . . . There is great originality in these narratives. . . . But the generosity and personal sacrifices of the people are as universal as the stars at night."

—*Publishers Weekly* (starred review)

"Gloriously vivid stories about the human heart."

—*Kirkus Reviews*

"Claire Vaye Watkins is never, ever satisfied with the ordinary. Each story in this brilliant debut surprises. Watkins offers us amazing visions of a funny, savage, haunted West—and one of the most outstanding short story collections in recent memory."

—Christopher Coake, author of
We're in Trouble and *You Came Back*

"As if Watkins's prose embodies the desert landscape of Nevada itself, the stories are stony, unkind, and harsh, though never unattractive. . . . Beneath these confessions runs a spiritual undertow—that salvific beauty can arise when brutality is brought to light. . . . All of her stories left me feeling purged and oddly cleansed, easily making *Battleborn* one of the strongest collections I've read in years."　　　—*The Millions*

"Claire Watkins's astonishing, thrilling collection could not have been more aptly named. Like Nevada, the 'Battleborn' state where most of these stories are set, the characters here are fierce, sometimes desperate, born out of struggle and ambition and frantic, driven hope. Written in gorgeous prose and animated with an exceptionally rich vision, these stories are searing portraits of the places our hungers will drive us, and the battles that await us there."
　　　—Erin McGraw, author of *The Seamstress of Hollywood Boulevard*

"Readers . . . will find much to admire in this arresting collection, which one hopes is merely the first stop along the way for a writer who deserves a sustained literary life."　　　—*Library Journal* (starred review)

"Dazzling."　　　—*O, The Oprah Magazine*

"A real treat . . . Through remarkably assured writing that manages to be both bristly and brittle, Watkins chronicles despair and loneliness, catalogs valiant fights for survival and desperate pleas to be heard, and every time has us rooting for her underdogs."
　　　—*San Francisco Chronicle*

BATTLEBORN

Claire Vaye Watkins

RIVERHEAD BOOKS
New York

RIVERHEAD BOOKS
Published by the Penguin Group
Penguin Group (USA) Inc.
375 Hudson Street, New York, New York 10014, USA

USA | Canada | UK | Ireland | Australia | New Zealand | India | South Africa | China

Penguin Books Ltd., Registered Offices: 80 Strand, London WC2R 0RL, England
For more information about the Penguin Group, visit penguin.com.

The following stories have been previously published, in slightly different form:
"Ghosts, Cowboys" (*The Hopkins Review*), "The Last Thing We Need" (*Granta*),
"Rondine al Nido" (*The Chicago Tribune Printers Row*), "The Past Perfect,
the Past Continuous, the Simple Past" (*The Paris Review*), "Wish You Were Here"
(*The Sycamore Review*), "Man-O-War" (*One Story*), "The Archivist" (*Glimmer Train*),
"Virginia City" (*Las Vegas City Life*), "Graceland" (*Hobart*).

The Library of Congress has catalogued the Riverhead hardcover edition as follows:

Watkins, Claire Vaye.
Battleborn / Claire Vaye Watkins.
p.   cm.
ISBN 978-1-59448-825-2
1. Nevada—Fiction. I. Title.
PS3623.A869426B38   2012   2012009175
813'.6—dc23

First Riverhead hardcover edition: August 2012
First Riverhead trade paperback edition: August 2013
Riverhead trade paperback ISBN: 978-1-59463-145-0

PRINTED IN THE UNITED STATES OF AMERICA

10 9 8 7 6 5 4 3 2 1

Cover design by Helen Yentus
Cover image by Jack Pierson / Art + Commerce
Book design by Amanda Dewey

for my parents

In the desert
I saw a creature, naked, bestial,
Who, squatting upon the ground,
Held his heart in his hands,
And ate of it.
I said, "Is it good, friend?"
"It is bitter—bitter," he answered;

"But I like it
Because it is bitter,
And because it is my heart."

STEPHEN CRANE

Contents

GHOSTS, COWBOYS

The day my mom checked out, Razor Blade Baby moved in. At the end, I can't stop thinking about beginnings.

The city of Reno, Nevada, was founded in 1859 when Charles Fuller built a log toll bridge across the Truckee River and charged prospectors to haul their Comstock silver across the narrow but swift-moving current. Two years later, Fuller sold the bridge to the ambitious Myron Lake. Lake, swift himself, added a gristmill, kiln and livery stable to his Silver Queen Hotel and Eating House. Not a bashful man, he named the community Lake's Crossing, had the name painted on Fuller's bridge, bright blue as the sky.

The 1860s were boom times in the western Utah Territory: Americans still had the brackish taste of Sutter's soil on their tongues, ten-year-old gold still glinting in their eyes. The curse of the Comstock Lode had not yet leaked from the silver vein, not seeped into the water table. The silver itself had not yet been stripped from the mountains, and steaming water had not yet flooded the mine shafts. Henry T. P. Comstock—most opportune of the opportunists, snatcher of land, greatest claim jumper of all time—had not yet lost his love Adelaide, his first cousin, who drowned in Lake Tahoe. He had not yet traded his share of the lode for a bottle of whiskey and an old, blind mare, not yet blown his brains out with a borrowed revolver near Bozeman, Montana.

Boom times.

Lake's Crossing grew. At statehood in 1864, the district of Lake's Crossing, Washoe County, was consolidated with Roop County. By then, Lake's Crossing was the largest city in either. The curse, excavated from the silver vein and weighted by the heavy ore, settled on the nation's newest free state.

O r begin the story here:
In 1881 Himmel Green, an architect, came to Reno from San Francisco to quietly divorce Mary Ann Cohen Magnin of the upscale women's clothing store I. Magnin and Company. Himmel took a liking to Reno and decided to stay. He started designing buildings for his friends, newly rich silver families.

Reno's Newlands Heights neighborhood is choked with Green's work. In 1909, 315 Lake Street was erected. A stout building made of brick, it was one of Himmel's first residential buildings, a modest design, small porch off the back, simple awnings, thoroughly mediocre in every way. Some say construction at 315 Lake stirred up the cursed dust of the Comstock Lode. Though it contaminated everyone (and though we Nevadans still breathe it into ourselves today), they say it got to Himmel particularly, stuck to his blueprints, his clothing, formed a microscopic layer of silver dust on his skin. Glinting silver film or no, after his divorce was finalized Himmel moved in with Leopold Karpeles, editor of the *B'nai B'rith Messenger*. Their relationship was rumored a tumultuous one, mottled with abuse and infidelity. Still, they lived together until 1932, when the two were burned to death in a fire at Karpeles's home, smoke rising from the house smelling like those miners boiled alive up in Virginia City mine shafts.

O r here. Here is as good a place as any:
In March 1941, George Spahn, a dairyman and amateur beekeeper from Pennsylvania, signed over the deed to his sixty-acre farm to his son, Henry, packed four suitcases, his wife, Helen, and their old, foul-tempered calico cat, Bottles, into the car, and drove west to California, to the ocean.

He was to retire, bow out of the ranching business, bury his tired feet in the warm Western sand. But retirement didn't suit George. After two months he came home to their ticky-tacky rental on the beach and presented Helen with plans to buy a 511-acre ranch at 1200 Santa Susana Pass Road in the Santa Susana Mountains. The ranch was up for sale by its owner, the aging silent-film star William S. Hart.

The Santa Susana Mountains are drier than the more picturesque Santa Monica Mountains that line the California coast. Because they are not privy to the moist winds rolling in off the sea, they are susceptible to fires. Twelve hundred Santa Susana Pass Road is tucked up in the Santa Susanas north of Los Angeles, off what is now called the Ronald Reagan Freeway. Back in 1941, when George was persuading Helen to move again, taking her knobby hand in his, begging her to uproot the tendrils she'd so far managed to anchor into the loose beige sand of Manhattan Beach—*Just a bit east this time, sweet pea*—the city of Chatsworth was little more than a Baptist church, a dirt-clogged filling station, and the Palomino Horse Association's main stables, birthplace of Mr. Ed. Years later, in 1961, my father, still a boy, would start a wildfire in the hills above the PHA stables. He would be eleven, crouched in the dry brush, sneaking a cigarette. But let's not get ahead of ourselves.

At the heart of the ranch was a movie set, a thoroughfare of a Western boomtown: bank, saloon, blacksmith, wood-planked boardwalk, side streets and alleys, a jail. Perhaps the set dazzled Helen. Perhaps she—a prematurely arthritic woman—recalled the aching cold of Pennsylvania winters. Perhaps she spoiled her husband, as her children claim. Whatever the reason, Helen laid her hand on her husband's brow and said, "All right, George." And though by all accounts Helen came to like the ranch, on the day George took her out to view the property for the first time her journal reads:

> *The property is quite expansive, surrounded by mountains.*
> *G. giddy as a boy. Not such a view as the beach, though. The*
> *road out is windy and narrow, sheer canyon walls on either side.*
> *Seems I am to be once again separated from the sea. And what*
> *a brief affair it was! Looking west I felt a twinge like something*
> *had been taken from me, something a part of me but never truly*
> *mine.*

Within a week of the Spahns' move up to 1200 Santa Susana Pass Road, Bottles the cat ran away.

But George was more adaptable than Bottles, and luckier. In 1941, Westerns were still Hollywood's bread and butter. George ran his movie set like he'd run his dairy ranch, building strong relationships with decision makers, underpricing the competition. It certainly didn't hurt business when Malibu Bluff State Recreation Area annexed Trancas Canyon and sold off its many sets, making Spahn's Ranch the only privately owned— and therefore zero-permit—outdoor set for seventy-five miles. The Spahns enjoyed a steady stream of business from the major studios, charging them a pretty penny to rent horses and shoot films at the ranch, among them *High Noon*, *The Comstock Boys*, and David O. Selznick's 1946 classic *Duel in the Sun*, starring Gregory Peck. TV shows were also shot at the ranch, including most episodes of *The Lone Ranger* and—before Warner Brothers, coaxed by Nevada's tax incentives and the habits of its big-name directors, moved production to the Ponderosa Ranch at Lake Tahoe—*Bonanza*.

W e might start at my mother's first memory:
It's 1962. She is three. She sits on her stepfather's lap on a plastic lawn chair on the roof of their trailer. Her older brother and sister sit cross-legged on a bath towel they've laid atop the chintzy two-tab roof, the terry cloth dimpling their skin. They each wear a pair of their mother's—my grandmother's—oversize Jackie O. sunglasses. It is dusk; in the eastern sky stars are coming into view—yes, back then you could still see stars over Las Vegas—but the family faces northwest, as do their neighbors and the teenage boys hired to cut and water the grass at the new golf courses and the city bus drivers who have pulled over to the side of the roads and the tourists up in their hotel rooms with their faces pressed to the windows. As does the whole city.

Their stepfather points to the desert. "There," he says. A flash of light across the basin. An orange mushroom cloud erupts, rolling and boiling. Seconds later, she hears the *boom* of it, like a firework, and the trailer begins to sway. Impossibly, the heat warms my mother's face. "Makes you think," her stepfather says softly in her ear. "Maybe there's something godly out there after all."

The blast is a 104-kiloton nuclear explosion. It blows a hole into the desert rock, creating the deepest crater of all the Nevada

Test Site's 1,021 detonations: 320 feet deep. The crater displaces seven hundred tons of dirt and rock, including two tons of sediment from a vein of H. T. P. Comstock's cursed soil, a finger reaching all the way down the state, now blown sky-high in the blast. The July breeze is gentle, indecisive. It blows the radiation northeast, as it always does, to future cancer clusters in Fallon and Cedar City, Utah, to the mitosing cells of small-town down-winders. But today it also blows the curse southeast, toward Las Vegas, to my mother's small chest, her lungs and her heart. And it blows southwest, across the state line, all the way to the dry yellow mountains above Los Angeles. These particles settle, finally, at 1200 Santa Susana Pass Road.

W e might start with George's longest year:
For nearly twenty years, George's letters to his son, Henry, back home in Pennsylvania were characteristically dry, questions about herd count, tips for working the swarm at honey harvest; he hardly mentioned his own ranch, which to his son would not have seemed a ranch at all.

But by the early 1960s the demand for Westerns began to wane and George Spahn blamed, among others, Alfred Hitch-cock. He increasingly ended his notes about farm business with aggravated rants about "cut-'em-ups," and "sex-crazed" moviego-ers' fixation on horror films, probably meaning Hitchcock's *Psycho*, the second-highest-grossing film of 1960, after *Swiss Family Robinson*. On the first day of February 1966, George Spahn filed for bankruptcy. By then, unbeknownst to George, his wife's kidneys were marbled with tumors. Six weeks later, at UCLA Medical Center, Helen died from renal failure on the same floor where my father would die thirty-four years later. The coroner's report noted that her tumors were visible, and in the glaring light of the microscope seemed "like hundreds of hairlike silver ribbons."

After Helen's death, George neglected the few already tenuous ties he had at the big studios. He wrote Henry often, spoke of the ranch deteriorating, of weeds pushing up through the soil in the corrals.

"I'm tired," he wrote to his son on July 23, 1966. "Let most everyone [three part-time ranch hands] go. It is hot here. So hot I have to wait for dusk to feed the horses. They get impatient down in the stalls and kick the empty troughs over. Boy, you wouldn't believe the noise of their hoofs against the metal . . ."

In the end it was the horses, thirsty or not, that kept Spahn's Ranch afloat. Spahn rented the horses to tourists for self-guided rides through the hills. Occasionally, a few of George's old studio friends would throw business his way, sending for six or eight paints when a scene couldn't have needed more than two. And so the horses became George's main source of income, meager as it was. The Los Angeles County tax records show Spahn's annual income in 1967 to be $13,120, less than a quarter of what it was in 1956.

In previous letters, George rarely wrote of Helen. When he did his lines were terse, referring to her only along with other ranch business: "Storm coming in. Your mother's knuckles would have swelled. Lord knows we need the rain."

That year, George continued to write even as his eyesight failed, his lines sometimes piling atop one another. He began to write of Helen more frequently, sometimes devoting an entire page to her blackberry cobbler or the fragrance of her bath talcum. These are the only letters in which George, otherwise a deliberate and correct writer, slips into the present tense.

In September, George reported discovering a tiny bleached skull in the hills above his cabin. "Bottles," he wrote, "picked clean by coyotes."

O r here. Begin here:
When a group of about ten young people—most of them teenagers, one of them my father—arrived at the ranch in January of 1968, having hitchhiked from San Francisco, George was nearly blind. Surely he smelled them, though, as they approached his porch—sweat, gasoline, the thick semisweet guff of marijuana. The group offered to help George with chores and maintenance in exchange for permission to camp out in the empty façaded set buildings. Though he'd broken down and hired a hand a couple weeks earlier—a nice kid, a bit macho, went by "Shorty," wanted to be, what else?, an actor—George agreed, perhaps because he wouldn't have to pay them. Or perhaps because the group's leader—a man named Charlie—offered to leave a young girl or two with George twenty-four-seven, to

cook his meals, tidy the house, keep up with the laundry, and bed him whenever he wanted.

My father didn't kill anyone. And he's not a hero. It isn't that kind of story.

Nearly everyone who spent time at Spahn's that summer wrote a book after it was over, Bugliosi's only the most lucrative. We know, from the books of those who noticed, that a baby was born at Spahn's Ranch, likely April ninth, though accounts vary. In her version, Olivia Hall, who'd been a senior at Pacific Palisades High School and an occasional participant in group sex at the ranch, wrote of the birth: "The mother, splayed out on the wood floor of the jail, struggled in labor for nearly fourteen hours, through the night and into the early morning, then gave up." In *The Manson Murders: One Woman's Escape*, Carla Shapiro, now a mother of four boys, says the struggling girl "let her head roll back onto a sleeping bag and would not push. Then Manson took over." My father's book reads, "Charlie held a cigarette lighter under a razor blade until the blade was hot and sliced the girl from vagina to anus." The baby girl slipped out, wailing, into Charlie's arms. My father: "The place was a mess. Blood and clothes everywhere. I don't know where he found the razor blade."

Charlie had a rule against couples. The group had nightly orgies at the ranch and before it in Topanga, Santa Barbara, Big Sur, Santa Cruz, Monterey, Oakland, San Francisco, the list goes on. You know this part, I'm sure. The drugs, the sex. People came and went. Tracing the child's paternity was impossible, even if the group had been interested in that sort of thing. "There was a birth, I know that," Tex Watson wrote to me from prison. "Hell, might've been mine. But we were all pretty gone, you know?"

Of the mother, the accounts mention only how young she was. No name, no explanation of how she came to the ranch. One calls her "dew-faced." In his account my father admits to having sex with her on several occasions. He says, "She was a good kid."

After police raided Spahn's on August sixteenth, California Child Protective Services placed the baby with foster parents, Al and Vaye Orlando of Orlando's Furniture Warehouse in Thousand Oaks. Vaye constantly fussed over the baby, worried at her calmness, what she called "a blankness in her face." During the child's first five years, Vaye had her examined for autism seven times, never trusting the results. She even hired a special nanny to play games with the child, encourage her cognitive development. Al thought this a waste of money.

Now the baby is a grown woman, forty. She is slender but not slight, and moves like liquid does. She has dark hair and the small brown eyes of a deer mouse. Not the eyes of those teenage girls my father met at Pali, the ones he invited to Spahn's and introduced to Charlie, the ones, later, with crosses cut into their foreheads, arms linked, singing down hallways, smiling into the camera in archived footage. I've looked. These are my father's brown eyes. Mine.

. . .

Ten years ago, Lake Street—the last surviving vanity land-
mark of poor Myron Lake, site of Reno's original iconic
arch (you know it, *Biggest Little City in the World*)—was lined
with slums: dumpy neglected mansions with fire escapes grafted
to their sides, bedsheets covering the windows, most of them
halfway houses. But soon people were calling Lake Street and
the surrounding neighborhood Newlands Heights. Op-ed col-
umns parleyed on the topic of redevelopment. Three Fifteen
Lake was converted from the single-family mansion envisioned
by Himmel Green to six one- and two-bedroom apartments in
2001, one of the last to go. By then, Newlands Heights (named,
of course, for Francis G. Newlands, Nevada senator, prudent
annexer of Hawaii, irrigator of the American West, and great
civilizer of savages) was lined with post–Comstock Lode Colo-
nials and Victorians, their lavish parlors and sunrooms parti-
tioned into open studio apartments and condos with hardwood
floors. They've even torn down the original arch—it attracted
vagrants and teenagers, they said. I was assured, back when things
like this meant anything to me, that the city was erecting a replica, in neon, across Virginia Street, closer to the big casinos.

These days, they say Newlands Heights is worth quite a
bit, and for all my bitching about gentrification, I don't mind
this. A person feels just as guilty living among the poor as she
does living among the rich, but at least you can be angry at the
rich. I can afford to live at 315 Lake only because the landlords,
Ben and Gloria (nice people, Burners turned bourgeois, role

models to us all) hired my boyfriend—ex-boyfriend—J to do the cabinetwork on the building. J ended up, as he does with so many of his business associates, smoking a bunch of pot with Ben. J considers marijuana the universal ambassador of goodwill, and himself its humble steward. Gloria was pregnant and Ben was desperate, pouring money into a building with no tenants. One afternoon, J and Ben sat on a pallet of bathroom tiles passing a joint between them, and J persuaded Ben to give me a deal on the only unit they'd finished, a studio on the first floor, number two. It was probably the last nice thing I let him do before he left.

I lived through nine months of construction noise and paint smells, the rest of the building a hollow skeleton. Once, I heard someone working in the unit right above me and went up there to see who it was. I was thinking if it was Ben I'd give him my rent check, see if he had any weed I could buy off him, or that he'd just give me. But it was Gloria, standing in a room painted a crisp robin's-egg blue, splotches of the paint on her hands and overalls, speckles in her blond hair. Clear plastic drop cloths billowed in the breeze from the open windows. She rested her hands on her globe of a belly and turned to me. I saw then that the room wasn't entirely painted. In front of her was a patch of wall the size of a playing card, dingy beige.

"I found it when we scraped the wallpaper," she said, her eyes teared up with sadness or paint fumes or both. She had a paintbrush in her right hand. "I've been avoiding this spot for a week." I bent to examine the patch of bare wall and saw there, scrawled in charcoal or heavy carpenter's pencil,

H. loves Leo, 1909.

"How can I do this?" said Gloria. And she said it again as she slopped a stripe of blue over the writing.

This was just before my mom died. Before Razor Blade Baby moved in. I didn't know what to say. Now I know better. I see Gloria in the yard, and I'd like to give her an answer. She's had her baby and puts a playpen under the willow tree and sings over to the girl while she gardens. She named her Marigold. I'd like to say: You do it because you have to. We all do.

And here we are.

The day my mom checked out, Razor Blade Baby moved in. Upstairs. Number four. Right above me. We are neighbors at 315 Lake Street, Newlands Heights, Reno, Nevada. That first day I heard the floorboards above my bed creak, then the hall stairs. When I opened the door, Razor Blade Baby invited me to see a three-dollar matinee at the old Hilton Theatre. Though I like their popcorn (stale and fluorescent yellow, salty enough to erode a gully in the roof of your mouth) and their hot dogs (all beef), I said what I would say every Sunday: No. No, thank you. I closed the door, and she sat on the stairs as she would every Sunday. She stayed there all day.

My father, Paul Watkins, met Charles Manson at a house party in San Francisco eleven months before Razor Blade Baby was born. He and Charlie wrote songs together and camped around the bay until December, when they set out for L.A., bored with the city, sick of the rain. Paul was eighteen and handsome. Or so my mother would tell me later.

At Spahn's, Paul moved his things into the old jail set: a sleeping bag, candles, his guitar and flute. He looked younger than his age, young enough to enroll himself in Pacific Palisades High School, though he'd already graduated the previous spring, a year early. He would become fond of pointing this out in interviews. (To Maureen Reagan on *Larry King Live*, August 23, 1987: "We were bright kids, Maureen. Not delinquents. I was the class president." Larry was out sick.) Paul went to Pali, home of the Dolphins, for two months to meet girls and bring them back to the ranch. He was good at it.

Years later, well after he was finally swallowed up by Hodgkin's disease, my mother, after one of her attempts to join him, wherever he was, called my father "Charlie's number one procurer of young girls." I couldn't tell whether she was ashamed or proud of him.

She also said, lying on her bed at University Medical Center, bandages on her wrists where she'd taken a steak knife to them, "When you go, all that matters is who's there with you. Believe me. I've been close enough enough times to know."

About once a year someone tracks me down. Occasionally it's one of Charlie's fans wanting to stand next to Paul Watkins's daughter, to rub up against all that's left, to put a picture up on his red-text-on-black-background website. Far more often, though, it's someone with a script. Producers, usually legit ones—I Google them: *True Lies*, *The Deer Hunter*. They offer to drive down from Lake Tahoe, take me out to dinner. They never want my permission to make their movie or input on who should play me (Winona Ryder); they just want to know how am I.

"How *are* you?" they say.

"I'm a receptionist," I say.

"Good," they say, long and slow, nodding as though my being a receptionist has given them everything they came for.

The day after Razor Blade Baby moved in, I rode my bike across the Truckee River to work. Razor Blade Baby followed, wearing a blazer, trailing behind me on a violet beach cruiser with a wicker basket, her long hair flapping behind her as though tugged by a hundred tiny kites. She followed me up the courthouse steps and sat in the lobby in front of my desk. She stayed there until lunch, when we sat on a bench beside the river, me eating a burrito from the cart, her dipping celery sticks into a Tupperware dish of tuna salad made with plain yogurt instead of mayonnaise. After lunch I went back to work, she back to the lobby. At five we rode home.

Some days she brings a roll of quarters and plugs the parking meters in front of the building. Others she crosses the street and browses the souvenir shops. I watch her from my office window, through the shop's glass front, running her fingers along the carousels of T-shirts. When the sun is very hot she simply sits on the courthouse's marble steps, drinking a cherry Slurpee, her palm pressed to the warm rock.

Some weekends I go out, and Razor Blade Baby comes along. One night, about three months after she moved in, I went to a dinner party to celebrate a friend's new condo, built high up in the hollowed-out bones of the renovated Flamingo. A row of one-legged bird silhouettes was still left on the building's façade.

It was a fine party, good food. I wore a poufy emerald green cocktail dress with pink flats, a pink ribbon in my hair. My friends, trying their very best for normalcy, sometimes pointed across the room and asked, "Claire, sweetheart, did you bring your auntie? You look just like her."

"Oh, no," I would say, swallowing the last bit of prosciutto or salmon dip or whatever it was. "That's Razor Blade Baby. She goes everywhere with me."

That night Razor Blade Baby and I left the party and started our walk back to 315 Lake. It had been raining heavily up in the Sierras for two days straight, and the Truckee was raging—the highest I'd ever seen it. The water was milky and opaque, and in it tumbled massive logs that had probably lain on the river's bed unmoved for years. Across the bridge two concrete stumps with rebar worming out the tops stood on either side of the street like sentinels, all that was left of the original arch. We stood there for a long while, Razor Blade Baby and I, sort of hypno-tized with the high water thrashing by, not sure whether it was safe to cross or what we'd do when we reached the other side. I imagined taking very small steps down the wet, slippery bank and wading into the current, my pockets weighed down with silver.

At home I got stoned and thought—as I often do after tracing my fingers over the frosted glass of my cabinets, my butcher-block countertops, sanded and varnished by his hands, all that's left of him, in my life anyway—of calling J. But I was no more capable of giving him what he needed than I was the day he left.

I didn't call. Instead I smoked myself deeper into oblivion and watched my hot breath billow at the ceiling, Razor Blade Baby no doubt on the other side, and fell asleep.

I believe I fell in love with one of them, these producers. He e-mailed me, said his name was Andrew, that he wanted to have dinner and talk about a film he wanted to make about my father, about how he was Charlie's number two in charge (true), how he came to live in an abandoned shack in the desert (true), how he got sober and testified against Charlie, then fell off the wagon again, blacked out, and woke up in a van, on fire (mostly true). I agreed to let him buy me dinner, as it is almost always my principle to do.

I met Andrew at Louis' Basque Corner on Fourth Street. Razor Blade Baby came along. I take all the movie guys to Louis', or I used to before Andrew. Now I take them to Miguel's off Mount Rose, also very tasty.

"What's good here?" he said. He had an easy, loose smile.

"Picon Punch," I said. "If you come here and don't order the Picon Punch, you didn't really come here." This was my bit. My Picon Punch bit.

Picon Punch is the deep brown of leather oil. Only the Basques know what's in it, but we all have a theory—rum, licorice root and gin; top-shelf rye with club soda and three drops of vanilla extract; well vodka, gin and a splash of apple juice; Seagram's, scotch and a ground-up Ricola cough drop— all theories equally plausible, none of them the truth. One Picon Punch will make you buy another. Two is too many. That night we had three each.

For dinner we ordered the sweetbreads and two Winne-mucca coffees and ate at the bar playing video poker, Deuces Wild. Razor Blade Baby played Ms. Pac-Man in the back.

We talked quietly, closely. Every once in a while Razor Blade Baby floated over and stood at my elbow. I did my best to shoo her away. I gave her another roll of quarters and found myself leaning into Andrew. He smelled of strong stinging cinnamon, like a smoker who tried hard to hide it.

A casino can make an average man lovely. The lights are dim, the ceiling low and mirrored. The machines light his face from below in a soft sweet blue. As they turn to reveal themselves on the screen, the electric playing cards reflect in his eyes as quick glints of light. The dense curtain of cigarette smoke filters the place fuzzy, as if what the two of you do there isn't actually happening. As if it were already in the past. As if your life wasn't a life but an old nostalgic movie. *Duel in the Sun*, perhaps. You don't want to know what a casino can do to a man already lovely.

It wasn't long before we were turned facing each other, and my right leg, dangling off my stool, found its way between his legs, nestled into his groin. We finished off the sweetbreads with our hands, sopping the small sinewy pieces of young lamb glands in onion sauce.

He asked about my father. I wanted to tell him what I told you, but that's nothing that can't be found in a book, a diary, a newspaper, a coroner's report. And there is still so much I'll never know, no matter how much history I weigh upon myself. I can tell you the shape of the stain left by H. T. P. Comstock's brain matter on the wooden walls of his cabin, but not whether he tasted the sour of the curse in his mouth just before he pulled the trigger. I can tell you the backward slant of Himmel Green's left-handed cursive, but not whether Leo loved him back. I can tell you of the silver gleam of Helen Spahn's tumors, but not whether she felt them growing inside her. I can tell you of the view from George's front porch, of the wide yellow valley below, but not what he saw after he went blind. I can tell you the things my father said to lure the Manson girls back to Spahn's Ranch, but I can't say whether he believed them. I can tell you the length and width and number of the cuts on my mother's wrists, and the colors her skin turned as they healed, but I couldn't say whether she would do it again, or when. Everything I can say about what it means to lose, what it means to do without, the inadequate weight of the past, you already know.

But the whiskey in our coffees was doing its job. I was feeling loose. So I told him what I could. I told him of the heavy earth scent after a desert rain, three or four times a year. That it smelled like the breathing of every thankful desert plant, every plot of soil, every unfound scrap of silver. That it had a way of softening you, of making you vulnerable. That it could redeem.

After dinner we watched Razor Blade Baby until she killed

off her last life. Andrew walked us out to our bikes and helped us unchain them. He kissed me then, or rather we kissed each other, right in front of Razor Blade Baby. It was an inevitable kiss. A kiss like I had caught the hem of my skirt on the seat of my bike while trying to mount it, and toppled. A kiss like we had fallen into each other, which I suppose we had.

Afterward, Razor Blade Baby and I rode home to 315 Lake, headlights lighting us from behind. When I closed my front door, my cell phone rang.

"Come outside." It was Andrew, his voice breathy, sweetly slurred.

"What?"

My doorbell buzzed. I pulled the curtain of my living room window aside, saw him swaying slightly on the porch, glowing phone pressed to his ear.

"Or come and live with me," he said.

"You're drunk," I said.

"So are you. Let me in. We'll move to L.A., down by the ocean. You can ride your bike up and down the coast. Or forget L.A., we can live here, in the mountains. In the desert. Whatever this is. That thing you said about the rain. You and me, Claire. Just let me in."

And I wanted to let him in. It wasn't that I didn't want to. I was swaying now and reached for the wall to steady myself, trying to stop the swirl of Picon in my head, my chest. Tried not to think of the words written there under the paint. *When you go, all that matters is who's there with you. Believe me.* I rested my head against the front door and wanted badly to open it.

But the story was too much, wherever I began: the borrowed revolver on the floor of a cabin near Bozeman, Montana. The sweet sizzle of Himmel Green's skin as it melted into Leopold's. Helen Spahn's withering uprooted tendrils. Bottles's dry bleached bones. My parents' own toxic and silver-gilded love. Razor Blade Baby, the simple fact of her.

"Good night, Andy," I said. "Please don't call me again."

When I hung up, I heard the sound I had already come to know: a quick creak in the floorboards above me. Razor Blade Baby's body shifting. The unpressing of her ear from the floor.

When Razor Blade Baby came to my door the next morning—this morning—I did not say, No. No, thank you. We rode our bicycles to the old Hilton Theatre, down Lake Street. Her hair flapped behind her as though lifted by George Spahn's Pennsylvanian swarm.

I bought a hot dog before the matinee from the concession stand. I covered it with mustard, onions, kraut, jalapeños. Razor Blade Baby nervously fingered a Ziploc bag of peeled carrot sticks hidden in her purse.

Here in the theater I know I ought to try, ought to carry that weight, ought to paint over the past. But I can only do my best. I hold my hot dog near her face. "Want a bite, Razor Blade Baby?"

"Claire," she says. "I could be your sister."

And though we have known this since she moved in—well before—this is the first time either of us has said it aloud. And

I admit now, it sounds softer than it felt. There is something thankful in the saying.

I nod. "Half sister."

The lights in the theater dim. Technicolor figures—ghosts, cowboys, Gregory Peck—move across the screen. In *Duel in the Sun* Pearl Chavez asks, "Oh, Vashti, why are you so slow?"

"I don't rightly know, Miss Pearl, except I always have so much to remember."

THE LAST THING
WE NEED

July 28

Duane Moser
4077 Pincay Drive
Henderson, Nevada 89015

Dear Mr. Moser,

On the afternoon of June 25, while on my last outing to Rhyolite, I was driving down Cane Springs Road some ten miles outside Beatty and happened upon what looked to be the debris left over from an auto accident. I got out of my truck and took a look around. The valley was bone dry. A hot west wind took the puffs of dust from where I stepped and curled them away like

ash. Near the wash I found broken glass, deep gouges
in the dirt running off the side of the road and an array of
freshly bought groceries tumbled among the creosote.
Coke cans (some full, some open and empty, some with
the tab intact but dented and half-full and leaking). Bud
Light cans in the same shape as the Coke. Fritos. Meat.
Et cetera. Of particular interest to me were the two
almost-full prescriptions that had been filled at the
pharmacy in Tonopah only three days before, and a
sealed Ziploc bag full of letters signed *M*. I also took
notice of a bundle of photos of an old car, part primer,
part rust, that I presume was or is going to be restored.
The car was a Chevy Chevelle, a '66, I believe. I once
knew a man who drove a Chevelle. Both medications had
bright yellow stickers on their sides warning
against drinking alcohol while taking them. Enter
the Bud Light, and the gouges in the dirt, possibly. I
copied your address off the prescription bottles. What
happened out there? Where is your car? Why were the
medications, food and other supplies left behind? Who
are you, Duane Moser? What were you looking for out at
Rhyolite?

I hope this letter finds you, and finds you well.
Please write back.

Truly,
Thomas Grey
P.O. Box 1230
Verdi, Nevada 89439

P.S. I left most of the debris in the desert, save for the medications, pictures and letters from M. I also took the plastic grocery bags, which I untangled from the bushes and recycled on my way through Reno. It didn't feel right to just leave them out there.

— —

August 16

Duane Moser
4077 Pincay Drive
Henderson, Nevada 89015

Dear Mr. Moser,

This morning as I fed the horses, clouds were just beginning to slide down the slope of the Sierras, and I was reminded once again of Rhyolite. When I came inside I borrowed my father's old copy of the *Physician's Desk Reference* from his room. From that book I have gathered that before driving out to Rhyolite you may have been feeling out of control, alone or hopeless. You were possibly in a state of extreme depression; perhaps you were even considering hurting yourself. Judging by the date the prescriptions were filled and the number of pills left in the bottles—which I have counted, sitting out in the fields atop a tractor that I let sputter and die, eating the sandwich my wife fixed me for lunch—you had not been taking the medications long enough for them to counteract your possible feelings of despair. "Despair," "depression," "hopeless," "alone." These are the words of the *PDR*, forty-first edition, which I returned to my father promptly, as per his request. My father can be difficult. He spends his days shut up in his room, reading old crime novels populated by dames and Negroes, or watching the TV we bought him with the volume up too high. Some days he refuses to eat. Duane Moser, my father never thought he would live this long.

I think there will be lightning tonight; the air has that feel. Please, write back.

Truly,
Thomas Grey
P.O. Box 1230
Verdi, Nevada 89439

— —

September 1

Duane Moser
4077 Pincay Drive
Henderson, Nevada 89015

Dear Mr. Moser,

I slept terribly last night, dreamed dreams not easily identified as such. Had I told my wife about them, she might have given me a small quartz crystal or amethyst and insisted I carry it around in my pocket all day, to cleanse my mind and spirit. She comes from California. Here is a story she likes to tell. On one of our first dates, we walked arm in arm around downtown Reno, where she was a clerk at a grocery store and I was a student of agriculture and business. There she tried to pull me down a little flight of steps to the red-lit underground residence of a palm reader and psychic. I declined. Damn near an hour she pulled on me, saying what was I afraid of, asking what was the big deal. I am not a religious man but, as I told her then, there are some things I'd rather not fuck with. Now she likes to say it's a good thing I wouldn't go in, because if that psychic had told her she'd be stuck with me for going on fourteen years now, she would have turned and headed for the hills. Ha! And I say, Honey, not as fast as I would've, ha, ha! This is our old joke. Like all our memories, we like to take it out once in a while and lay it flat on the kitchen table, the way my wife does with her sewing patterns, where we line up the shape of our life against that which we thought it would be by now.

I'll tell you what I don't tell her, that there is something shameful in this, the buoying of our sinking spirits with old stories.

I imagine you a man alone, Duane Moser, with no one asking after your dreams in the morning, no one slipping healing rocks into your pockets. A bachelor. It was the Fritos, finally, which reminded me of the gas

station in Beatty where I worked when I was in high
school and where I knew a man who owned a Chevelle
like yours, a '66. But it occurs to me that perhaps this
assumption is foolish; surely there are wives out there
who have not banned trans fats and processed sugar, as
mine has. I haven't had a Frito in eleven years. Regardless,
I write to inquire about your family, should you reply.

Our children came to us later in life than most.
My oldest, Danielle, has just started school. Her little
sister, Layla, is having a hard time with it. She wants so
badly to go to school with Danielle that she screams and
cries as the school bus pulls away in the morning.
Sometimes she throws herself down to the ground,
embedding little pieces of rock in the flesh of her fists.
Then she is sullen and forlorn for the rest of the day.
My wife worries for her, but truth be told, I am
encouraged. The sooner Layla understands that we are
nothing but the sum of that which we endure, the better.
But my father has taken to walking Layla to the end of
our gravel road in the afternoon to wait for Danielle at the
bus stop. Layla likes to go as early as she is allowed, as if
her being there will bring the bus sooner. She would stand
at the end of the road all day if we let her. She pesters my
father so that he sometimes stands there in the heat with
her for an hour or more, though his heart is in no
condition to be doing so. In many ways he is better to my
girls than I am. He is far better to them than he was to
me. I am not a religious man but I do thank God for that.

I am beginning to think I dreamed you up. Please, write soon.

> *Truly,*
> *Thomas Grey*
> P.O. Box 1230
> Verdi, Nevada 89439

— —

October 16

Duane Moser
4077 Pincay Drive
Henderson, Nevada 89015

Dear Mr. Moser,

I have read the letters from M, the ones you kept folded in the Ziploc bag. Forgive me, but for all I know you may be dead, and I could not resist. I read them in my shed, where the stink and thickness of the air were almost unbearable, and then again in my truck in the parking lot of the Verdi post office. I was struck, as I was when I first found them out near Rhyolite on Cane Springs Road, by how new the letters looked. Though most were written nearly twenty years ago, the paper is clean, the creases sharp. Duane Moser, what I do not understand is this: why a Ziploc bag? Did you worry they might get wet on your journey through the desert in the

middle of summer? Then again, I am reminded of the
Coke and Bud Light. Or am I to take the Ziploc bag as
an indication of your fierce, protective love for M? Is it a
sign, as M suggests, that little by little you sealed your
whole self off, until there was nothing left for her?
Furthermore, I have to ask whether you committed this
sealing purposefully. She says she thinks she was always
asking too much of you. She is generous that way, isn't
she? She says you didn't mean to become "so very alien"
to her. I am not so sure. I love my wife. But I've never
told her how I once knew a man in Beatty with a '66
Chevelle. I know what men like us are capable of.

Duane Moser, what I come back to is this: how
could you have left M's letters by the side of Cane
Springs Road near the ghost town Rhyolite where
hardly anyone goes anymore? (In fact, I have never seen
another man out on Cane Springs Road. I drive out there
to be alone. Maybe you do, too. Or you did, anyway.) Did
you not realize that someone just like you might find
them?

I have called the phone number listed on the
prescription bottles, finally, though all I heard was the
steady rising tones of the disconnected signal. Still, I
found myself listening for you there. Please, write soon.

Truly,
Thomas Grey
P.O. Box 1230
Verdi, Nevada 89439

P.S. On second thought, perhaps sometimes these things are best left by the side of the road, as it were. Sometimes a person wants a part of you that's no good. Sometimes love is a wound that opens and closes, opens and closes, all our lives.

— —

November 2

Duane Moser
4077 Pincay Drive
Henderson, Nevada 89015

Dear Mr. Moser,

My wife found your pictures, the ones of the Chevelle. The one you maybe got from a junkyard or from a friend, or maybe it's been in your family for years, rotting in a garage somewhere because after what happened nobody wanted to look at it. I kept the pictures tucked behind the visor in my truck, bound with a rubber band. I don't know why I kept them. I don't know why I've kept your letters from M, or your medications. I don't know what I would do if I found what I am looking for.

When I was in high school I worked the graveyard shift at a gas station in Beatty. It's still there, on the corner of I-95 and Highway 374, near the hot springs.

Maybe you've been there. It's a Shell station now, but back then it was called Hadley's Fuel. I worked there forty, fifty hours a week. Bill Hadley was a friend of my father's. He was a crazy son of a bitch, as my father would say, who kept a shotgun under the counter and always accused me of stealing from the till or sleeping on the job when I did neither. I liked the graveyard shift, liked being up at night, away from Pop, listening to the tremors of the big walk-in coolers, the hum of the fluorescent lights outside.

Late that spring, a swarm of grasshoppers moved through Beatty on their way out to the alfalfa fields down south. They were thick and fierce, roaring like a thunderstorm in your head. The hoppers ate anything green. In two days they stripped the leaves from all the cottonwoods and willows in town, then they moved on to the juniper and pine, the cheatgrass and bitter salt cedar. A swarm of them ate the wool right off of Abel Prince's live sheep. Things got so bad that the trains out to the mines shut down for a week because the guts of the bugs made the rails too slippery.

The grasshoppers were drawn to the fluorescent lights at Hadley's. For weeks the parking lot pulsed with them. I would have felt them crunch under my feet when I walked out to the pumps that night, dead and dying under my shoes, only I never made it out to the pumps. I was doing schoolwork at the counter. Calculus, for God's sake. I looked up and the guy was already coming through the door at me. I looked outside and saw the '66 Chevelle, gleaming under the lights, grasshoppers falling all around it like rain.

I tried to stop him but he muscled back behind the counter. He had a gun, held it like it was his own hand. He said, You see this?

There was a bandanna over his face. But Beatty is a small town, and it was even smaller then. I knew who he was. I knew his mother worked as a waitress at the Stagecoach and that his sister had graduated the year before me. The money, he was saying. His name was Frankie. The fucking money, Frankie said.

I'd barely touched a gun before that night. I don't know how I did it. I only felt my breath go out of me and reached under the counter to where the shotgun was and tried. I shot him in the head.

Afterward, I called the cops. I did the right thing, they told me, the cops and Bill Hadley in his pajamas, even my father. They said it over and over again. I sat on the curb outside the store, listening to them inside, their boots squeaking on the tile. The deputy sheriff, Dale Sullivan, who was also the assistant coach of the basketball team, came and sat beside me. I had my hands over my head to keep the grasshoppers away. Kid, it was bound to happen, Dale said. The boy was a troublemaker. A waste of skin.

He told me I could go on home. I didn't ask what would happen to the car.

That night, I drove out on Cane Springs Road to
Rhyolite. I drove around that old ghost town with the
windows rolled down, listening to the gravel pop under
my tires. The sun was coming up. There, in the milky
light of dawn, I hated Beatty more than I ever had.
The Stagecoach, the hot springs, all the trees looking so
naked against the sky. I never wanted to see any of it
ever again.

I was already on my way to college and everyone
knew it. I didn't belong in Beatty. The boy's family, his
mother and sister and stepfather, moved away soon
after it happened. I'd never see them around town, or at
Hadley's. For those last few weeks of school no one
talked about it, at least not to me. Soon it was as though
it had never happened. But—and I think I realized
this then, up in Rhyolite, that dead town picked
clean—Beatty would never be a place I could come
home to.

When my wife asked about your pictures, she said
she didn't realize I knew so much about cars. I said,
Yeah, sure. Well, some. See the vents there? On the
hood? See the blackout grille? That's how you know it's a
'66. I told her I'd been thinking about buying an old car,
fixing it up, maybe this one. Right then she just started
laughing her head off. Sure, she managed through all her
laughter, fix up a car. She kept on laughing. She tossed
the bundle of photos on the seat of the truck and said,
You're shitting me, Tommy.

It's not her fault. That man, the one who knows a '66 when he sees one, that's not the man she married. That's how it has to be. You understand, don't you?

I smiled at her. No, ma'am, I said. I wouldn't shit you. You're my favorite turd.

She laughed—she's generous that way—and said, A car. That's the last thing we need around here.

When I was a boy, my father took me hunting. Quail mostly and, one time, elk. But I was no good at it and he gave up. I didn't have it in me, my father said, sad and plain as if it were a birth defect, the way I was. Even now, deer come down from the mountains and root in our garden, stripping our tomatoes from the vine, eating the hearts of our baby cabbages. My father says, Kill one. String it up. They'll learn. I tell him I can't do that. I spend my Sundays patching the holes in the fence, or putting up a taller one. The Church of the Compassionate Heart, my wife calls it. It makes her happy, this life of ours, the man I am. Layla helps me mend the fence. She stands behind me and hands me my pliers or my wire cutters when I let her.

But here's the truth, Duane Moser. Sometimes I see his eyes above that bandanna, see the grasshoppers leaping in the lights, hear them vibrating. I feel the kick of the rifle butt in my sternum. I would do it again.

> *Truly,*
> *Thomas Grey*
> P.O. Box 1230
> Verdi, Nevada 89439

- —

December 20

Duane Moser
4077 Pincay Drive
Henderson, Nevada 89015

Dear Duane Moser,

This will be the last I write to you. I went back to
Rhyolite. I told my wife I was headed south to camp and
hike for a few days. She said, Why don't you take Layla
with you? It would be good for her.

Layla slept nearly the whole drive. Six hours. When
I slowed the car and pulled onto Cane Springs Road she
sat up and said, Dad, where are we?

I said, We're here.

I helped her with her coat and mittens, and we took a
walk through the ruins. I told her what they once were.
Here, I said, was the schoolhouse. They finished it in 1909.
By then there weren't enough children in town to fill it. It
burned the next year. She wanted to go closer.

I said, Stay where I can see you.

Why? she said.

I didn't know how to say it. Crumbling buildings,
rotted-out floors, sinkholes, open mine shafts. Coyotes,
rattlesnakes, mountain lions.

Because, I said. It's not safe for little girls.

We went on. There behind the fence is the post office, completed in 1908. This slab, these beams, that wall of brick, that was the train station. It used to have marble floors, mahogany woodworking, one of the first telephones in the state. But those have been sold or stolen over the years.

Why? she said.

That's what happens when a town dies.

Why?

Because, sweetheart. Because.

At dusk I tried to show Layla how to set up a tent and build a fire, but she wasn't interested. Instead, she concentrated on filling her pink vinyl backpack with stones and using them to build little pyramids along the path that led out to the town. She squatted over them, gingerly turning the stones to find a flat side, a stable base. What are those for? I asked.

For if we get lost, she said. Pop Pop showed me.

When it got dark we sat together, listening to the hiss of the hot dogs at the ends of our sticks, the violent sizzle of sap escaping the firewood. Layla fell asleep in my lap. I carried her to the tent and zipped her inside a sleeping bag. I stayed and watched her there, her chest rising and falling, hers the small uncertain breath of a bird.

When I bent to step out through the opening of the tent something fell from the pocket of my overalls. I held it up in the firelight. It was a cloudy stump of amethyst, as big as a horse's tooth.

I've tried, Duane Moser, but I can't picture you at 4077 Pincay Drive. I can't see you in Henderson, period, out in the suburbs, on a cul-de-sac, in one of those prefab houses with the stucco and the garage gaping off the front like a mouth. I can't see you standing like a bug under those streetlights the color of antibacterial soap. At home at night I sit on my porch and watch the lights of Reno over the hills, the city marching out at us like an army. It's no accident that the first step in what they call developing a plot of land is to put a fence around it.

I can't see you behind a fence. When I see you, I see you here, at Rhyolite, harvesting sticks of charcoal from the half-burnt schoolhouse and writing your name on the exposed concrete foundation. Closing one eye to look through the walls of Jim Kelly's bottle house. No, that's my daughter. That's me as a boy getting charcoal stains on my blue jeans. That's you in your Chevelle, the '66, coming up Cane Springs Road, tearing past what was once the Porter brothers' store. I see you with M, flinging Fritos and meat and half-full cans of Coke and Bud Light from the car like a goddamn celebration, a shedding of your old selves.

It's almost Christmas. I've looked at the prescriptions, the letters, the photos. You're not Frankie, I know this. It's just a coincidence, a packet of pictures flung from a car out in the middle of nowhere. The car is just a car. The world is full of Chevelles, a whole year's worth of the '66. You know nothing of Hadley's Fuel in Beatty, of a boy who was killed there one night in late spring when the grasshoppers sounded like a thunderstorm in your head. I don't owe you anything.

When I woke this morning there was snow on the ground and Layla was gone. She'd left no tracks. I pulled on my boots and walked around the camp. A layer of white covered the hills and the valley and the skeletons of the old buildings, lighting the valley fluorescent. It was blinding. I called my daughter's name. I listened, pressing the sole of my shoe against the blackened rocks lining the fire pit. I watched the snow go watery within my boot print. There was no answer.

I checked the truck. It was empty. In the tent I found her coat and mittens. Her shoes had been taken. I scrambled up a small hill and looked for her from there. I scanned for the shape of her among the old buildings, on the hills, along Cane Springs Road. Fence posts, black with moisture, strung across the valley like tombstones. Sickness thickened in my gut and my throat. She was gone.

I called for her again and again. I heard nothing, though surely my own voice echoed back to me. Surely the snow creaked under my feet when I walked through our camp and out to the ruins. Surely the frozen tendrils of creosote whipped against my legs when I began to run through the ghost town, up and down the gravel path. But all sound had left me except for a low, steady roaring, the sound of my own blood in my ears, of a car rumbling up the old road.

Suddenly my chest was burning. I couldn't breathe. *Layla. Layla.* I crouched and pressed my bare palms against the frozen earth. The knees of my long johns soaked through, my fingers began to sting.

Then I saw a shape near the burnt remains of the schoolhouse. A panic as hot and fierce as anything— fiercer—rose in me. The slick pink vinyl of her backpack. I ran to it.

When I bent to pick it up, I heard something on the wind. Something like the high, breathy language my daughters speak to each other when they play. I followed the sound around behind the schoolhouse and found Layla squatting there in her pajamas, softly stacking one of her stone markers in the snow.

Hi, Dad, she said. The snow had reddened her hands and cheeks as though she'd been burned. She handed me a stone. Here you go, she said.

I took my daughter by the shoulders and stood her up. I raised her sweet chin so her eyes met mine, and then I slapped her across the face. She began to cry. I held her. The Chevelle drove up and down Cane Springs Road, the gravel under its tires going *pop pop pop*. I said, Shh. That's enough. A child means nothing out here.

Truly,
Thomas Grey

RONDINE AL NIDO

Now I am become Death,
the destroyer of worlds.

—*Bhagavad Gita*

She will be thirty when she walks out on a man who in the end, she'll decide, didn't love her enough, though he in fact did love her, but his love wrenched something inside him, and this caused him to hurt her. She'll move to an apartment downtown and soon—very soon, people will say, admiringly at times, skeptically at others—she will have a date with a sensible man working as an attorney, the profession of his father and brothers, in the office where she is a typist. They will share a dinner, and the next weekend another, then drinks, a midday walk through the upheaved brick sidewalks of her neighborhood, a Sunday-morning garden tour of his. On their fifth date she will allow him to take her to bed.

Before they met, he'll have been a social worker, and after they make love he will tell her this, and about the terrible things he saw in that other life. He'll begin—At CPS, there was this woman. She had this little girl. Beautiful. Two years old—then stop and lean down and put his lips to her hair. Do you really want to hear this? he'll ask, as though just remembering that she was listening. He'll feel her head nod where it rests on his chest and go on. About the Mexican woman who let her beautiful, bright two-year-old daughter starve to death in a motel room near the freeway. About the teenage boy, high on coke, who broke into the apartment next door and slit his neighbor's throat. About the man who worked at the snack bar at the Sparks Marina, who lured a retarded girl into the men's bathroom with a lemonade. About the father who made his son live under their porch in Sun Valley, about the hole the boy bored up through the floor so he could watch his stepmother brush her hair in the morning.

He will talk, and she will listen. It will be as though she's finally found someone else willing to see the worst in the world. Someone who can't help but see it. For the first time in her life, she will feel understood. When he finishes one story she'll ask for another, then another, wanting to stack them like bricks, build walls of sorrow around the two of them, seal them up together. An uncontrollable feeling—like falling—will be growing in her: they could build a love this way.

Then, feigning lightness, she'll ask him to tell her about something he did, something terrible. When he was a boy, maybe. It will be late. Watery light from a waxing moon will catch the corner of the bed, setting the white sheets aglow. Two candles—the man's idea—will flicker feebly on the nightstand, drawing moths against the window screen. He will tell her about his younger brother and a firecracker and a neighbor's farmhouse in Chatsworth, of straw insulation and old dry wood that went up like *whoosh* so fast it didn't seem fair, of running around to the front door and ringing the bell—she will find this curious, the bell—and helping the neighbor, an elderly woman, down the front steps. Now you show me yours, he'll say, and laugh. He will have a devastating laugh.

By then, there will be much to tell—too much. A pair of expensive tropical lizards she'd begged for, then abandoned in a field to die when their care became tedious. Birthstone rings and a real gold bracelet plucked from a friend's jewelry box at a sleepover. Asking an ugly, wretched boy with circles of ringworm strung like little galaxies across his head to meet her for a kiss at the flagpole, laughing wildly when he showed. These she'll have been carrying since girlhood like very small stones in her pocket. The sensible man will be waiting. Who can say why we offer the parts of ourselves we do, and when.

O ur girl is sixteen years old. Her palms press against the stinging metal of a heat rack. Her best friend, Lena, a large-toothed girl from Minnesota, stands across from her, palms pressed against the rack, too. Their eyes are locked, and a skin scent rises between them. This is their game, one of many. In the pocket of our girl's apron rests a stack of fleshy pepperoni, their edges curling in the swelter. Behind her, the slat-mouthed pizza oven bellows steadily. A blackened sheet of baking parchment floats in a dish of hot grease. The grease has a name, and as our girl tells the story this name will return to her, along with other details of this place, which had until now left her—the flatulent smell from a newly opened bag of sausage, the flimsy yellowed plastic covering the computer keyboards and phone keypads, the serrated edge of a cardboard box slicing her index finger nearly to the bone. Naked in her own bed with a man for whom she feels too much too soon, our girl will recall the name of the grease—Whirl, it was called—and the then-exquisite possibility of searing off her fingerprints.

Lena, her friend, finally pulls her hands from the rack, shaking the sting from them. You win, she says.

Our girl waits a beat, gloating, then lifts her palms from the surface, lustrous with heat. She folds a pepperoni disk into her mouth. Let's go again, she says.

Soon, our girl is cut loose for the night by the manager, a brick-faced, wire-haired woman named Suzie. She goes to the back of the restaurant, to a bathroom constructed from Sheetrock as an afterthought. At a row of metal sinks outside the bathroom, two delivery boys wash dishes. One of the boys, a nineteen-year-old named Jeremy, has convinced himself that he loves our girl, though she has already once declined an invitation to watch *Dawn of the Dead* in the single-wide trailer he has all to himself on his mother's boyfriend's property.

In the bathroom the plastic shelves are stocked with fluorescent lightbulbs and printer paper and a dozen two-gallon plastic tubs once used to store a cream sauce the franchise no longer offers. She removes her hat, her apron, her once-white tennis shoes and ankle socks. She unpins her name tag from her patriotically colored collared shirt, and pulls the shirt off over her head. Yellow grains of cornmeal sprinkle into her eyelashes and along the part in her hair. She steps out of her khaki pants, stiff with dried doughwater and dark, unidentified oils.

She stands before the mirror in her bra and underwear, listening to the hollow, slow-motion clangs at the triple sinks. She steps out of her underwear. Suzie bellows from up front, and someone's nonmarking sole screeches against the tile. In the sink, using the granulated pink soap from the dispenser, our girl scrubs the smell of herself from her panties. Later, the dampness left from this washing will remind her of the pizza parlor and of poor pathetic Jeremy the delivery boy, and other remnants of a life she already wishes she could forget.

She waits for Lena on the bench in front of the counter, watching carryout mothers waddle from and to their idling cars with their pizzas and their slippery, foil-wrapped cheese sticks. Six and a half hours ago, in the parking lot of the Wal-Mart across the highway, Kyle Peterson, a tenor sax in their school's jazz band, dumped Lena, his girlfriend of nearly a year, for the first-chair flutist, a freshman and a thinner, looser version of Lena. Two hours later, our girl wiped mascara from under Lena's rubbed-raw eyes in the Sheetrock bathroom and asked her whether she wanted to get the fuck out of this shit town. Two hours after that, when she was certain her mother and stepfather had left for their Friday-night twelve-step meeting, our girl dialed her own phone number. She told the machine, I'm going to Lena's after work to stay the night, and, I love you, which is what she always says after she lies to them. By the time Lena gets off, they've both got an uneventful adolescence's worth of recklessness welling inside them, and one of them has a driver's license and a like-new Dodge Neon and it's just the tip of summer, which means there are college boys from places like Chicago and Florida and New York City wandering the Strip, sixty miles away, boys who came to Las Vegas looking for girls willing to do the things she and Lena think they are willing to do.

At eight o'clock Lena changes out of her uniform and wets her hair and underarms at the bathroom sink and then the two walk out into the parking lot with their soiled uniforms balled under their arms, their apron strings trailing along the asphalt, as though they don't have to be back for tomorrow's dinner rush, as though they don't have to be back ever again.

On the road, all there is is desert and night and the taillights of the cars ahead of them. The radio comes in and out. Once, without taking her eyes off the road, Lena says, I should have done it with him. I don't know why I didn't. Our girl says nothing, only nods. When Lena swings the Neon around the final curve of the mountain range separating their town from Las Vegas, they see light sweeping across the valley floor like a blanket made of lights, like light is a liquid and the city is a great glistening lake.

Lena sucks a little saliva from her over-large teeth and asks is it okay if they turn the radio off. She has never driven in the city. Our girl says, That's cool, because the radio is suddenly nothing compared to the billboards and limos and rented convertibles and speakers embedded in the sidewalks emitting their own music into the air, and because she'll say anything to soothe Lena, to keep her driving.

Our girl directs Lena to park on the top floor of the parking garage at the New York New York. It is June 2001. This is the Las Vegas that has recently given up on becoming what they were calling a family-friendly vacation destination. The waterslides and roller coasters and ice-skating rinks that were once part of the megaresorts have been torn down to make room for additional hotel towers, floor space, and parking garages like this one. Lena pulls hard on the parking brake, the way her mother taught her. She moved from Minnesota her freshman year, when her mom was offered a job as the Nye County health nurse. Her parents have been divorced since before she can remember. She sees her father, an accountant, on Christmas and Easter, and lives with him in St. Paul for five weeks during the summer. Lena doesn't know anything about what was once Wet 'n' Wild or MGM Grand Adventures. Our girl spent her birthdays and end-of-year field trips in such places and could be saddened by their vanishing, could consider it the demolition of her childhood. But thoughts like these will not come to her for years.

Lena has a tube of waterproof mascara and a peacock blue eyeliner pencil in her purse. Our girl has vanilla-bean body spray and kiwi-strawberry lip gloss and gum in three different incarnations of mint. All these they trade in the front seat of the Neon until both are eyelined and fragrant and fresh-mouthed. From the parking structure they walk through the New York New York. The shops in the casino are façaded with half-scale fire escapes and newsstands and mailboxes with graffiti replicated on the side. They sell Nathan's Famous hot dogs or tiny Statue of Liberty erasers and key-chain taxicabs and all varieties of shot glasses.

Our girl leads the way. The floor is busy carpet or plastic cobble. Tacky, her mother would call it, dully. The ceiling is lit to suggest stars glittering at twilight, as is popular along the Strip at this time. A bulbous red glittered apple rotates above a stand of slots. Our girl ignores the directional signs, which point down circuitous routes pitted with pocket bars and sports books. Once, Lena touches her lightly, thinking they've lost their way. Our girl says, Trust me, and Lena does.

Outside there is a breeze threading through the warm night and a jubilant honking of cars and all those billions of bulbs flashing in time, signaling to the girls that they are, at long last, alive. Across Las Vegas Boulevard is an enormous gold lion posing regally in the mist of a fountain. The lion is the property's second; the original—a formidable openmouthed beast forged in midroar—was replaced because it frightened some Chinese tourists and was considered bad luck by others. Down the expansive block is an unimpressive aging Camelot, and beyond that a black glass pyramid, the apex of which emits a thick rope of light supposedly visible from space. The girls set off in the opposite direction, toward an ever-expanding ancient Rome and, across the palm-lined, traffic-clogged boulevard, the Eiffel Tower, where our girl's stepfather poured concrete during phase two. They cross a Brooklyn Bridge, its waters strewn with coins, and pass before the wood-toothed mouth of a grinning Coney clown that will be demolished long before either girl reveals the happenings of this night to anyone.

The weekend crowds are dense on the sidewalks and mostly foreign or Midwestern. This allows the girls to amuse themselves at intersections by grasping hands, stepping off the curb against a red light, and glancing backward to see the crowd follow in their wake, taxicabs honking wildly. They have a teenage sense of their surroundings: They wander unknowingly into the photos of strangers, and twice Lena tramples the heel of a Japanese tourist walking in front of her. But they feel men and boys before they see them, poking each other in the ribs, perking for button-ups and baseball caps and oversize jerseys, whirling around at the sound of a skateboard.

Soon, propped on the rubber handrail of a down-bound outdoor escalator, our girl stares unblinkingly at a cluster of young men headed in the opposite direction. When they pass, Lena turns and waves to them, but our girl dismounts the escalator coolly and without turning, wielding the fearsome magnetism of ambivalence. When they reach the top, the young men turn and descend the escalator.

The young men outnumber the girls by two. Our girl likes the way the four of them form a slowly closing semicircle around her and her friend. She likes, too, how they all look the same, in their baggy jeans and pastel collared shirts. They are dressed as most boys their age or slightly older dress, as though their tops and bottoms were mismatched pieces from two separate puzzles, one marked boy and the other man. One of them introduces himself as Brad, another as Tom, another Greg, and the last,

Allen. Except for Allen, they say these names too often and like candies too large for their mouths—This is *Brad*. *Brad*, shake her hand. Don't be rude, *Brad*—and because of this it becomes clear to everyone that these are not their real names. Everyone except Lena, who waves and says, Nice to meet you, Brad.

The one who calls himself Tom suggests they walk up to the Bellagio to watch the fountain show. The girls glance at each other and say, Sure, as they do again at the show when one young man—Greg, is it?—offers them a cup of orange soda clandestinely cut with vodka. Lena's mouth twists as she releases the straw, but our girl urges the straw up to her lips again, and Lena drinks more heartily. They pass the cup back and forth. This is what they came for.

Soon, the industrial fountain spigots emerge from the glassy black surface of the water, and somewhere strings begin to hum. The song is "Rondine al Nido," which pleases our girl, not because she recognizes it as such—she doesn't—but because she wants Lena to experience the pure painful awe of the bright-lit Bellagio fountains and she believes this is best conveyed when the cannon blasts are paired with something classical, something like the agony of ill-fated love.

After the show, the boy who calls himself Greg turns to them. He is large, with the overexpressed muscles that come from a university rec center, so unlike the aching, striated parts of a man who works for a living, as our girl's stepfather would say. Greg asks, How old are you guys?

Old enough, says Lena, and this makes our girl proud.

Greg laughs. We'll see about that.

The boys ask them more questions—where they live, where they go to school—and meanwhile, one of them replenishes the soda cup. Our girl lies up a city life for them: moves them into adjacent two-story houses near the Galleria Mall, skips them ahead to senior year and enrolls them in a school whose football team once came out and trounced their own.

They drink. They walk. The boys say they go to UCSB, though our girl will misremember it as UCSC, so that in the coming years, these boys and what they do to them will combine with far-off Santa Cruz, California, and years later, lying beside the sensible man with the devastating laugh—the first man she will not see beyond—the boys will have the scent of damp redwood and the sharp angles of that region's mountain lions, which she once read about.

In her bed, the candles dimming behind her, she will say nothing of these associations. She will be barely aware of them. She'll tug the top sheet out from under her, absently touch her fingers to the dampness left between her legs, and say, They had a room.

But the sensible man—being who he is—will find the angles in her face. The redwood wet will be in his throat when he asks her, You went there? Alone? You were just a girl.

I had Lena, she'll say. My friend.

Because he'll know what's coming, this will only make it worse.

. . .

The boys lead the girls to their hotel, where entering once meant passing through the jaws of a fearsome gold lion and now means nothing. Warm with sugar and liquor, our girl wants badly to tell Lena this—about the original lion and the superstitious Chinese tourists—because tonight's lion is the only lion Lena has ever known. It seems, for an instant, that if Lena knew about the old lion then at last the miles between Minnesota and Nevada might fold like a sheet, the distance crumpling into closeness, and they would tell each other everything, always.

But the time for telling passes. In its place is the sudden chemical smell of chlorine and a flash of the too-blue water encircling the statue, and then the girls are met with a blast of air-conditioning and stale cigarette smoke and the noise of the machines inside the MGM Grand.

The six of them make their way across the floor, toward the hotel's two towers. The boy called Tom lays his hand on the back of our girl's neck. As they pass a security guard standing beside a golden trash can, she is possessed by the impulse to sink her fingers deep into the glittering black sand of the ashtray atop it, but she resists this. Behind her, Lena stumbles, rights herself, then stumbles again. The boy called Brad grips her upper arm. Bitch, be cool, he says through his slick teeth.

Lena walks steadily for several steps, then stops. She has felt his words, more than understood them. She says, I have to pee. Our girl tells Tom, We'll be right back, and follows her friend to the ladies' room.

Lena locks herself in the handicapped stall at the far end of the bathroom and sits on the toilet without taking down her pants. Our girl goes into the stall beside Lena's and shuts the door. She sits on the toilet in the same way. A woman is washing her hands at the sink, and the automatic faucet blasts in spurts. Lena breathes heavily through her mouth. The woman at the sink dries her hands partially and leaves, the door opening and closing behind the blast of the dryer.

Our girl reaches her hand underneath the wall dividing them. Lena considers the fingers extended toward her, then laces her own between them. They say nothing for a long time, only hold hands under the stall. Lena begins to cry, softly. Aside from the dim noise of the casino making its way back to them, the wet efforts of Lena's nose and throat are the only sounds heard.

I don't feel good, says Lena. I miss Kyle.

Are you going to throw up?

No, says Lena. Then, Yes. Our girl releases Lena's hand and leaves her stall, allowing the door to swing shut behind her. She gets on all fours, the tile cool against her palms, and crawls under the partition into Lena's big handicapped cube. Lena is on her knees leaning over the bowl, her purse on the floor beside her.

Our girl says, Here, reaching over to lift the toilet seat. As Lena begins to vomit, our girl gathers her friend's wavy hair in her hand and holds it. Get it out, she says. All out. Between purges Lena emits a mournful language intelligible only to herself, the main theme of which is certainly Kyle.

Our girl fingers the soft baby hairs at Lena's nape and says, Shh.

Eventually, Lena lifts her head slightly. I think I'm ready to go home, she says.

As though the word has materialized the cloth on her, our girl becomes instantly sensitive to the persisting dampness of her underwear. She sees the Sheetrock bathroom in the back of the pizza parlor. Jeremy the delivery boy. Her stepfather. His long commute to job sites in Vegas. The empty and near-empty potato chip bags swirling around the backseat of his car like deflated Mylar balloons. Then, her memory lurching from shape to shape, there is her mother, hands shaking, unable to sit through a meal without popping up to get him seconds or refill his glass with milk.

Lena heaves again. Our girl tucks Lena's hair into her shirt collar. She quickly removes her own shoes, her pants, and then her still-damp underpants. She folds the panties in half and half again and tucks them in the paper-lined metal bin meant for soiled feminine hygiene products and their wrappings.

Lena moans into the toilet bowl. I want to go home, she says.

Naked from the waist down, our girl stoops and fishes the car keys from Lena's purse.

No, you don't, she says, and begins re-dressing.

As the girls wash and reassemble themselves at the sinks, their eyes meet in the mirror. Our girl nods and says, You're fine. Let's have a good time.

Lena smiles weakly. I'm fine, she repeats. They return to the casino.

. . .

In her bed, she'll go on. The room, she'll begin, remembering two queen-size beds with thin synthetic quilted coverlets in mauve and gold. All the lights turned on. No, the light was from the TV. Beer from cans in a torn box sitting on its side at the bottom of a small black refrigerator. But the sensible man will interrupt her.

Was it all four of them?

No. And she'll see in his face relief, the excess of which will force her to turn from him, to the window and the pinkening dawn. One of them left to get pancakes, she'll say. Allen. I gave him directions to IHOP.

Three, then, he'll say, his voice blank as a dead thing. And you two girls.

We started watching a movie. Something with Halle Berry. Lena said she'd almost done it once with her boyfriend in Minnesota. But.

Had she?

No. I told her she had to get it over with.

Had you?

Yes, she'll say. But not like that.

What did they do to you?

She will shake her head, a movement nearly imperceptible. It wasn't like that. Afterward, mine asked for my phone number. Tom, I think. He said, I really like you. Or something.

Did he ever call you?

This question will surprise her, and she will have to pause, trying to remember. No, she'll say eventually. I gave him the wrong area code. They thought we lived in the city.

And your friend?

Lena. She passed out on the other bed. I thought maybe she was faking. I don't know why. During the movie the big one got on top of her. Brad. He took off her clothes. Her eyes were shut but she was mumbling something. I don't know what. The other one spread her out, kind of. The big one spit into his hand. I remember that. I was on the other bed, with mine.

Jesus.

The other one put his dick by her face. He hit her with it, softly. They called her names. Drunk cunt. Fuck rag.

Jesus Christ.

Here, she will stop. Are you sure you want to hear this? she'll ask. Though she won't be able to stop even if he asks her to. He'll nod, slowly.

Lena woke up, she'll say, during. She got out of the bed and stood by it. They didn't try to stop her. She was naked, looking at the floor around her. For her clothes, maybe. Or the keys. But then she stopped and just stood there, looking at me. Tom—or whatever—was already inside me. She was just standing there.

Now Lena is limp in the light from the hotel television, as though, underneath her splotchy skin, her bones are no longer adequately bound together. She stares at our girl from between the two beds, her naked body like a question she can't ask, a prayer she can't recall. Behind Lena, the two young men look to our girl. The big one is shirtless, with his pants splayed open.

The other has removed his pants, though he still wears his collared shirt, buttoned up. His bare ass glows blue in the light from the TV and he holds his dick in his hand. She forces herself to wonder what they want from her, though she knows. Permission.

Once, before Lena got her license, the girls were waiting at the county clinic for Lena's mother to drive them home, and they found a file folder filled with pictures of diseased genitals mounted on heavy card stock. Lena said her mother used them when she gave sex-ed talks at the high school. Our girl flipped through them. Lena giggled and looked away, saying the pictures were gross. Our girl went on. They *were* gross, but in a curious, enthralling way, like a topographical map of a place she would never visit. But then there was one photograph in which the photographer, or the doctor—Who takes these pictures? she had wondered suddenly, then thought, A nurse, probably, or an intern—had captured the patient's thumb and index finger where they held the penis. She could see the man's grooved thumbnail and a little rind of skin peeling back from the cuticle. It made her wish she weren't a woman.

In the hotel room, Lena reaches for her friend. She says her name. The boys look to her too, even the one called Tom, above her. Our girl takes Lena's hand.

It's okay, she says. We're having fun.

She urges her friend back to the bed, gently, as though pulling the last bit of something shameful and malignant out through the tips of Lena's limp fingers.

Afterward, on the way down to the lobby, our girl watches

her own face in the polished doors of the elevator, and then Lena's, puffed around the eyes and mouth, her hair clumped to one side where they'd poured something on her. Through the summer, the tight circles in which the girls circumnavigate the pizza parlor will overlap less and less each day. Sometimes our girl will be at the oven, watching Lena's back as she works the line, and the heat will well up in her and she'll want to cry out. But what would she say? Sometimes, as she cuts a pizza, boiling grease cupped in a piece of pepperoni will spatter up and burn the back of her hand, or her bare forearm. This will bring her some relief.

That summer, Lena will shrink and yellow. Her eyes will develop a milky film. Even her big teeth will seem to recede into their gums, as though the whole of her is gradually succumbing to the dimensions of their town, its unpaved streets, its irrigation ditches and fields of stinking alfalfa. The four walls of the pizza parlor, the low popcorned ceiling of her mother's manufactured home. When Jeremy the delivery boy shuffles back to the walk-in where Lena stocks the commissary and asks her to come over to watch his band practice, she'll say yes, her voice wet with inevitability and exhaustion. The master bedroom of his trailer will start to feel like her own. Jeremy's love for her will be an unquestioning and simple thing, with rising swells of covetousness. It will be this particular strain of love—that's what he'll call it—that makes him hit her for the first time, on the Fourth of July, on the darkened plot of packed dirt in front of a house party where she'd danced too closely with a friend of his. Our girl will watch this from the porch of the house, where a crowd will have gathered. She will do nothing.

By September, she and Lena will not even nod in the halls. When the announcement comes over the intercom first period, our girl will try to make herself feel the things she is supposed to feel: grief for dead people in buildings she didn't know existed, sorrow for a place she can't envision. Deadened, but afraid of the deadening, she will look across the classroom to Lena, hoping to inflict upon herself that sickly shame that the sight of her old friend now evokes, thinking it the least she could do. But Lena— standing humped beside her left-handed desk with her right hand over her heart, crying—will be barely recognizable. This will bring our girl a sturdy rising comfort, a swelling buoyancy: A person can change in an instant. This, almost solely, will take her away from here.

The loudspeaker will emit a disembodied human breath. Things will never be the same, it will say, as if she needs to be told this. As if she doesn't know the instability of a tall tower, a city's hunger for ruin. As if this weren't what she came for.

THE PAST PERFECT,
THE PAST CONTINUOUS,
THE SIMPLE PAST

This happens every summer. A tourist hikes into the desert outside Las Vegas without enough water and gets lost. Most of them die. This summer it's an Italian, a student, twenty years old, according to the *Nye County Register*. Manny, the manager of the Cherry Patch Ranch, reads the story to Darla, his best girl, while they tan beside the pool in the long late sun.

"His friend found his way back and told the authorities, thank God. Seven days they give this kid to live out here." Manny checks his watch. "Well, six. Paper's a day old."

"Fucking tourists," says Darla, lifting her head from *Us Weekly*. She lies facedown, topless, on a beach towel laid over the sun-warped wooden picnic table she pulled next to Manny's cracking plastic lounger. Darla has worked at the ranch for two years, nothing to Manny's fifteen, but longer than most girls last out here, long enough to be called a veteran. She may have tits like a gymnast but she's smart for twenty and has a round, bright face with a gap between her front teeth that makes her look five years younger—a true asset in this business. Straight men eat her shit up.

Once, she and Lacy dyed their hair together, the same shade of coppery strawberry blond. Manny warned them it was a mistake. "Bad for business," he said. "Men want variety." But he marveled as the very next client to pass through the front door pointed to the two new redheads and asked, "How much for a mother-daughter party?"

Poor Lacy's lip began to quiver—as if she just realized she was old enough to be the girl's mother—but Darla simply slipped her fingers through Lacy's and said, "What do you think, Momma? Four grand?"

"Put that shit away," she says now. "You're depressing me."

Manny lingers on the story of the missing foreigner for a moment longer, more exhilarated than is respectful to a boy likely dying of thirst. He scans the other goings-on of the rednecks and dirt farmers and Jesus freaks in Nye. The Lady Spartans win the three-A state softball championship. Ponderosa Dairy petitions BLM for more land. He can't be blamed for wanting some excitement around here. He puts the paper under his chair.

Darla checks her phone and turns over on the picnic table, exposing her small stark breasts to the sun. She folds her magazine back along its spine and leans over to Manny, tapping a picture of a shirtless movie star standing in the Malibu surf, dripping wet. "I met him," she says. "In L.A. He used to come into Spearmint all the time. One of my girlfriends gave him a lap dance. Said he had a huge cock."

"Girl, don't tell me that. I'm so horny I could rape the Schwan's man."

"I'll trade you," she says, slipping her hand gingerly between her legs. "My twat is sore." She goes back to her magazine. Manny watches the heat waves warp and wobble the mountains in the distance. Six days. Poor kid. Soon, Darla lifts her sunglasses and presses two fingers to her left breast. "Am I burning?"

Manny presses his fingers to her tit. "A little."

"Good."

That evening, as the sun sets, a cab drops Michele at the ranch. He is twenty, the same age as his missing comrade. He's a student of civil engineering, a field he chose because he did not have the grades for medicine or the head for law. In a family like his, a boy has only so many options.

He pauses at the gate and looks up at the sky. A dense swath of stars cuts diagonally across it. If this trip had gone as it was supposed to, he and Renzo would be at the Grand Canyon right now. If everything had not in an instant become so horrifically and hopelessly fucked, they would have flown home in August, and when friends asked about his summer he would have told them of the unfathomable American landscape, the innumerable

American drugs, the indefatigable American girls. Or, if he was feeling wistful, he might have said simply, *It was beautiful. There were more stars out there than I've ever seen.*

Instead, here he stands, listening for helicopters searching for his friend, lost somewhere in the Nevada desert. But the helicopters wouldn't be searching at night; the police had said that at the station. It wouldn't do any good.

He imagines Renzo tilting his head back in the darkness. Looking up at the faraway mechanics of the galaxy, listening for helicopters that aren't there. The night before he disappeared, Renzo had pointed to the stars, an arm of the Milky Way adjacent to their own. He called it proof of something. He expounded on the ideas put forth in the books he read, about futility and hopelessness, ideas Michele had long since tired of. Renzo fancied himself a person with a cruel intellect and an unceasing sense of scale.

The cabdriver shouts from his window, saying something over and over again. But he's speaking English, and Michele understands only when the driver jabs his index finger, pantomiming pushing a button. *Where am I?* he wonders. *And what kind of bar has a doorbell?*

The buzz of the bell reverberates deep inside Manny's throat. The girls—showered, shaved, plucked, bleached, perfumed, lotioned, and powdered—arrange themselves in the neon-lit lobby facing the front door, waiting for him to open it, introduce each of them, and encourage the client to pick a date.

Darla hangs back, waiting for her place at the end of the line. She thinks she gets picked most from that spot, Manny knows. Every girl would rather be picked from the lineup than have to go push for a date in the bar, even Darla, who's a damn good pusher. Being picked from the lineup is a sure thing, cash in hand. This is how Manny convinced Darla to quit dancing in the first place. "Girl," he said, shouting to her over the squeal of distorted electric guitar inside Spearmint Rhino. "Stripping is like waiting tables, okay? Come work for me and you'll never have to beg for tips again."

Manny claps his hands. "All right, ladies. Remember, they don't come in here for interesting, okay? They come for *interested*." This is the first client they've had all night and they need the business. He opens the door. "Welcome to the Cherry Patch Ranch."

On the front step stands a good-looking kid with smooth olive skin, glossy black curls and eyes as bright and blue as the swimming pool out back. Manny hands him a packet of brochures and a menu, ushering him across the threshold. "Is this your first visit to the ranch?"

"Hello," says the kid softly, reaching to shake Manny's hand. "It is nice to, ah, meet you."

"Well. It's nice to meet you, too. You're welcome to have a drink at the bar or choose a girl and let her take you on a tour. All these lovely ladies are here to make you feel at home." Manny introduces the girls by their working names, the only names known here, a rule they need never be reminded of. Down the line they each say hello. They give a little wave and smile, and Manny can almost hear it in the space between their clenched teeth, louder than ever before for this polite, smooth-skinned kid with an exotic accent. *Pick me.*

First is Chyna, a heavy half-breed Shoshone in a plaid ruffled jumper outfit. Geoff, one of her regulars, brought the outfit for her as a present, hoping she'd give him an extra date for free, which she did, straddling him near dawn in the bed of his truck where they wouldn't be heard on the intercom system wired throughout the trailers, where they thought Manny wouldn't find out.

Next in line is Trish, a part-time beautician who does most of the girls' waxing in a heavily wallpapered salon in Nye called Serendipity. She charges them half price, and they tip her accordingly. Bianca is beside Trish, her hair painstakingly straightened and oiled, her waxy pink C-section scar peeking out from under her red panties. Her two daughters, preteens now, live with their grandmother during the week. They think their mother is a masseuse at a spa in Summerlin.

Lacy is next in line, and though Manny can't smell her from where he is, she's no doubt spritzed on too much Victoria's Secret Love Spell body spray. Beside her is Army Amy, wearing silver hoop earrings, frayed Daisy Dukes, and a squarish camouflage hat. She's topless, except for a pair of blue sparkly pasties shaped like stars stuck to her big nipples with eyelash glue. Amy is the ranch's big name, the only girl here who's done porn. It's her picture on the billboards, the cab signs, the snapper cards passed out by illegals on the Strip.

Next to Amy, Darla wears a black bustier and a dusting of

silver glitter around her eyes. She put the glitter on to satisfy Manny, who made her change out of the satin pajamas she wanted to wear. "Honey," he said, "those things makes you look—and I'm only telling you this because I love you—like a lesbian." She pretends to fidget with her garters now, looking innocent and eager at the same time. Her niche.

The girls are all angles: the apex of their plastic pointed heels, the thrust of their wet-looking lips, their jaws extended in stiff smiles, the jut of their nipples made erect from a hard, quick pinch just before Manny opened the door. Each angle is a beacon emitting its own version of the same signal. *Pick me, want me.* But the kid is fumbling with the brochures, not getting the message.

A lot of young kids drive out here on their eighteenth birthdays. They ring the bell long and hard in front of their friends, drunk on machismo and MGD from the mini fridges in their fathers' garages. *Watch me become a man.* How quickly they turn to boys again when they come inside and see the girls in the lineup, all tits and perk like they think they've always wanted. Most kids pretend to be lost, ask for directions back to Nye or Vegas, as if they weren't born and lived all their days within seventy miles of here. As if they didn't know what this was.

But this kid has no idea; that much is clear. He looks queerer here than Manny did his first time, and Manny *is* queer. Vegas cabbies are as attentive as any to the fresh currency plugging the pockets of overstimulated tourists. They drive them out to the brothels without telling them what they are, just to get the fare. Manny doesn't condone it, but when he hears the boy's velvety European accent he thanks God for doing whatever it took to set this fine white-toothed boy down in front of him.

Michele isn't sure how he ended up out here. He thinks he asked the cabdriver, back in Vegas, to take him to a bar where they wouldn't check his age. And the way the driver nodded and tapped the meter, asking whether he had cash, Michele assumed he'd been understood. In Italy, the legal drinking age is sixteen. The first time a clerk denied him and Renzo, they had been in San Francisco for two days. Renzo stormed out of the store, flailing his short thick arms in the air, shouting in Italian, "You Americans too moral for booze all of a sudden? We will just have to steal it then, like damn little children." Stupid, stubborn Renzo.

Michele shifts his weight from one foot to the other, the bulky white Nikes he bought at an outdoor shopping mall in Los Angeles looking too bright, like the shoes of a character on a children's television program. He looks over the papers he was handed, front and back, absently pushing his hair from his eyes. He recognizes vocabulary words but can't make sense of them in these odd couplings. Straight Lay. Chair Party. Reversed Half-and-Half. Not for the first time since he arrived in America four weeks ago, he wishes he had taken his language classes more seriously.

He turns to the man who answered the door—who, it seems, has been talking incredibly fast. Michele tries to explain himself but doesn't have the English. He makes useless gestures with his big hands and says finally, "No, ah, I am not . . . I am Italian."

"That's okay," Manny says, his hand on the boy's shoulder.

This, Michele understands. "Okay," he replies.

"Have a drink." Manny shows him across the room to the bar.

"Ah, yes. A drink." Finally. "I like Budweiser. How do you say, King of Beer?"

Manny doesn't card him. It's a slow night, better to keep him around than lose the customer. Better for business. You never make money on people leaving you. Jim taught him that.

Most of the girls see no business in the scared-looking teenager and return to the karaoke machine they'd paused when the doorbell rang. But Darla, Army Amy, and Lacy follow him to the bar. Manny fixes them their drinks. They jostle sweetly for a place at the boy's elbows, but Darla jostles sweetest.

"How do you say your name?" she asks, leaning into him.

"*Meh-kay-lay*," he says, drumming the syllables on the bar with his long middle finger.

"Meh-kay-lay. Like that?"

"That is it." He bends to kiss her hand. "Very smart lady."

Darla reddens. "Shut the fuck up."

"What is . . . ?"

"'Shut the fuck up'? It's like 'be quiet,' or 'I don't believe you.'"

"Who you don't believe?"

"You," she says.

"No, you," he says. "You shut the fuck up."

The boy drinks steadily. He pays for each beer with a smooth new twenty, gesturing for Manny to keep the change. Later, after the boy has gone, Manny will overhear Lacy and Darla gossiping in the hallway. Lacy will say, "Jeez. That kid must have spent eighty bucks on Budweiser."

Darla will correct her. "A hundred and twenty."

At the bar the girls ask Michele all about Italy, the fashion, the tiny cars, the Mafia. They make like they hang on his every word, but if you were to run into one of these girls on her next day out in Nye, at the grocery store or having a smoke outside Serendipity, not one would be able to tell you a thing about the climate of Milan or where Michele was when Italy won the World Cup. Because while he is talking they stare at him and nod in all the right places but think only this: *Pick me, pick me. Oh, God, let him pick me.*

Manny hasn't been much better. He lets his eyes rest on the boy too often, watching that full flush mouth having trouble with its English. The hands. The curve of the chest. He polishes the same pint glass for five minutes, sets it down, then picks it up again. He needs to keep busy or his thoughts slide into forbidden territory. Is it the heat that does it, or the dehydration? What does forty-eight hours without water do to a body?

He can't take it anymore. He sets the gleaming pint glass on the bar too loudly. "What were you doing out there?"

Michele tells them in slow, hesitant English how he lost Renzo. They'd gone to see the endangered desert pupfish, which their guidebook said live only at Devil's Hole, a supposedly bottomless geothermal spring outside Nye. "*Foro del diavolo*," Renzo had said, the danger dancing in his eyes.

But Devil's Hole was not anything, Michele says now, only a bathtub-size pool of hot water in the middle of nowhere, the rare fish just guppy-looking glimmers in the shadows. Renzo thought so, too. At the spring he was ill-tempered, railing that their entire trip had been ruined. He suggested—no, insisted—that they at least salvage the day by hiking out to the nearby sand dunes. "Go without me," Michele had wanted to say. But he could see the ochre peaks of the dunes swooping across the horizon; they seemed that close. And there was a trail even, meandering through the crumbly bentonite hills. Renzo had complained of this too, the trail; he wanted authentic desert, pristine wilderness. He kept asking, "Why must Americans turn everything into an advertisement?" That was the last thing Michele heard him say.

They'd been hiking only an hour, Renzo charging forward, Michele struggling to keep up, neither speaking to the other. Michele stopped to take a drink of water, to shake a rock from his shoe. When he stood up, his friend was gone.

He called for Renzo to wait, but there was no answer. He spit on the ground and watched the earth swallow the moisture. It was too hot for this. He followed the trail back and waited for Renzo in the air-conditioned rental car. But Renzo never came.

A nd we, ah, are, ah, separate," the boy says.

"You were separated," Manny says.

"Now, I wait." He nods to the bar, the brothel, the girls, as if they all have some arrangement.

"Wait for what?" Amy asks dully.

Michele is quiet for a moment, looking down at his large hands. "I wait, ah, for my friend," he says. "For his return."

Darla says, "Oh, you poor thing," and puts her arms around his neck. She says, "Don't you worry; they'll find him." She can probably smell him there, his cologne, his hotel soap. Cheap beer. Clean sweat. Salt.

Michele takes a swig of his Budweiser. "Yes, yes," he says, then swallows. "Then I go home. With Renzo."

Michele doesn't go back with Darla that night. It's slow. Geoff comes for Chyna, and afterward he presents her with another gift, a hideous gold-plated charm bracelet. Amy and Bianca take care of a pair of mortgage brokers from New Jersey, in Vegas for a conference. But Michele and Darla simply sit at the bar, talking. Under normal circumstances this would piss Manny off, one of his girls spending an entire evening with a man without taking him back. Under normal circumstances he would sit her down in his office and tell her, "You know I don't like being the bad guy, but at the end of the day I don't give two shits about making friends. Because, honey, if you don't get paid, I don't get paid, okay? Ask for the fucking order."

That's the way it has to be. These bitches would run all over him if he let them.

But tonight circumstances aren't normal. Tonight the thought of Darla—or any of the girls—taking the Italian back to a trailer for an hour, maybe two, makes him feel sick with something like jealousy. It must be pure hormones—he hasn't been laid in longer than he'd like to admit. Or perhaps it's the terribly familiar way the boy looks at Darla, his face flushed with booze and all the want and wonder of a child. He's seen that look before, on men two and three times this kid's age, men who knew better. He's seen Darla take everything they were willing to give, and more. That's what he's always loved about her.

When the cab honks in the parking lot at five a.m., Manny helps the drunk, sweet-faced boy down the front steps. As the sun comes up, he stands alone on the porch and watches the red taillights of the taxi shrink down Homestead Road, then up the hill toward Vegas. There's nothing but the lolling violet mountain range and spiny yucca and creosote and that taut ribbon of road as far as the eye can see. Poor Renzo doesn't have a chance out here, and sooner or later that beautiful boy is going to realize it.

Manny imagines the Italian looking back at him through the rear window of the cab. The ranch the boy would see looks like a dollhouse, down to its dormer windows hung with boxes of poppies and desert primrose. The wood siding is painted the bright fuchsia of deep flesh, the country trim a chalky lavender. Back east this building would be a bed-and-breakfast; in the Midwest it would be an antique store. But here there is a red light attached to the weather vane, rotating in the dawn. Here, it is what it is. Manny makes his way out back to the peacock coop.

Manny was hired to manage the Cherry Patch Ranch one day when he drove out from Las Vegas, where he grew up. He was eighteen, had been hustling for three years and always knew he was destined for something bigger, though it took a tranny john whipping him across the face with a stiletto for him to act on that instinct. Jim Hart—fifty then, with the girth and slope of an aging athlete and a full head of black hair just starting to gray—happened to be working the door that day, a stroke of luck, because Jim never worked his own door. Bad for business. Jim took one look at Manny and waved the girls off, saying, "Sorry, guy. We don't have men in here."

And Manny, prepared for this, said, "Why not? You're losing money, honey. You want to know what I get for a hand job with Rentboys? Three fifty. A hand job. And that's off-Strip, okay?"

Jim took him straight back to his office with Gladys, Jim's assistant. After an hour Jim said, "Look, guy, bottom line: Every other Tuesday I load the girls into the van and we go down to Nye County Health and get them all looked at. Every other Tuesday. And no legal hooker, not in the entire state of Nevada, has *ever* tested positive for an STD. Not even crabs. It's safe, clean sex. That's the brand. I bring men in here . . . I'm not messing with a good thing. That's all." He tipped back in his chair and put his pen into his mouth. "But a fag madam. That's unique."

That was fifteen years ago. Manny walks past the girls' fifth wheels lined in two rows behind the main house like eggs in a carton, with the courtyard and swimming pool between them. Beyond the fifth wheels are the single-wide trailers they call suites. The Oriental Room, the Hot Tub Room, British Campaign. The thick black wires of the intercom system droop between the buildings. The pool is ringed with knobby salt cedars and adolescent pomegranate trees. Manny drags Darla's picnic table back to the courtyard where it belongs, in the rocky dirt peppered with screwbean mesquites and young cottonwoods. He plucks a cigarette butt rimmed with lipstick from a struggling patch of sod, puts it in his breast pocket; then he slips out to the coop.

On paper, Jim Hart raised Indian blue peacocks until 1970, when he got his operating license. Prior to that, as far as the government was concerned, Hart Ranches made its modest living selling the birds to zoos and private collectors. In reality, Jim hated selling the birds and found reason to do so as seldom as possible. When the cost of the food and upkeep was considered, the peacock business barely broke even.

The girls always brought in more money than the birds, but it was a long time before the Cherry Patch Ranch was much more than two single-wide trailers on either side of the wide, airy coop. Then, in 1970, as Jim and his friends in Carson City had suspected it might, the state legislature outlawed prostitution in

Clark County. Jim remodeled, making the ranch straddle the county line, with the trailers and main house in rural Nye County, and the peacocks technically residents of Clark. By the time Manny arrived, the Cherry Patch was the closest a brothel could get to Vegas.

His second week, a courier came out and picked up three sedated chicks destined to roam some movie producer's estate in the Pacific Palisades. Manny found Jim sitting on an overturned feed bucket by the coop, bawling into his hands. When he noticed Manny standing there watching, Jim leaned back against the chicken wire. "Goddamn it," he said, and pressed the heels of his hands against his eye sockets as though he could stop his tears that way.

Manny squatted in front of the older man. "It's all right."

"I know that, kid," Jim managed to say, before he crumpled forward again, crying and hiccuping like a child. Manny held him, stiff and awkward as a Joshua tree, half-stroking his head. He was no good at these things.

They stayed like this a while, and just as Manny's thighs began to burn from squatting for so long, Jim calmed and his breath steadied, but he did not lift his face. Instead, he put his hand on the back of Manny's neck and urged Manny's head down toward his groin.

Working Jim's belt buckle loose with one hand, Manny was grateful as a pet: here was something he knew how to do. Jim finished in Manny's mouth, with a string of quick jerks that scraped the feed bucket along the ground, then zipped his

Wranglers and wiped his eyes. He squinted out across the sage-brush. "Jesus H.," he said. "It's like selling off one of your kids."

From that day on, Jim never sold another peacock. He named the remaining sixteen after Nevada's sixteen counties. Washoe, the eldest female, died in the winter of 2003, when coyotes got into the coop. One of her mates, Lander, died of old age shortly thereafter, though on darker days it's not hard for Manny to convince himself that Lander died of a broken heart. Now there are four females and ten males, including White Pine, a rare albino, red eyed and completely white, down to his feet and the tip of his thick, five-foot train.

After two years, Jim moved to Brazil. Retirement, he called it, though he was only fifty-two. He took his wife with him. When he left he said only, "Take good care of my babies, Manny boy. And the girls, too." When Jim comes out for the annual audit, wheelchair-bound these days, he spends most of his time in the shady coop, the fiscal year's ledger book open on his lap, his face tilted to the sun.

Manny, too, has come to love these birds. He feeds them at sunrise before he goes to bed, and again at dusk, after break-fast. At least once a week he takes a heavy-duty rake and cleans out the stalls, sifting out rocks and piss clods with the sturdy iron teeth. Sometimes he wakes and comes out to the shade of the coop at midday, when the girls are still asleep. He likes to watch the iridescent shimmer of blue all down the throats of the males, their shake and strut, the bobbing of their crests, the green and gold and red eyes spread across their fans. He admires the great effort with which they display, that they try so damn hard. Though a few of the girls complain about it, it soothes Manny to fall asleep to the trill and *ca-ca-caw* of the regal peacocks, the shades in his fifth wheel drawn against the desert sun.

He keeps a rosary in the coop, looped through chicken wire, and though he hasn't been to mass since he was thirteen years old, he's taken to praying out there some mornings, alone. To his mind, the coop at dawn is as close to holy land as there is.

That night, when the cab finally arrives at Michele's motel, the driver turns back to Michele and asks him whether he'd like to do it again sometime. And Michele manages, "Yes, I like very much."

The driver says, "Tomorrow, then?" Michele suspects this is meant to be a joke, but still he hesitates. Of course he's realized the place isn't just a bar. There are whorehouses in Genoa, and he's no altar boy. But the people there are friendly, and they don't ask his age. If he doesn't go back to the ranch, what would he do instead? Unpack and repack Renzo's bag, as he had the night before. Stare at the cell phone the police gave him, willing it both to ring and not to. Fiddle with the canteen—the only one they'd brought with them—that he was carrying when he abandoned Renzo. Try to imagine the feeling of three days thirsty.

The driver waits for an answer. God knows Michele can afford another run. Nevada Search & Rescue have given him a debit card for his living expenses. They said the money would come from the embassy, because he was foreign, that it was a loophole, a word he had to look up. The room he and Renzo had been sharing at the La Quinta on Tropicana was covered too. But before they'd explained all that, before they'd handed him the debit card, they gave him an international phone card and asked him to call Renzo's parents and explain what had happened. They were sorry to ask that of him, they said, but none of them spoke the language. An officer showed him to a little room with a phone on a desk beside a stained instant-coffee machine. The officer said Michele had better advise Renzo's parents to fly to the U.S. Then he shut the door softly behind him.

Michele wove the coils of the phone cord between his fingers for a moment. Then he lifted the phone, input the codes from the phone card, and dialed his own parents instead. His mother answered and asked whether everything was okay. She sounded more exposed than a mother ought to. He told her yes, everything was fine. More lies came warmly to him then. "Actually, something happened," he said in Italian. He told his mother he'd left his wallet out on the beach in Los Angeles and someone had taken his money. Not his ID, just the money. His mother comforted him. She teased him gently for being so naive. She thanked God that it was only that. She said she would have his father wire him more spending money. I love you, his mother said before she hung up. Be good.

Afterward, the officer returned and set his hand kindly on Michele's shoulder. He nodded at the phone and said, "We appreciate that." Michele said nothing.

The next morning, Michele used the debit card he'd been given at the ATM in the gas station across from the motel. He halfheartedly withdrew stacks of twenties until the machine beeped and spit out a warm, smooth sheet of paper. On his walk across the parking lot he was dully surprised to count five hundred dollars in his palm. Once in his room, he used his pocket dictionary to translate the words from the sheet of paper, eventually understanding that five hundred dollars was the maximum amount he was permitted to withdraw in a single day.

Since then, Michele has gone to the gas station every morning, buying a sugary Honey Bun and a squat carton of orange juice and withdrawing another five hundred dollars. Each morning he expects the machine to reject the card. If confronted about the money, he plans to say it was an accident, that he was confused about the machine or the currency, and hand the rest of it over.

On good days, he looks forward to spending the money on very good pot and Ecstasy that he and Renzo will take in the Grand Canyon. Even now, in the back of the cab, he imagines Renzo's face flickered by a campfire, the Colorado River sliding by. Renzo laughs hard at something, barely able to get his words out. A girl sits beside him, laughing too, and looking at Michele lovingly, with silver glitter dancing around her eyes.

"Tell it again," they are begging in Italian, tears rolling down their cheeks. "Tell us how you fucked the American cops for all their money."

"Yes," Michele says to the cabdriver now. "Please, you will come tomorrow?"

So the next day, as the streetlights come on and the shadows of the mountains grow long through the city, the taxicab returns and takes exit thirty-three west, spiriting Michele from Las Vegas up and over the Spring Mountains, out of that valley always saturated with light.

Manny watches from the peacock coop as a pair of head-lights turn off the highway. Hot, immediate hope for the Italian boy blooms inside him, though he knows enough about the tricks of lust and loneliness to recognize his thoughts as pure fantasy. He returns to the birds; Gladys can handle the lineup. But soon, over the scrape of his rake against the gravel, he hears the front door open and the breeze carries to him the famil-iar squeals of surprise that Darla releases for all her regulars.

Manny stops in his trailer to change his shirt, wipe the sweat from his forehead and armpits with a bouquet of toilet paper, and reapply deodorant. By the time he steps into the main house, Darla is refilling Michele's Budweiser. She flits and chat-ters around him like a hummingbird, finally perching herself on the upholstered stool beside him. Her legs dangle, not reach-ing the floor even with the added inches of her slick, clear-plastic heels.

"Did you go to the oh-six Olympics?" she asks. "In Turin?"

"Oh, ah, no." Michele laughs. "I live far from there. But I watch on the TV."

"Hella," says Darla. "I love the Olympics. I like the Summer Olympics best, swimming, diving, all of it. I would love to go sometime. I've never been to Europe. I've been to Mexico, Canada, Australia, and Costa Rica, but never Europe." This is a lie, one Manny must have heard a thousand times. Aside from the year she spent stripping in L.A., the girl's barely traveled as far as Lake Havasu for spring break. But the line impresses tourists and townies alike. They're pleased by the prospect of bedding a cosmopolitan whore.

"Yes, Europe is the best place for to visit. Take the train, when you go. The train is best."

"You know, if you had enough fucking money, and spent it, like, in one of those weird sports like riflery or table tennis or the ribbon routine—shit like that—anyone could be an Olympian. That's what I'm gonna do. Get a good trainer, a famous one, fucking quit my job."

She babbles on like that, and the boy seems to like it. That's the difference between the ranch and a strip club. Here, some men come in just to talk. Sure, they want a piece of ass so bad that they're coming out of their skin to pay for it. But there's something that brings out the lonesomeness in them. Maybe it's being so far from civilization. Manny's heard them afterward, over the intercom. Old men, young men, men with wives or steady girlfriends, men who've never had anybody in their whole pathetic lives. They listen to their date chatter until the hour is up, and when she reaches for her clothes or the white wedge of towel on the nightstand to wipe herself, they hold her tightly and say, so softly it might be mistaken for a blip of static over the wires, *Wait*.

The Italian returns the next night, and the next. Manny

watches him and Darla get closer. They talk at the bar, then huddled together on the couch in the lobby, then with their feet dipped in the pool, splitting pomegranates on the concrete and spitting the seeds and pith into the dirt.

The other girls are talking. One morning before bed, Amy's voice spills from the hall bathroom. "If Michele was one of these old farts, Manny would have pried him from that girl's titty on day one. He's just glad to finally have some ass around here."

Jim would not stand for this. But Manny cannot bring himself to throw the kid out. Amy is right: He likes having Michele around, and, yes, a part of him thinks, *Why not me?* His last hookup—in the hot soak room at the Tecopa baths, Mormon crickets shrieking in the eaves—was a forlorn, unmemorable thing, as all since Jim have been.

Manny spends more and more time out with his birds, away from the trouble swelling indoors. He knows he can't go on ignoring it forever, but he tries. He scrubs the salt deposits from the water troughs, hand-feeds the birds sardines and apple slices, and watches them strip a whole cooked chicken to the bone. He rakes and rakes the sand as the sun comes up, drawing intricate patterns like the monks on a show he saw once, as if the dirt were an offering to God.

On the sixth night, Michele is sitting close to Darla on the cheap red sofa in the corner, watching the other girls sing karaoke, when the buzz of the doorbell sounds throughout the bar. Michele notices for the first time small black blocks—they must be speakers—arranged throughout the room: above the glass shelves behind the bar, over the neon-lit lounge area, tucked up where the low ceiling meets the wall. The girls ebb to the front lobby, running their hands all over themselves while they walk, checking hooks and ties and the backs of earrings, adjusting their panty hose and breasts and hairdos. Darla stands up, runs her tongue over her teeth, and rolls something oily and fruit-scented onto her lips.

"Where you are going?" he asks the back of her.

Army Amy calls over the clacking of plastic heels on the laminate dance floor, "Don't you worry, sugar. We'll take care of you." She winks.

Without leaving the couch, Michele watches a thick-armed man step through the front doorway. Plastic mirrored sunglasses dangle from the man's neck by a fluorescent-colored cord. Flecks of cement speckle his work boots. He points to Darla and says her name. The two walk by the bar, arm in arm. She grins like a pageant contestant, a beauty queen. When the man isn't looking, she blows Michele a kiss. This girl is trouble. Renzo would have loved her. Renzo was always looking for trouble.

Listen to him: *Renzo was.* This is what unsettles him, how easily the past tense comes now. The police had said, *There is a chance. Maybe if the heat doesn't get too bad.* Even as Michele nodded, his tongue rolled silently through conjugation exercises. *He's young,* the cops have kept saying. *He's athletic.* And in his head, each time Michele has corrected them: He *was* young. He *was* athletic. Just this morning, Michele called the police station, and the woman who answers the phone said she was sorry, that there was no news, they would call the cell phone as soon as they found his friend. "But don't you worry," she said. "God works in mysterious ways."

And as if he dreamed in English, Michele replied, "Yes, He did."

All those years confusing the past perfect, the past continuous, the simple past, and now it comes to him, here. Now he thinks in the frantic notes he took before he quit trying altogether. *Simple past: use when an action started and finished at a specific time in the past. The speaker may not actually mention the specific time, but he does have one in mind.*

After the lineup, Manny returns to the bar with Army Amy. Michele joins them. Amy sets her overtanned tits on the bar, and they rest there like two globes in a skin sac. "I need a goddamn date," she says.

Michele smiles broadly at her—the big, openmouthed smile of a foreigner pretending to know what's going on.

Amy traces her finger up and down the boy's forearm. "Why don't you pour this kid a real beer, Manny?" Manny fixes Michele a pint of Boddingtons. The kid looks at the cloud of head billowing to the top of his new beer, mildly bewildered.

"Budweiser is piss," Amy says. "It's a joke here."

Michele takes a long swallow of his new beer. "When she will, ah, return?"

"Darla? Depends," says Manny. He calls back to the office. "Gladys, what'd she log?"

When he first started, Manny had asked Gladys whether she ever listened in on the suites, "You know, for fun?" Gladys only scoffed and said, "Fun? Baby, I've seen it all. My best client was a county commissioner. He used to drive his Buick all the way down from Tonopah once a month, just to have me tap on the floor with his dead wife's peg leg. This was before you were even born."

"Hold on," she says now. They hear the click of the old intercom buttons as Gladys patches in to the suite. "Nothing special, baby," she calls. "Just a suck and fuck. A grand."

Manny whistles. Half of that is his. "Damn. That girl's got a gold mine between her legs."

"Big deal," says Amy. Through her tank top she grips a breast in each hand and lifts them to Michele's face, first one and then the other. "Think what she could do with some assets." Michele looks away, and who could blame him? No one outside the industry would call Amy a beauty. She has big biceps and a bench-press chest left over from her time in the army, where she was supposedly a Green Beret. Whenever a new ad comes out, she flashes the proofs to anyone who will look, listing all the places the billboards will go up: off I-15 near Indian Springs, by the turnoff to the test site, on 395 in Stateline for all those rich, horny Californians. On the latest, Amy is saluting and smiling above the words, *Visit Army Amy for an honorable discharge!*

Amy swirls her finger in the foam of Michele's beer. "When I was her age, I had to work for my money. I was hosting big parties. I'm talking twelve, thirteen hours of straight fucking. You learn a lot that way." She sticks the finger deep in her mouth and licks it clean. "You want me to teach you, Luigi?"

Michele shakes his head.

"Come on. Won't cost you no grand."

He takes a drink of the Boddingtons and says, "Shut the fuck up, you."

Amy straightens on her stool. "I know you want to make an honest woman out of her, Luigi, but your little prom date is—how do you say?—sucking some Teamster's cock right now. Get it?"

Michele knocks his pint glass over, and beer soaks her wife-beater. Amy jumps back, dripping.

"I am sorry," he says. "Very sorry." He lays cocktail napkins impotently on the spreading puddle of beer.

She sets her jaw and leans in close to him. "I bet you'll fuck me now, you wop drunk."

"That's enough," says Manny.

"Me?" says Amy.

He wipes the spill with a dry rag. "Go change."

Amy gathers the hem of her shirt and wrings it out. "I know what you're thinking, Manny. Don't bother. She's got this kid's dick on a string. And you?" She laughs. "You're shit out of luck."

The empty pint glass rolls off the bar and shatters on the laminate.

Manny looks straight at her. "Go change or go home."

Amy stomps out the back door. Manny comes around and helps Michele pick up the glass from the floor. A few girls have gathered around. Lacy tries to help, but he waves her and the others back to the couch, to a pair of Southern truck drivers they called in off the road with the CB in the office. Something tortured and twangy and sour rises from the jukebox.

Michele, squatting on the floor, leans into Manny, so close that Manny can feel the boy's breath on him. "When she will finish?" Michele asks.

Looking back, this is the moment when he should have known how truly fucked he was. But this is closer to the boy than he's ever been, and he can't help himself. He only wants to touch him. He presses his rag to Michele's wet T-shirt. It's impossible, but he feels the boy's warmth underneath, the striations in the muscles of his chest. He feels his heartbeat. "One hour." He removes the rag and holds his index finger in the air between them. "One hour."

Michele finishes his replacement beer, and another. By the time Darla says good-bye to her Teamster, logs her cash with Gladys, and joins the boy at the bar, he's a heavy, lethargic kind of drunk, leaning on his elbows, his eyelids wilted. Manny watches Darla rest her head on his shoulder, chewing on the stir straw poking out from her cranberry juice. No doubt she can feel the warmth of him, the pulse of blood in his neck. "Did you know that tug-of-war used to be an Olympic sport?" she says. "I could do that."

With his mouth half in his new pint glass, Michele says, "You can do anything. You are a gold mine."

And then Darla does something Manny's never seen her

do. She takes Michele's face in her hands and bends him down to her. She kisses him softly on the forehead.

D ay seven. At the motel Michele lies staring at the untouched bed across from him. He hasn't slept in days, not really. When the red-orange glow of sunset permeates the crack between the two heavy panels of curtain covering the west-facing window, he gets out of bed and showers without soap or shampoo, though there are fresh supplies of both on the shelf in the shower, still sealed in their waxy sanitary paper. He keeps the water so hot that when he finally steps onto the linoleum and wipes the condensation from the bathroom mirror with his palm, his skin is flushed pink where the water began to burn his back and shoulders, his stomach and buttocks and balls. He sits on the edge of the bed, naked.

He and Renzo have been friends since they were boys playing for the same youth football club. They went to university together, took the same classes, shared a room in the dormitory, then in a basement apartment near campus. Every morning for three years Michele woke up to the shape of Renzo against the opposite wall, or stepped over piles of his soiled clothes to get to the toilet. But already Michele cannot recall Renzo's hands, or the sound of his laugh, or the exact expression on his face when he was angry. All he can see is this smooth quilted square of bed, this worn white sheet pulled taut over these too-full pillows like dead open eyes in the daylight. All he can hear is the chug of the air-conditioning unit along the west wall, the underwater sound of cars idling in traffic along Tropicana Avenue, and the Search & Rescue cell phone on the nightstand ringing ringing—at long last—ringing.

That night the doorbell buzzes, and Manny looks over his lineup before opening the door. Darla is nowhere to be found. He last saw her on the couch with Michele, who's missing, too. Manny does not open the door. Instead, he leaves the other girls standing there and finds Gladys in her office. She sits with headphones to her ears, half smiling, her mouth hanging loosely open. The light of Darla's fifth wheel glows on the switchboard. "Young love," says Gladys.

The doorbell buzzes again. "Come *on*, Manny," calls Amy from the lobby. "Let's get this show on the road."

Manny motions to Gladys. With the same reluctance with which she pauses her tape of the previous day's *General Hospital* to log cash, Gladys takes the headphones off and stretches them over Manny's head, nestling the coarse black foam over his small ears. Darla's voice comes through the crackle and fuzz of the old intercom.

"You don't have the fucking Academy Awards in Italy? That's crazy. I love the Academy Awards. Ask me a year."

"I don't, ah . . ."

"A year, a year. Ask me. Go on." A game she plays with all of them.

"Nineteen ah, seventy . . . four?"

"*Godfather II.*" A pause. Manny pictures Michele's smooth, perpetually puzzled face. "That's what won Best Picture that year. Ask me another."

"Okay. Nineteen ninety . . . one?"

"Easy. *Silence of the Lambs.* Too easy, none from the nineties."

"Nineteen fifty-two?"

"That would be . . . *The Greatest Show on Earth.* DeMille."

"Nineteen thirty-eight?"

"*You Can't Take It With You.* Fucking classic Capra. Funny. Sad. Optimistic. One of my favorites."

"You are very good."

She can do Best Actor and Best Actress, too. The boy wouldn't know the difference if she were making them up, but she's not. She can list them all, every single year, forward and backward, which she does, she says, in her head when she's standing in the lineup or straddling a new client or lying in bed trying to sleep, listening to the shrieks of the peacocks chasing one another around the coop.

There's a faint rustling sound in the headphones. Manny hears Darla gasp, then say, "Shit, Mikey, where'd you get that?"

"They gave it to me, to live, to wait for Renzo."

"How much do you have?" The intercom crackles.

"I am not sure. Here." A longer pause. The doorbell buzzes again.

"There must be nine, ten grand here. What—"

The connection fizzles, submerging Darla's voice in static.

Manny shakes the cord furiously. He presses the headset to his ears so hard they sting. When the connection returns Michele is saying, "Come, ah, with me. To Italy."

Manny presses his hand to his heart. That stupid boy.

The doorbell buzzes, long and loud, and for a moment it is all Manny can hear.

"I will come tomorrow," Michele says. "And we will go." Dumb, big-eyed Michele. "We, ah, fly home," he is saying. "Tomorrow."

Before she can answer, Manny presses the speaker button. "Darla," he says. "The lineup. Now."

When Manny finally opens the door, the chunky man who's been buzzing spins his keys on his index finger and steps inside, tonguing a monstrous divot of tobacco down in his bottom lip. He picks Darla, though she barely bothers to look at him. What did Manny expect? Michele, this fat fuck, they're all the same, stumbling in from the middle of nowhere, trying to fill the empty space in them with her.

In the morning, after feeding the peacocks, Manny says a little prayer and then steps into Darla's room, where she's watching a black-and-white movie. She motions him to her and they lie together on the twin bed, head to toe. He says, "What are we watching?"

"*You Were Never Lovelier*," she says. "Fred Astaire. Rita Hayworth. It's public access."

Manny rests his cheek on the tops of her bony feet. Rita Hayworth spins through Buenos Aires, all sheen and tinsel. "Honey," he says finally, "you really like this boy?"

Darla keeps her eyes on the screen. "Is that why you came in here?"

"He's been through some shit."

She shrugs. "Him and everyone else around here." She shifts her feet under the blanket. "You know I love you, Manny. You've been hella good to me. But that boy is my ticket out of here."

"Girl, this is for real. You're gonna hurt somebody."

"Hurt somebody? What happened to 'Give 'em a little attention'? What happened to 'Make them feel better than their girlfriends, better than their wives, better than they are'? You don't have to touch these men, Manny. You don't have to fuck their sorry asses. You sit out there stroking your goddamn peacocks, writing letters to Jim about what a good boy you've been, how much money you've made him, hoping he won't die on you. You come inside to sign the paychecks, to tell me I might hurt somebody? Too late, old man. I been hurting them. And you taught me how."

When Michele leaves the La Quinta the next night, he leaves it for good, Renzo's backpack laid out on his bed. Amy opens the door before he buzzes, and takes him to the bar. "Have a seat, baby. Budweiser?"

"Yes. Please."

She puts a beer on a napkin and beside it sets a little shot glass filled to the top with brown liquor. "For courage," she says. Michele drinks it and pats the bundles of twenty-dollar bills in the pockets of his cargo shorts. It's all there, the Search &

Rescue money from the teller machine, the two thousand dollars his parents wired him, his own money. Renzo's money. He's made up his mind. He can't go back to Genoa. His flight leaves in the morning. He'll buy a plane ticket for Darla. An engagement ring. Put a security deposit on an apartment in another city, away from his family. Away from Renzo's friends. God, Renzo's family. He feels his new life folded inside his pockets. Yes, a whole new life for nine thousand American dollars, he believes this. A new life with a woman there to busy his hands, to pour his drinks, to help him forget. A life where he came to America alone. Or not at all.

He waits. The night pulls on. He reaches around the bar for the tap and refills his own glass when he needs it. Men come and go around him, but each time the bell reverberates through the building it's the old woman who opens the door for them. He waits for Darla, but she never comes. When he asks about her, none of the girls will answer him. His head is hot and clouded and his cab isn't coming until morning. He doesn't know what else to do. He walks outside through the dust and gravel to Darla's fifth wheel and knocks on the door and then the windows. The lights are off but through the blinds he can see the paper-lined drawers of her dresser pulled half-open and empty, and the bed where he last saw her, stripped bare. He looks in the other trailers. He calls for her. There is no answer.

Somewhere in the night Amy comes and pours more shots. She lines them up on the bar like tiny monuments. They drink them together, one after another. "Where is she?" he says finally, a stinging in his voice.

She pours them another round. "Here."

"Tell me."

"I don't know," she says. "She was just gone. I swear."

Near dawn, Manny appears from the darkness of the hall-way and puts his hands on Michele's shoulders. "Walk with me, honey."

As he follows Manny out the back door, beyond the lights and sounds of the compound and into the desert, Michele looks to the sky. So this is what Renzo looked upon as he died, naked and faceup in the dirt: the wide brightening sky, the fading stars, the waning moon white like a jaw on the horizon. A peacock caws. A part of him—the part that speaks in a ghost's voice—knows he'll never see Darla again.

The peacock coop is shaded from the pink-purple of dawn by palm leaves and canvas overhead. The air is thick with the scents of seed and dust and bird.

The boy hesitates before coming inside. "These are, ah, your pets?"

"Not mine, my boss's. I hear you're headed out of town. You're leaving."

"Yes, I go back to Italy."

"And you think you're taking Darla with you."

"She, ah, would like to leave. She has told me." A bird rustles in its nest. "I, ah, like Darla."

"I liked her, too," says Manny.

"I love her."

"Honey, I know. But she didn't love you, okay?"

"She does," he says, though he says it like a question.

"American girls, you don't know how they are. All they care about is money, okay? Especially these girls. Don't you know? It's all business. Even with Darla."

"Where is she?"

Manny combs his fingers through a trough of seeds, letting the breeze winnow away the empty shells. "Don't worry about it."

"Tell me where is she."

"This is a business, kid. She had somewhere else to be." There is a stillness pulled tight between them. Outside, dawn lightens the landscape but the last dregs of night linger in the coop. "They found your friend, didn't they?"

Michele picks at the chicken wire. "Yes." Then quickly, "No. They said he is dead. They stopped looking."

He turns away and hooks his fingers through the chicken wire. His broad shoulders start to tremble. He begins to shake the entire wall of the coop back and forth, harder and harder, until Manny fears he might snap the old two-by-fours. The birds, startled from their roosts, squawk and dart around, frenzied, among them the bright albino flash of White Pine. All the while Michele wails, a feral, guttural sound.

"Fuck, kid," says Manny, too quiet to be heard. "Come on." He pulls Michele back and turns the boy to face him. Michele's face is wet and slick where he's bloodied his nose against the fence. Manny embraces him. The boy writhes at first, then goes limp and lets his head fall to Manny's shoulder. He is sobbing.

"My boss, Jim," Manny says, maybe just to have something to say. "The one who owns these birds? He's dying, too. Half the time he doesn't even know who I am. You think it's not going to happen, and then. But these girls—"

"I, ah, have to take her," Michele says, shrugging him off. "I love her."

Manny takes Michele by his shoulders and turns him gently to face the yellow lights of the ranch in the distance. "Kid," he says softly. "Look. There's no love in there. Trust me."

Manny lets his arms wrap around the boy's waist and presses him close again, from behind. For a moment—just a moment—the birds are still and Manny feels warmth against him.

Michele wrenches away, shaking his head. "No—"

"She never cared about you," says Manny, hot with want, walking toward the kid. Burning. Michele shoves him back, hard. The peacocks are screeching now, and flapping, but there's nowhere for them to go. Manny comes at him still. "She didn't. You're a kid." The boy tries to leave, groping drunk for the gate in the half-light. "A stupid, sad, foreign kid with a dead friend and too much money. That's all you are, understand? I did you a favor."

Later, Manny will say it happened quick—the swing so fast it was a blur, the boy all sweet inertia, a dervish, and the rake's prongs just a flash. Then he left, waited for his cab on the side of the road and never came back. But in truth Manny sees everything slow. The boy's arched back. The contours of his ribs through his T-shirt. The blood around his nose and mouth already maroon with coagulate. His triceps made taut by the weight of the tool. The swing misses Manny so wildly that he doesn't even move his feet. Michele wrenches the rake's metal teeth into White Pine's chest.

For an instant the air is filled with the report of the sternum snapping. Michele's never seen a bird like this. The snowy feathers redden as blood wells up around the prongs. He feels the give of the meat as he plies the rake from the bird's breast. Its beak opens and closes, leaking the tight sorrowful cry of a baby, a cry that will come to mean America.

WISH YOU WERE HERE

It begins with a man and a woman. They are young, but not so young as they would like. They fall in love. They marry. They have a child. They buy an adobe house in a small town where all the houses are adobe. The McDonald's is adobe. The young man is named Carter. Carter often points to the adobe McDonald's as proof of what a good decision they made in moving away from the city. The woman, Marin, is also glad they've moved here, but she misses her friends, and the constant sound of city traffic whispering like the sea. She feels this little town tries too hard.

As soon as Carter and Marin learn they've conceived the child, they begin to argue about it. What will they feed it, what will they teach it, what of this world will they allow it to see? They fight about these things before the child is more than a wafer of cells. Before the child is anything, it is a catalyst for fights.

All the fights are the same fight: Carter wants to be sure Marin will change for their child. She has irresponsible habits. She eats poorly. She never exercises. She is terrible with money. She smokes and watches too much TV and gets bored easily and antagonizes people at parties.

Carter used to be fine with her habits. They were the things he once loved about her. Marin points this out, many times. She asks who it is he thinks he married. A child changes things, he says. A child is sacrifice. This is inarguable, and eventually she gives up arguing it. Each day he has a new stream of questions about what kind of mother she will be.

Does she plan on using disposable diapers?

Of course not.

Will she allow the child to watch television?

Only in small amounts. No. No. Not at all.

Will she use a microwave to heat the child's food?

Never.

When he was a boy, Carter says, his family had a garden where they grew fresh fruits and vegetables. He's told Marin about this garden, many times. The garden was monstrously fecund. His mother spent days and days in their basement, canning its yields. He wants to know, Will she garden? Will she can?

Of course, she says.

Why does she say this? She doesn't know. She is not willing to can.

Marin never cooks. For dinner, she likes to make herself

cereal or cheese and crackers or half an English muffin with mayonnaise and a microwaved egg on top. This is another thing that will have to change. Carter never cooks either, but this is not something that will have to change. Carter has seven brothers and sisters and when he was a boy, he says, his mother made them all a healthy, hot meal, every single night. She never used a microwave.

When he was a boy, Carter says, his family never ate out. He and Marin are always eating out. Their refrigerator is crammed with wire-handled Chinese takeout boxes and containers of pasta with the lids pinched on and Styrofoam clamshells of crab cakes and vegetable quesadillas and leftover restaurant steaks wrapped in aluminum foil. Marin pretends to be apologetic about these—it's just that they're so busy, she says. But she likes eating out. She is comforted by the choreography of a restaurant. And she likes to bring the leftover steaks to bed and gnaw on them, cold, while she watches TV.

A memory Marin often excavates during their arguments:

They'd been dating only three months when Carter asked her to meet his parents. It had just rained and the two of them were walking to the BART station, trading easy jokes about the terrible, bombastic movie they'd just seen. Carter stopped on the shining, still-wet sidewalk and took her hand. Come home with me, he said. She loved the urgency of the question, and how fearlessly he asked it.

The next morning they drove from San Francisco to Seattle, then continued north to a suburb of Seattle. It was his mother's fiftieth birthday, and their visit was a surprise. When they arrived, Carter's mother held Marin as though she were her own baby. His mother did not have a bank account, Marin learned. His mother did not have a driver's license. She was cooking her own birthday dinner.

In the kitchen, Marin wanted to seem helpful. She opened the door of the pantry to reveal a wall of hand-canned fruits and vegetables. The stained-glass colors of tomatoes, yellow squash, zucchini and green beans. Carrot spears, halved beets, apricots, rings of apple. Small shriveled pickles and relish and a row of homogeneous dun-colored jams. Pearl onions like eyeballs.

In the pantry Marin said, I need some air. No one heard her.

She walked to the tennis courts across the street and smoked just a tiny bit of a stale joint she kept in her compact. Small white moths flitted silently in the halos of the court lights, and she watched these until she felt a little better. She returned to the house and over dinner she saw quite clearly that she was attending the birthday celebration of a fifty-year-old woman who had never had an orgasm.

On the long drive home, Marin sat silently with her anxieties, turning them over in her head. She had a tendency to be self-destructive, she knew. Before Carter, her life had been a string of beautiful, aloof men with names like the four legs of a very sturdy table. Even now she had the urge to call one of them up and see if he still knew his way around her. She could pass a whole day inflaming the listlessness inside her with erotic fantasies of men who, for the most part, had been unkind to her.

When was she going to grow up?

She looked at Carter. He smiled, bleary-eyed from the drive, and put his hand on the back of her neck. She was twenty-nine. He would be a good husband. A wonderful father. He loved her as though it had never occurred to him that he could feel otherwise. She wanted to be someone who deserved a love like that. She smiled back at him and cracked her window, feeling the stale air sucked from the rental car. She inhaled deeply, and when she exhaled she let her doubts slip out the window with her breath, littered them all along I-5.

Six months later, in April, Marin and Carter were married beneath a copse of papery crab-apple blossoms in Golden Gate Park. Carter had already found an impressive job in the progressive high desert town with the strict zoning laws. A place to raise a child. They bought their first car and hitched it to their moving truck and towed it out of California. Every hundred miles or so Marin asked Carter to pull over, and when he did she opened the door of the U-Haul and vomited on the side of the road.

They arrived in the adobe town and the questions began. Now Carter comes home from work and wants to know, what has she eaten today?

Has she exercised?

How much water has she drunk?

What is her temperature?

Did she nap?

In what position did she sleep?

I don't want to talk about it, she sometimes says.

We have to talk about it, he says.

He's right, she knows. They are going to have a child together. They have to talk about everything. They will always have to talk about everything.

The baby grows inside her. Carter brings home fruit and leafy greens and obscure whole grains Marin has never heard of. Before bed—when once he would have touched her—he leans down and speaks to her midsection. He insists on massaging her neck and feet, which do not bother her, and the knots running along either side of her spine, which do. Under his hands Marin cannot help but return to his mother's pantry. Everycolor walls of foodstuff close in around her. White moths flit around the watty bulb dangling from the ceiling. How briefly her life was her own.

Then, when the child is born, something unexpected happens. Carter's questions cease. Now the child has been here for eleven weeks and it is as though his points are moot. Or if not moot, then at least he does not raise them. She can tell he would like to—she can see their shadows traveling occasionally across his face—but he does not. Perhaps he finally loves her for who she is. Perhaps he sees that she is trying. Perhaps he is as tired as she is.

The weeks since the child was born have been exhausting but rewarding, too. The child lifts its head. He smiles. He sleeps on his father's chest. Marin takes photos. The child will want to see this someday.

This weekend they are taking their first trip as a family, meeting up with married friends from the city to go camping at Lake Tahoe. On the plane the baby sleeps and Carter sleeps and in this peace Marin thinks for the first time how good it will feel to see these old friends from when they were young. She opens the in-flight magazine and there in the center spread are photos of the lake and captions which compare its waters to precious gems. Emerald. Sapphire. Aquamarine. She can see them there on the white ring of shore. Val. Jake. Old friends from before the child. How she's looked forward to sitting beside them on the shore of the largest alpine lake in North America.

They meet their friends at the campsite. Val and Jake have children of their own. They also have a dog. The children are four and six. The dog is a reddish color, a copper retriever. The group goes down to the water: Carter and Marin, Val and Jake, the children, the infant and the dog.

The beach is rockier than Marin would have liked, but the water is clearer than she could have imagined. Val and Carter swim with the children. Carter makes a spirited effort to teach the boy the front crawl—It starts with a glide, he says. The glide is everything—but the boy loses interest. Marin sits with the baby on a blanket under an umbrella. The baby wears a hat.

The dog runs wild wild wild. Runs like it's never run in its whole dog life. Jake throws a tennis ball and the dog brings it back. The dog wants so bad it doesn't know what it wants, and each time it returns Jake must wrest the ball from the folds of its wet black lipflesh. Jake throws the ball out into the water. He wears a baseball cap with white sweat lines creeping up the band. Once, the dog jumps up and knocks the bill of the hat, and Jake lifts it slightly to reposition it. Marin is shocked to see he's lost most of the hair on the top of his head. His thick, sandy blond hair, once hearty as dune grass. She cannot imagine when this would have happened.

Each time the dog emerges from the lake it shakes itself violently, spraying Marin and the baby with stinking dog water. Jake ought to do something about this but doesn't. Marin tries to position the umbrella so as to protect the baby from both the dog and the sun, but the maneuver is impossible. She grows to hate the dog. The damn dog's name is Mingus. In her head she calls it Dingus. In her head she says, *Go away, Dingus. Dingus, go lay down. Bad Dingus.* Down the beach, a young couple is lying wrapped together in a single towel, kissing. Dingus bounds up to them and begins to growl. Jake calls to the dog, ineffectually. Sorry, he calls down the beach.

Poor kids, says Marin.

They're young, Jake says. Plenty of time for that.

Marin scoffs and Jake turns to her. He nods to the baby in its hat and says, Been a while?

Marin looks up at him, squinting. Too long, she says.

Carter and Jake had been on the diving team together in college. Of course, she ended up with Carter, years later. But it was Jake first. Marin can still remember the first time she saw him, in the backyard at a house party, standing barefoot in the moist grass, shifting his weight gently from one foot to the other. There was a crowd gathered around him. He rubbed his hands together and pursed his fine lips. His eyes met Marin's for a moment; then he flung himself backward, landing sturdy and fantastic on his bare feet. His audience applauded, begging drunkenly for more as Jake slipped back into his shoes.

By sunset the gang returns to camp. Jake and Carter walk to the store to get beer and marshmallows. Despite their considerable protests, the children are forced to stay behind. Val and Marin start dinner. The baby sleeps faceup on a blanket in the shade. The children throw rocks and bark chips at Dingus. They scream at each other constantly. Val does not seem to hear them. A snaky twilight settles over the lake basin. There is a smell of wood smoke and the fires of adjacent campsites visible between the branchless trunks of pine.

The men return. Hatless now and rosy headed, Jake sets a twelve-pack of IPA on the picnic table, where Marin is shucking corn. Carter goes to the baby and lifts him from the blanket. Nearby, reddening charcoal biscuits throb in the campsite grill. Val sorts through the groceries the men brought. She turns to Jake, wagging a wet package of hot dogs at him. Why did you buy these?

You like them, Jake says. Remember? We had them in Mammoth. You were surprised how much flavor could fit into such a skinny frank.

But I have chicken, says Val, gesturing to a plastic bowl where breasts, legs, thighs and wings have been marinating in blood-colored barbecue sauce.

The boy says, Get over it, Mom. Chicken is old cabbage.

Yeah, says the girl. Old cabbage.

The boy says, She's copying me.

Val is a sport. She looks at Marin and shrugs. Old cabbage, she says. I don't know where he got that.

Marin has a beer with her frank. She catches Carter

glancing at the beer from across the table. She has not had a drink in nearly a year. But she can tonight. Marin stopped breast-feeding a week ago. She was an underproducer. When the child was born she could pump just an ounce from the right breast, two from the left. Carter kept a chart. The pediatrician told her to drink more water. She did, constantly, but it was never enough. The baby had to get fifty-one percent of his milk from the breast, Carter said. Fifty-one *at least*. Marin tried Mother's Milk herbal tea. She tried blessed thistle. One fenugreek capsule a day. Two. Three. A prescription for Reglan. Still, she was expressing only three ounces on the right and two on the left. His word, *expressing*. Finally, they went to formula entirely. Another disappointment her husband has endured silently.

Or silently until today. In the rental car on the drive up from Reno he asked whether she was experiencing any pain from stopping. Any pressure.

No, she said.

No, said Carter, thoughtfully. I guess you wouldn't.

After dinner the troop roasts marshmallows. The boy inevitably pokes his sister with his roasting stick. She cries and pouts and is not satisfied until Val puts him in time-out in the cabin of the RV. In the commotion of discipline and fairness, Marin retrieves another beer from the cooler.

Carter fetches the diaper bag and mixes a bottle using the jug of distilled water he bought at the store. He feeds his son, burps him, and passes the child to Marin. She paces with him around the site, waiting for him to fall asleep. Val, Jake and Carter sit in camp chairs near the fire. Jake smokes a cigar.

The little girl—Sophie is her name—climbs into her mother's lap and squirms there. She asks, What does that baby like?

Val strokes her hair. I don't know, Bug. Why don't you ask Marin?

Who's Marin?

The baby's mommy.

The girl considers this and then takes leave of Val, scrambling into dusty stride with Marin. Marin? she says. What does your baby like?

Marin considers the question. He likes milk, she says. And baths in the sink. And binkies.

And toys? asks Sophie.

And toys, says Marin.

What does he do?

Not much, really. Eats and sleeps, mostly. Poops.

Marin thought this would make the girl laugh, but it doesn't. Sophie considers the information, then says, Because he's just a baby.

That's right.

Can I hold him?

Marin glances at Carter. He is watching them. Of course you can, says Marin.

Marin directs Sophie to sit in her folding chair and extend her arms along her lap. She lays the child in this cradle and rotates the girl's hands at the wrist so they curl around the baby. There, she says. Just like that. Carter watches. Sophie is stern faced, taking this responsibility seriously. Though her feet swing a little, gleefully.

Marin retrieves her beer from the mesh pouch of the chair. You're good at that, she says, then immediately regrets it when the girl smiles a smile so wide it requires the active involvement of all her facial features. Christ, thinks Marin, what a thing to say.

Just then, Sophie's brother emerges from time-out. The boy processes the scene—the baby in his sister's lap, all adult eyes on her—and says, No fair. I want to hold the baby.

Sophie is pure joy. You can't, Aidan, she says. *I* am.

Aidan says, But—

Carter stands. The baby has to go to sleep now, he says. It's his bedtime.

Marin scoops the child from Sophie's lap and follows Carter to the RV. Inside, Carter tries to set up the Pack 'n Play they've brought—never *playpen*—so the baby can sleep there. Val and Jake have two tents, one for themselves and one for the children. It will be too cold for the baby to sleep outside, which is why Carter and Marin were offered the RV in the first place. But now it appears the Pack 'n Play is too wide, the space in the RV too narrow. Carter allows the half-expanded structure to fall noisily to the floor.

Now what are we supposed to do? he says.

As though Marin designed the Pack 'n Play. As though she engineered the RV. She says, What about the bed?

Carter considers the bed Val has folded out for them, converted from two bench seats and the dining table. Will he roll? he asks.

How surprised Marin is to be asked this. How satisfying it feels that Carter does not have the answer.

No, she says, shaking her head casually. He can't roll.

Okay, Carter says. He builds a barrier of pillows and sleeping bags at the edge of the bed. He swaddles the child and lays him on his back—always on his back—in the center of the bed. As Carter pulls the door of the RV quietly closed, he pauses with a hand still on the knob. The smell of Jake's cigar has made its way to them. Those pillows, says Carter. You sure he'll be okay?

He'll be *fine*, she says. He can't roll.

Of course he can't roll. She wouldn't have suggested putting him on the bed if he could. The baby is too young to roll. He won't roll for weeks. The books say so. The pediatrician says so. He can reach his arms above his head and sometimes he sort of scissor-kicks his legs inside his sacklike pajamas, but he cannot roll.

But the baby *can* roll. Once, she laid him on his back in the center of their bed back home, in the adobe house. He was asleep. Carter was at work. She hopped into the shower. She had to. She had a cheesy something behind her ears and in the creases of her knees. She washed her hair and used the lather from the shampoo to wash her body. She did not use conditioner. She did not shave. She kept the bathroom door open. Five minutes, tops. She stepped out of the shower and looked into the bedroom and the baby was not where she'd left him.

She ran to the bed, naked, dripping wet. Then she saw him.

Half wedged beneath her own plump pillow. Still breathing. Thank *God*, still breathing. She lifted the pillow. He must have rolled in his sleep. How true, she thought, once the panic began to recede, once the baby was laid safely in the Pack 'n Play, once she was dry and dressing. To be capable of a thing only in a dream-world. This was two weeks ago, nearly. She never told Carter.

Outside, Jake and Val put the children to bed in their tent, finally, and the adults settle into the story world of old friends. Marin gets another beer. Bent over the cooler, she can feel the warmth of the fire on her back and her husband watching her. She won't look to him. Not tonight. She won't see his once-fine face drooped with disappointment. She will not, *will not* look to him. She feels as though she has been looking to him her entire life.

Around the fire it is old times. Remember? they ask. Remember walking home through South Campus? Remember filling Sandy's mailbox with crushed beer cans? Remember our illiterate landlord on the Strand? Remember that note he left us; oh, how did it end? They all say it together, roaring: *I will not be tolerated*.

Jake brings out a pipe and a baggie from a cloth coin purse. He offers it to Carter.

Carter says, No, thanks, man.

Jake extends the pipe to Marin. Em?

Em. He used to call her that.

Marin takes it. What the hell? They smoke a bit, Marin, Val and Jake. After some time, Marin exhales and says, Remember when we used to climb up on my roof and smoke?

Jake smiles and says, Remember watching the fireworks from up there?

Marin says, Remember Tarv?

Christ, Tarv!

Jake's roommate. Tarv had gotten fucked up and was doing a happy jig to celebrate how fucked up he'd gotten when he stomped through the rotted roof of Marin's apartment building. Marin and Jake climbed down the ladder as fast as their laughter would allow them. They left Tarv wedged in the building, his leg dangling through a neighbor's bedroom ceiling. Remember, remember, remember. Whatever happened to Tarv? How did they turn out to be anyone other than who they were on that roof?

There is a little stretch of quiet and in this they can hear the distant voices of other campers and the hoot of a night bird. On the ground at Jake's feet Dingus runs a dream run, then whimpers, then is still. Val stands and announces she's going to bed. Everyone tells her good night. Marin looks at Carter, the firelight making long shadows on his face. He ignores her. For a moment she cannot remember why. She grows afraid. He is staring into the fire and she looks at it too. Her *husband* will not even *look* at her. Why? Where is he?

Marin tamps down her fear and goes to pee in the darkness. She can see stars while she's peeing, and these stars remind her of the town they will return to. She realizes she has no one there and grows afraid again, out in the trees with her pants down.

Once, early on, Marin took Carter to visit her hometown, the T of two state routes in the Mojave desert. They drove there and spent a night at the motel where she and her childhood friends used to jump the fence to swim in the kidney-shaped swimming pool. He was the first man she'd brought home in a very long time. Jake had not been interested in that sort of thing.

That night, Marin and Carter swam in the pool, alone. He held her in the soft water and kissed her, the rough beginnings of his beard chafing against her neck and her jaw and her collarbone. When the pool lights turned off, he lifted her to the edge and untied the knot at the back of her neck. He took her nipples into his mouth, first one, then the other, and after he said, I've been wanting to do that all night. Then he pulled the crotch of her bathing suit to one side and fucked her like he hasn't since.

We used to play a game here, she told him, when they were finished. I forget what it was called. But the premise was this: Marco Polo without the calls. Someone was It and the rest of them would say nothing. The pool was small, but it hadn't seemed so then. Back then it seemed extravagant. Of course, visiting with Carter she saw that it was the least the town could do.

In the game, the It would have to *feel* where they were. No talking. No calling. Just old friends in the too-warm water. There were times when the It would be right in front of you, and you would be holding your breath, and It would reach out and touch the lip of the pool instead of you. To get away you had to slip down into that silky chlorinated dream. How inadequate that felt, to It. To be so sure you were reaching for a friend. Someone who knew you. And to touch only concrete. The lip of a swimming pool. It ought to mean something.

She has to get back. She finds a firelight in the night and makes her way to it, hoping it is theirs.

Jake is there, alone. She sits beside him. Hey, she says.

Hey, he says.

Carter go to bed?

Jake nods to the RV. Baby was crying, he said. You didn't hear?

I never do.

Well. Jake stands. He laughs a little, to himself.

What? she says, standing and stepping toward him.

Remember when you pushed Miles into the fishpond? he says. At Corinne's parents'. Remember?

Marin nods. She remembers everything. She moves closer to Jake. She can smell cigar on him. She can see miniature reflections of the fire in his eyes. She can see herself underneath him.

He provoked me, she says, and hooks her fingers in the waist of his shorts.

Jake smiles and tilts his head to the right slightly, the way a curious bird might. Then he steps back, allowing her hands to fall from his waistband, shaking his head. He tosses something—a twig? a pine needle?—into the fire. My God, he says, kindly. What a nightmare you must be.

Jake goes to bed and Marin sits in his chair and props her feet on the warm rocks near the fire. She puts her face in her hands. She lived alone once, for a year and a half, in the building where Tarv fell through the roof. Sometimes, in that aloneness, she did weird things. She walked around her apartment wearing a piece from a Halloween costume—a pair of white silk gloves, usually, or an eye patch—or as many pieces of jewelry as she could, or a bathing suit under her regular clothes. She took pieces of metal into her mouth to get a feel for them. A coin, a pin, an earring. In her bathroom mirror she flicked her eyeliner pencil twice on her upper lip to make the two tines of a dashing, charcoal-colored mustache. She would say words that she liked out loud. *Pith. Coalesce. Dirigible.* She wasn't lonely. It wasn't that. She was the opposite of lonely.

It has gotten late, somehow. Marin kicks dirt inadequately over the coals of the fire and goes to bed.

In the RV she wedges herself on one side of the bed. Carter is on the other. Between them, the child. Eleven weeks old tomorrow. As long as Carter's forearm. What does the child do? Lift his head. Reach. Speak in a tonguey language of all *l*s and *o*s. Lie between them. On the drive to the airport this morning, the sun still not risen from the horizon, Carter said, quietly, This is not how I pictured things.

There is so little room on this arrow of bed. She can feel the bundle of child beside her. She is light with youth, with once-love, and also heavy with the disintegration of these. In this specific gravity she slides into sleep.

She dreams she is wrestling with the copper retriever, groping in its mouth for the tennis ball. Grappling with Dingus on a rockless beach. Rolling through reeds. Green-gray follicles succumbing in the wind. They tumble. She is up to her elbows in the warm, wet lining of Dingus's dog cheeks. She is laughing, rolling over mounds of perfect hot white sand. In her sleep she says, What does your baby like? In her sleep she says, This is not how I pictured things. In her sleep she rolls on top of the child and suffocates him.

She wakes, too terrified to scream, and begins to dig at the blankets. There are so many of them—hundreds. The soft, papery blankets of babies, the substantial bulky blankets of adults. They all smell of wet dog. Carter is there. Right there. He moans. Between them—somewhere—is the mass of her child. Their child.

Then her hands touch skin. A very small body. She feels it in the dark.

Breathing. Alive. Yes, alive.

She lifts the baby, not gently, and presses him to her. The child begins to cry.

Carter sits up in the darkness. Where? he says, thick-tongued and sleepstruck. Not what. Not who. Where? *Where are you?*

MAN-O-WAR

The fifth of July. Milo slunk out and sniffed around the dry lake bed while Harris loaded his find into the truck. The bitch was a pound mutt—mostly Lab, was the old man's guess—and the abandoned stash was a good one, like last night's festivities never got to it. At least fifteen Pyro Pulverizer thirty-three-shot repeaters, a load of Black Cat artilleries and Screamin' Meamies, some Fortress of Fire and Molten Core mortars, probably three dozen Wizard of Ahhhs and one Man-O-War, a hard-to-find professional-grade shell pack, banned even on Paiute land after an Indian boy blew his brother's face off in '99. It was a couple grand worth of artillery, all told. The largest pile Harris had ever found.

Every Fourth of July kids from Gerlach, Nixon, Lovelock, and Indian kids from the Paiute res came out to the Black Rock with their lawn chairs, coolers of Miller, bottles of carnival-colored Boone's Farm for the girls. They built themselves a bonfire, got thoroughly loaded, and shot off fireworks. The lake bed had no trees, no brush, no weeds to catch fire, just the bald bottom of an ancient inland sea. They dumped their Roman candles and Missile Heads and Comet Cluster shells and Komodo 3000 fountains in a heap away from their encampments, out of range of the fires, then trotted out there whenever they wanted to light them off.

Except out here the night got so dark and the kids got so loaded they'd forget where they stowed their fireworks. They'd forget they even had fireworks. They'd drink like men, like their fathers and uncles, like George fucking Washington, take off their shirts and thump their chests and scream into the wide black space. Pass out in their truck beds and let their tipsy girlfriends drive them home all in a line. Leave their stash for an old man to scavenge come sunup.

Harris moved quickly now, working up a sweat as the sun burned the haze from the valley. He unbuttoned his shirt. Finished loading and ready to leave, he called Milo. He slapped his thigh. He whistled. But Milo didn't come.

Scanning, Harris could barely make out a shape in the distance, warped by the heat waves already rising from the ground. He drove to it, keeping an eye on Ruby Peak so he'd know his way home. Out here a person could get turned around and lose his own trail, each stretch of nothing looking like the next, east looking like south looking like west, not knowing where he came on the lake bed, and not knowing how to get home.

The shape in the distance was Milo, as Harris thought it would be, bent over and sniffing at a heap of something. The truck rolled closer and stopped. Harris got out, softly shutting the door behind him.

"Come here, dog," he said. But Milo stayed, nosing the pile.

It was a girl—a young girl, Mexican—lying on her side, unconscious. Maybe dead. Harris circled her. She wore cutoffs, the white flaps of pockets sticking out the frayed bottoms. She was missing a shoe, a thick-soled flip-flop. A white button-up man's shirt tied in a knot exposed her pouchy belly. Her navel was pierced, had one of those dangly pink jewels nestled inside. Rising below the jewel was a bruise, inky purple, the size of a baseball. Or a fist.

Milo licked at the vomit in the girl's black hair, matted to her head. Harris pushed the dog away with his boot and crouched over her. He laid his hand on the curve of her calf. Her skin was hot; the early morning sun had begun to burn her. She was breathing, he saw then, but barely. Her lips were dry and cracked white as the lake bed itself. No doubt she hadn't had any water in God knows how long. Her dark fingernail polish was chipped. Fifteen years old, maybe sixteen, but she was wearing a truckload of makeup and he couldn't tell with these kids anymore.

Harris shook the girl gently, trying to wake her. He looked around and saw no one, only dirt and mountain and sky. He poured some water from his jug and wet her lips with it. It was an hour and a half to the trailer clinic in Gerlach, and they couldn't do much more for her than he could. His knees popped as he hoisted the girl and positioned her body across the seat of the truck.

"Let's go," he said, and slapped his thigh. Milo came then, slowly: sharp ears, bad eyes, bad hips, a limp of one variety or another in all four legs. Harris squatted and lifted the dog to the bed of the truck.

The truck sped for six, seven miles over the white salt crust of the lake bed. Harris watched absently for dark spots of wet earth. When it had the chance, the Black Rock held moisture as if it remembered when Nevada was mostly ocean, as if it was trying its damnedest to get the Great Basin back underwater. It would be near impossible to dig the truck out of the mud by himself, even with the squares of carpet he kept in the bed for traction. And there was no time for that.

The tires of the Ford crunched the dirt, leaving a pair of faint tracks. Harris turned and followed two tire-wide ruts of crushed sagebrush. The road shifted from weed to dirt to gravel. Harris bent and put his face to the girl's. He felt her breath against his cheek. He turned once to check on Milo, her tail wagging against the fireworks he'd forgotten he'd come for.

The road shifted twice more: to State Route 40, that hot belt of shoulderless asphalt, and then to Red's Road, the ten-mile stretch of gravel that led up the alluvial fan to Harris's slumped brick house.

Harris carried the girl inside. She didn't stir when he laid her on the couch, nor when he slipped her remaining sandal from her softly curled toes. Milo milled underfoot, sniffing at the sandal on the floor where Harris set it. "Don't even think about it," he said. The dog retreated to sulk in front of the swamp cooler.

Figuring it would make her more comfortable, Harris unknotted the girl's shirt. Though he'd already seen the twin juts of her pelvis and the slope of her stomach—she wasn't leaving much to the imagination—his hands fumbled and his breath went shallow while he buttoned the wrinkled flaps back together, not sure what he would say if, at that moment, she woke.

But she woke only once that afternoon, delirious. It was all he could do to make her drink, tap water from the mason jar sliding down her stretched neck, wetting her chest, pooling in the divots above her collarbones. While she slept he checked on her often, felt for a fever, held a moist washcloth to her forehead and cheeks. He cleaned the puke out of her hair by dabbing at it with damp paper towels. All the while the bruise on her abdomen seemed to throb, to shape-shift.

There was only so much he could do. He tidied up the house while she slept, washed the dishes, made his bed, trimmed Milo's nails. He could not remember the last time he'd had a house-guest, if the girl could be considered such. At least sixteen years. And though she was unconscious, having the girl there cultivated a bead of shame in him for the years of clutter he'd accumulated, with no one to get after him. The living room was walled with hutches and shelves and curio cabinets that had once been full of trinkets long since removed by Carrie Ann, off for another extended stay at her sister's while he sat smoking on the porch, too angry or afraid to ask what she needed with her Kewpie dolls in Fallon.

And then she was gone for good. The shelves now held his rock collection: igneous feldspars, quartzes, olivines and micas on the east wall; sedimentary gneiss and granoblastics on the built-in along the north; shale, siltstones, breccias and most conglomerates along the west wall, minus the limestones, gemstones and his few opals, which he kept in the bedroom.

Plastic milk crates lined the edges of the room, full mostly of chrysocolla chunks pickaxed from the frozen rock above Nixon the previous winter. A few were marbled with nearly microscopic arteries of gold. Dusty, splitting cardboard boxes were stacked four and five tall near the coat closet and in front of it, full of samples to be sent to the lab in Reno for testing, to tell whether or not his claims had finally paid off, whether he might augment his miner's pension. The rusted oil barrels on the porch and wheelbarrows out front overflowed with dirty schorl and turquoise and raw malachite in need of cutting and tumbling, specimens enough to supply a chain of rock shops from here to San Francisco.

Harris tried straightening up, but there was nowhere to put it all. Even the single drawer of his nightstand was filled with soapstone and milky, translucent chunks of ulexcite waiting to be labeled.

He kept an eye on the lake bed too, though whoever left the girl would most likely know better than to come looking for her. It was a hundred and six degrees by ten a.m. The only person with any business out here this time of year was Harvey Bowman, a Jack Mormon from Battle Mountain, and that was because the government paid him for it. But Harris knew full well that

Bowman kept his BLM Jeep parked at the Mustang Ranch, a hundred and fifty miles away, where the trailers had swamp coolers chugging on the roofs and it was never too hot for sex. Bowman got laid more than Brigham Young himself.

The lake bed was dead. Whoever left the girl out there wasn't coming back, and anyone who wanted to find her didn't know where to look. For this Harris found himself strangely pleased.

For dinner he fixed a fried bologna sandwich and a bowl of tomato soup. He was in the kitchen, fishing a dill pickle from the jar with his fingers when the girl woke.

"Where's my shoe?" she said, propping herself up with her arm.

"That is your shoe," said Harris.

She looked down. "So it is." Her face turned sickly and Harris rushed to her just in time for her to dry-heave into the pickle jar. The girl lifted her head and looked at Harris squatting in front of her. Her face hardened. Out of nowhere she stiff-armed him in the gut, toppling him back on his haunches. Biled pickle juice sloshed down the front of him.

The girl looked wildly to the door.

"Relax," said Harris, rubbing his ribs where she'd hit him. "I'm not going to hurt you. I found you on the lake bed. This is my house. I live here. You've been out all day."

He got to his feet and slowly handed her the mason jar from the windowsill, and a dishrag to wipe her mouth. "Here." She eyed the jar, then took it. Three times she drained it, sometimes coughing softly, and each time he refilled it.

"Thanks," she said finally. "What's your name?"

"Edwin Harris," he said. "Bud," he added, though he hadn't been called that in years.

She looked around, assessing, it seemed, the house and its contents in light of their belonging to an old fart who wanted to be called Bud. Harris asked her name. "Magda," she said. "Magdalena. My mom's a religious freak."

"Magda, you're lucky to be alive," he said. "The hell you doing out there alone?"

She dabbed her mouth with the dishrag and looked lazily about the living room, swirling the last bit of water around the bottom of the jar. "Drank too much, I guess," she said, giving a little shrug. "Happy birthday, America."

He nodded, and went to his bedroom for a clean shirt. Drank too much. That's what he'd figured, at first. Kids partied on the lake bed year-round. Harris often heard the echoes of screeching and thumping they called music. Out here they could see the headlights of Bowman's BLM Jeep coming from fifty miles away, if it came at all. The whole area was off-limits, but most kids knew as well as Harris did that paying one man to patrol the entire basin, from the north edge of the lake bed all the way to the Quinn River Sink, almost a thousand square miles, was the same as paying nobody.

He returned to the kitchen. This girl seemed different from those kids, somehow. She was beautiful, or could have been. Her features were too weary for someone her age.

Magda motioned to the dog, lying in front of the swamp cooler. "Who's this?"

"Milo," he said. "She found you. You likely got heatstroke. You should eat." He brought her a mug of the soup and refilled her water.

She took a bit of soup up to her lips, nodding politely to the dog. "Thanks, Milo." She looked around, not eating, spooning at her soup as though she expected to find a secret at the bottom of the mug. "You're a real rock hound, no?"

"I do some lapidary work," he said.

"You at the mine?"

"Used to be. I retired."

Magda set her soup on the coffee table. She picked up a dusty piece of smoky quartz the size of a spark plug from the shelf beside her and let it rest in her palm. "So, what do you do out here?" she asked.

"I make by," he said. "I got a few claims."

"Gold?"

He nodded and she laughed, showing her metal fillings, a solid silver molar. "This place is sapped," she said, and laughed again. She had a great laugh, widemouthed and toothy. "The gold's gone, old-timer."

"Gold ain't all gone," Harris said. "Just got to know where to look." He pushed the mug toward her. "You should eat."

Magda regarded the soup. "I don't feel good. Hungover."

Milo lifted herself and settled at Harris's feet. Harris scratched the soft place behind her ear. "I drove you in from the lake bed," he said, gesturing out front. "I got a standard cab. Small. You didn't smell like you drank too much. Didn't smell like you drank at all."

Magda set the quartz roughly on the coffee table and leaned back into the couch. "That's sweet," she said dryly.

Harris walked to the pantry and returned. He set an unopened sleeve of saltine crackers in Magda's lap. "My ex-wife ate boxes of these things."

"Good for her," said Magda.

"Especially when she was pregnant," he said. "I suppose they were the only thing that settled her stomach. Used to keep them everywhere, on her nightstand, in the medicine cabinet, the glove box of my truck."

Magda touched her belly, then quickly moved her hand away. She considered the saltines for a moment, then opened the package. She took out a cracker and pressed the salted side against her tongue. "You can tell?" she asked, her mouth full.

Harris nodded. "What, twelve weeks or so?"

The question bored Magda, it seemed. She shrugged as though he'd asked whether she wanted to bust open a geode with a hammer and see what was inside.

Carrie Ann had taken a hundred pictures of herself at twelve weeks. Polaroids. The film had cost a fortune. She wanted to send them out to family, but, as with so many of her projects, she never got around to it. So for months the photos slid around the house like sheets of gypsum. After she lost the baby, when he couldn't stand the sight of them anymore, he collected every last one, took them to work and, when no one was around, threw them into the incinerator.

He took the quartz into his own hand now and pointed it at Magda's abdomen. "You want to tell me who did this to you?"

He spit on the crystal and with his thumb buffed the spot where the saliva landed.

"It was my boyfriend," she said. She snapped another cracker in half with her tongue. "But he only did it because I asked him to."

Harris felt instantly sick. "Why'd he leave you then?"

"Because he's a fucking momma's boy. He'd just finished when we saw BLM coming. That ranger goes to Ronnie's church. We're not supposed to be together." She smiled. "He said he'd come back for me."

"Hell of a plan."

"You think I don't know that? He just took off." She folded another cracker into her mouth.

"He could have killed you, hitting you like that."

"What were we supposed to do? His mom was threatening to send him to Salt Lake to live with his grandma just for going out with me."

"What about your folks?"

"Forget it."

"Jesus," Harris said softly.

"I tried him." Magda laughed. "*La Virgen*, too. Nothing."

Harris decided to let the girl be a while. He turned on the AM jazz station and had his evening smoke on the porch. Through the screen door came Dizzy Gillespie, Charlie Parker, Fats Waller, Artie Shaw. When he returned, Magda was biting into the last saltine in the sleeve. "Can we turn this off?" she said, and without waiting for an answer hit the power button on the radio.

Harris went to the pantry and brought out the whole box of saltines. He set it on the coffee table. "You want, you can take these with you." She eyeballed the box. "I'll give you a ride," he said. "We got to get you home."

"I know. It's just . . . I'm still feeling a little sick." She combed her fingers through her hair. "I wonder would the ride upset my stomach even worse, you think? Probably I should stay here, just for the night. If that's okay with you, Bud."

This was a lie, he knew, though her face gave up nothing. He didn't like the prospect of explaining to the authorities why he was hiding a runaway. And there were her parents to consider. If he had a girl, he'd beat the living shit out of anyone who kept her overnight while he was looking for her. The county was full of men—fathers—who'd do the same or worse.

And yet he said nothing, only sat for a moment with his hands on his knees and then walked to the linen closet to get the girl a quilt and a clean pillowcase. He'd take her home. First thing in the morning. The girl smiled up at him as he handed her the linens. What was one night?

His sleep was fitful and often interrupted. He had to piss constantly these days and crossed the hall as quietly as he could, hoping the girl would not notice. When he did sleep he dreamed vile scenes of stomachs and fists, babies and blood. Once he woke sure he'd heard the throaty chafe of Magda's voice at his bedroom door. *Levántate.* Around four a.m. he started to a faint knock, imagined. An erection strained against his shorts. It'd been some time since he was blessed with such and so he quietly took advantage. After, he slept soundly through the remaining nighttime hours.

Harris rose in the early violet of the morning, antsy with a feeling like digging on a fresh plot of land. He dressed in clean blue jeans, white cotton socks, boots and a fresh white T-shirt. He tucked an unopened pack of filterless Camels into his breast pocket, poured himself a mug of coffee and walked quietly through the living room to the porch, so as not to wake the girl.

Carrie Ann had been gone since the spring of 1991, having cleared her Kewpie dolls and floral china out of the curio cabinets, wrapped them in newspaper, married a state trooper she'd met in Fallon while she was—yes—staying at her sister's. She'd long since moved with the man to Sacramento. Their miracle baby was almost sixteen. And still Harris accommodated her by smoking outside.

He'd stirred the shit a little when, a new bride, she forbade him from smoking in the house. He went on about a man's home being his own and hadn't he earned the right, but in truth he didn't mind being shooed outdoors. He was even patient later, when she implied that his smoking—combined with his single glass of bourbon in the evening—was the reason they were having such a hell of a time conceiving again, that he ought to take better care of himself, and finally that he didn't give a shit whether they made a baby or not. But it could not be said

that Harris made things easy for his young wife. He never held
Carrie Ann's temper against her—in his head he forgave her
before she even apologized—but just the same he never let on
how it soothed him when she let off steam, that seeing her angry
was effortless next to seeing her hurting. And where was the
harm, he figured, in letting his hotheaded wife guilt herself into
a steak dinner, a foot rub, a blow job?

Somewhere in their bickering Harris decided to cut back,
to exercise a grown man's discipline. But what was once discipline had over the years become mindless routine, four smokes
a day: morning, after lunch, midafternoon and sundown. His
cigarettes helped mark the passage of time, especially on days
that seemed all sun and sky, when he scolded poor Milo just to
hear the sound of his own voice. The dependable dwindling of
his cigarette supply reassured him that he hadn't been left out
here, that eventually he would have to ride into town and things
would still be there, that the world hadn't stopped whirling.

Magda was awake now, and he could hear her shifting on the
couch. He rubbed his cigarette out on the side of the Folgers can
he kept on the porch and dropped the butt inside. In the living
room, the sun was filtered through the yellowed paper window
shades, lighting the room warmly. Harris let the screen door
swing shut behind him. Magda's lids lifted at the soft *schwack*.

She arched her back, stretching catlike. "Morning," she said.

"Coffee?" he said.

She made a face and pulled the old quilt up under her arms.
She'd slept in her clothes. "Mind if I shower?"

"We should get you back."

"Come on, Bud. I reek." She looked up at him, smiling sweetly. "You don't want to ride in that cab with me."

It had been a long time since a woman had tried to convince him of anything. "Be quick," he said. "Hot water don't last but twenty minutes. Pump leaks." She shuffled down the hall, still wrapped in the quilt. He called down after her, "I apologize for the hard water."

"It's all right," she said, poking her head out the bathroom door, her shoulders already naked. "We got hard water, too."

Steam soon billowed from underneath the door, thickening the air in the hall. Water beaded on the metal doorknobs and hinges. Harris heard the squeak of her bare feet pivoting against the porcelain. From what he'd seen of her while she slept, it wasn't difficult to imagine the rest. He busied himself cleaning the coffeemaker and filling Milo's water dish, though the dog preferred to drink from the toilet.

Eventually, the pipes squealed closed and the bathroom door opened. Harris turned to see Magda standing in the doorway, one of his thin maroon bath towels tucked around her like a cocktail dress, her hair wet-black, curling at her shoulders, her bare collarbones. She held her dirty clothes in a wad under her arm. Milo limped to her. The girl bent and scratched the dog under the chin. Without looking up, she said, "Mind if I borrow some clothes?"

Harris was uneasy at the idea of her pilfering his drawers, her fingers running over the flecks of mica among his graying underwear. But better that than him choosing clothes for the girl. "Go ahead," he said. "Bedroom's on the left."

"Bud." She turned, smiling, strands of wet hair clinging to her skin. "This house's got four rooms. I been in three of them."

When Magda emerged from the bedroom she wore a black T-shirt, a pair of tall white socks pulled to her knees with the heels bulging above her ankles, and Bud's royal blue swim trunks. They were old, like everything in this place—except Magda herself—with yellow and white stripes running up the sides. They were short, even on her small frame. She must have hiked them up.

She stood in the doorway dipping the pad of her middle finger into one of his dented pots of Carmex and running the finger over her lips until they glistened.

"What are we doing today?" she said.

"Doing?"

"Let's go swimming," she said. "Bet you know all the hot springs."

"Swimming? Sweetheart, this ain't sleepaway camp."

She sat cross-legged in the recliner, setting it rocking and squeaking. "You're too busy?"

The only thing he'd been busy with in two years was her. "Somebody's bound to be looking for you."

"Nobody's gonna come looking for me," she said. She got up and walked out the door.

Harris wished something painful she was right. He wiped his hands dry on a dishrag and followed her out to the porch.

"Come on now. We have to get you home."

"I'm not going home."

"Why not? Because you did something dumb? Because your

novio's a son of a bitch? That don't mean nothing. Plenty of girls your age get into this situation."

"Bud," she said, turning to him and squinting in the sun.

"What about your parents? They're probably scared out of their minds."

"Bud," she said again.

But he went on, partly because she needed to hear it and partly because he didn't at all mind the sound of someone else's voice saying his name over and over again. "Shit, kid, if I was your dad—"

"You're not."

"I'm just trying to say—"

"Bud, you're a fucking idiot," she said, laughing that mean laugh into the open expanse of valley. "You think I'm worried about my *boyfriend*? The Mormon *virgin*?" She laughed again. "I told Ronnie we got pregnant by taking a fucking bath together. Want to know what he said? 'I heard that happens sometimes.'" She lifted the T-shirt and swept her hand across her belly, her bruise, the way a person might brush the dirt from a fossil to expose the mineralized bones underneath.

Harris said, "Who, then?"

"Don't ask me that." She put her middle finger into her mouth and scraped some of the black polish off with her bottom teeth. "Please don't."

They stood staring a long while, her at the valley and him at her. He watched her come right up against crying, then not, instead saying, "Fuck," which was what he wanted to say but his mouth had gone dry.

"It's all right," he said, finally. "Let's go for a swim."

She looked to him. "Really?"

"I'll get you some shoes."

They left Milo behind and took Route 40 in the direction of town for fifteen miles, and even though Harris kept saying, "It's all right," he could tell Magda didn't trust him. She sat stiff, with her right hand on the door handle, and wouldn't look him in the eye until he took the Burro Creek turnoff and Gerlach began to shrink behind them.

Some heifers were grazing on the long swaths of bluegrass and toadflax that had sprung up on either side of the spring, bright plastic tags dangling from their ears. The truck rolled to a stop at the edge of the alkali field, and a few of them lifted their heads to notice, but most kept their mouths pressed to the ground, chewing the dry grasses. Harris shut off the truck. "Here we are."

"It's beautiful, Bud. I didn't even know this was out here." Magda got out of the truck and shuffled through the tall grass in Harris's bed slippers. Harris followed her to where the water ran downhill from the spring to a clear, rock-bottomed pool.

"It's Indian land," he said. "Technically."

She pulled the slippers and socks from her feet. "Those Indians have all the luck."

He sat and watched her dip herself into the water, clothes and all. Wet to her waist, she turned to him. "You coming?"

"Nah."

She stumbled on a loose rock and slipped farther down into the water. "Come on. Aren't you hot?"

Harris shook his head, though he was burning up.

Magda pinched her nose and dipped her head under, pushing her hair from her face with her free hand. When she came up she said, "That feels good." She paddled a weak breast-stroke over to a half-submerged boulder and hoisted herself onto it. She lay there on her back, the wet clothes pasted to her body.

Harris looked away. He dug his fingers into the dirt around him—a habit—looking absently for something to catch the glint of the sun. Magda sat up and said, "What were you like as a kid, Bud?"

"Oh, I don't know."

"Come on. It's just us. What kind of stuff did you do?"

"Regular kid shit, I guess." He sifted a handful of dirt through his fingers.

"Like?"

"I used to sleep outside. With my friends. My best friends were these brothers. Lucas and Jimmy Hastings. Their folks had a cattle ranch, out by where the fairgrounds are now. We'd go out on their land."

"But what did you *do*?"

"We just talked, I guess. Shot the shit."

"About what?"

He pinched a dirt clod between his fingers. "About moving away. We were just kids."

"To where?"

"Reno, mostly. Or Salt Lake. Sacramento. San Francisco. New York. They were all the same to us back then. The big city." Harris laughed at himself a little, recalling. "We used to stay up all night, just listing the places you could take a girl in a city. One of us guys would say, 'To the park.' And another would say, 'A museum.' And another would say, 'The movies.' That was our favorite, the movies. Whenever somebody said the movies, we'd all together say, 'The movies,' all slow. Like a god-damn prayer."

Magda slipped from the rock into the water and went slowly under. Harris let himself watch this time, watched her belly submerge, her small breasts with his T-shirt clinging to them, then her shoulders, her jaw and lips. She arched her back under the water and pushed herself to the surface again, leading with her sternum, the ruts of her ribs visible beneath the soaked cloth, her nipples tight and buttonish. Drops dripped from her brows, her eyelashes, the tip of her nose, the outcropping of her bottom lip. She gathered her hair in her hand and wrung the water from it.

"What?" she said, like she didn't know.

Looking again to his fingers buried in the earth, he said, "I haven't thought of the Hastings brothers in thirty years. Sounds stupid, to say that's what we did around here."

"No, it doesn't," she said. "That's what we do now."

On the drive back, Magda unbuckled her seat belt and took off the slippers. She leaned against her door and stretched her bare legs across the seat between them. Soon she was asleep with her head against the window, one long line from her stretched neck down to the bottom of her bare feet. A damp mineral smell filled the cab. Their bodies bounced lightly from the washboard road, and her raisined toes sometimes touched his thigh. He went hard again. Good Lord, he thought, sixty-seven years old and behaving like an adolescent.

After a dinner of boiled hot dogs, Harris smoked his evening cigarette on the porch and watched the sunset burning in the distance. The sky settled into strata of pale blue atop gold and flame orange and a swath of clouds colored lavender and coral and an indigo so dark they seemed hunks of coal hovering above the range. Nearest the sun the sky was the wild red of a wound, like the thing had to be forced below the horizon. A single sandhill crane moved soundlessly across the sky. A sunset was nothing, Harris knew, dust particles, pollution, sunlight prismed by the slant of the world. Still, it was pretty.

Magda was trying with no luck to teach Milo to fetch a stick, oblivious to the dazzle going on behind her. When they'd dismounted from the truck that afternoon, Milo was sulking under the porch. It was Magda who finally coaxed her out. She'd used his Leatherman to cut the thorns off the mesquite branch she was now hurling into the rocky yard. But Milo only ambled over to the stick, lay down beside it and soothed her bloody gums by gnawing on it for a while. Magda was stubborn. She slapped her thighs and said, "Come, Milo. Milo, come!" over and over again. When the dog finally did come, she came slow and stickless. Finally, Magda lost hope. She sat beside Harris and looked out on the lake bed. "What were you doing out there?" she said.

"I live out here."

"You live *here*. What were you doing out *there*?"

He thought a while. "I'll show you," he said. "Stay right here. Don't move."

He went around the back of the truck and muscled the old tailgate down, an action that seemed to get more difficult each year. Harris had been coming out to the lake bed every July fifth, searching for fireworks near the burnt remains of plywood and grocer's pallets, since 1968, when he was one of those wild jackasses. Since he woke up with an ache behind his eyes and realized he'd left a paycheck's worth of Roman candles out on the lake bed and called his future ex-wife, Carrie Ann, and whispered into the phone so his mother wouldn't hear, "Morning, Honeybee. Where'd you stash my keys?" He told Magda all this, more or less.

"You had a wife?" she said. "Where is she now?"

"Doesn't matter," he said. Then, "Sacramento."

"City girl."

"I guess."

"I'm sorry."

"Don't be. It was a long time ago." He turned to the girl, gripping a shell pack as big as his torso. The Man-O-War.

For the next forty minutes, Harris scrambled up and down the adjacent hill setting the fireworks, sometimes returning to the shed for a tube of PVC pipe, sandpaper or duct tape. His back flared as he bent to wedge a stub of pipe into the ground or twist two fuses together. His sinuses stung with the brackish smell of sulfur. He glanced down the hill at Magda. She sat on the first porch step, leaning back, her arms propped behind her. He saw Carrie Ann sitting in that same spot, waiting for him to get home, passing her time knitting or shucking corn. Harris pressed the image below the horizon of his mind. They were fine now, him and Carrie. She'd gotten her baby. Harris sent the child birthday cards with fifty-dollar savings bonds inside. *Love, Uncle Bud*, they read. He couldn't complain, not in good conscience. They'd been given a second chance, Carrie and he, and were free to do with it what they pleased.

With the fuse hissing behind him, he hurried down the hill and sat beside Magda. She had her T-shirt lifted up under her breasts and one palm pressed to her bare stomach. She was bent, examining her midsection, looking for something.

"Watch," he said, nodding to his handiwork on the hill.

But she kept her face turned down to her abdomen. "It's probably dead, don't you think?"

"Come on, now," he said, too late to be of comfort. "Don't think like that."

"It is," she said. "I know it." He began to speak, but the first shell ignited then and shot into the air above them, sparks streaming behind it. They both started at the sound and Harris, with the quickness of a gasp, put his arm around Magda. The little comet went dark for a moment, then exploded—*boom*—into a sizzle so big it seemed to light the whole sky. The sound rico-cheted around the valley and returned to them—*boom*.

"See that?" he said. "That green? That's barium powder." He pressed her into him and held her there. She did not pull away.

Another shell rocketed into the sky—*boom*—raining down a brilliant hissing red.

He bent his face to her ear. "Strontium," he whispered.

"I'll be glad," she said. "If it's dead, this will all be over."

He held her tighter and said only, "Shh," before the next shell shot up, even higher than the others, as if propelled by the sound. It expanded—*boom*. Multicolored tendrils radiated from the center and made loops in the air like buzzards, descending. Silence took root between them.

A fourth shell and a fifth shot from the hill. They burst—*boom*—*boom*—into two spheres of light, one a steady-burning fountain of blue, and the other wiry spokes of purple turning orange.

"What's that one?" Magda whispered.

"The blue is copper," he said. "Pure ground copper."

The last four shells whizzed into the air, all at once. When they burst—*boom*—*boom*—*boom*—*boom*—Magda jumped a little and buried herself into him. Harris turned to see her face, his home, the whole wide valley lit by dazzling yellow light. He held her.

"And that one?" she whispered.

"That," he said. "That's gold."

. . .

That night, Harris watched her sleep. His own worn bed-sheet was roped around her, twisted through her arms and between her legs. Alone in his bed—he had insisted—she looked delicate as a salt crystal. Moonlight fell in through the window, catching the angles of the specimens on the nightstand. In this light her belly looked bigger. Was that possible? In these few days? Or was she right? His wife had said, *I knew it. I felt the baby go.* Had that stupid kid done the job? No. Though he'd seen what the boy did to her, saw with his own eyes the blood bloomed up under her skin—she looked bigger. She did. She would need a doctor. A hospital. He would make the calls. They would drive to Reno. The doctor would tell her, Yes, you are getting bigger. The doctor would tell her, It is not over. It is only just beginning. She would need vitamins. Though he knew better, deep down in the bedrock of himself, he couldn't help it. He thought, She will need a stroller. She will need a car seat. How the barren cling to the fertile. We, he thought, we will need a crib.

Harris took one last pull on his cigarette and stubbed it out on the sole of his boot. It was morning. He dropped the butt into the Folgers can. He would wake Magda soon, tell her to get dressed, that they were going to Reno. But instead of going inside, he scanned the lake bed, as he had every day since she came to him. From where the house was perched, high up on the alluvial fan, the valley below seemed to unfurl and flatten like a starched white sheet. The sun was rising, illuminating the peaks of the Last Chance Range to the west, starting its long trip across the Black Rock. He stopped. Something was different in the distance. A small white cloud of dust billowed on the horizon. It grew. At its eye was a speck. A truck.

"Morning," said Magda, startling Harris as she joined him on the porch. She caught sight of the dust cloud unfurling below them and squinted. "What's that?"

"You tell me," said Harris. "Probably been crossing the lake bed since sunup. Circling right about where I found you."

"Oh, fuck," she said. "It's my dad." She began to pace the porch like a wild animal. "Fuck, fuck. Fuck." She looked as though she might cry.

Then, as if it had heard her, the truck turned toward Route 40, toward Red's Road, the washed-out path that dead-ended at Harris's driveway. His heart beat like a herd of mustangs charging at his rib cage.

"Get in the house," he told her. "He doesn't know you're here. Go to the bedroom. Shut the door. Don't come out. I'll take care of it." He half believed this.

The truck lumbered up the long, steep gravel driveway, the way you'd drive if you were concerned about dusting out your neighbors. Harris rummaged frantically through a wheelbarrow. He found a large hunk of iron ore, heavy and angular, easy to grip.

He kept the ore in his right hand and sorted through the rocks with his left, wanting to seem busy when the man arrived. He organized the rocks in piles on the ground according to size.

The truck was halfway up the driveway—close enough to see them—when Harris heard the swing and *schwack* of the screen door. He tried not to turn too quickly, but jerked his head, panicked, only to see Milo ambling out to him. He almost hit her.

The truck—a black Ram, a dually with some sort of decal looping across the rear window—stopped at the edge of what Harris considered his yard. A man climbed out. He wore a rodeo buckle the size of a serving platter, a wide cream-colored Stetson, sunglasses and ornately tooled caiman shit kickers.

Harris knew the man. His name was Castaneda. Juan, Harris thought, though he couldn't be sure. He'd worked with him at the mine. He was a foreman, like Harris.

They'd spoken. On breaks in the pit. On the Newmont bus back into town. They'd talked sports—Pack football, March Madness. They'd discussed the fine tits on the teenage girl behind the counter at the Shell station where they parked. Castaneda had talked about his kids. Harris had seen pictures, grimy creased things pulled from a leather billfold. All girls. Beautiful, Harris had said, and meant. And this man, he'd smiled wide as the ocean and said, I know. Harris gripped the ore so tight his fingertips went white.

"Morning," said Harris. Then, too quickly, "Help you?"

"Morning," said Castaneda, removing his hat but leaving his sunglasses. There was not a gray hair on his head. "Hope so." He approached with a bounce. "Harris, right? How's the sweet life, brother?"

"Can't complain."

"You strike it rich yet?"

Harris kept sorting, kept his wieldy rock in his right hand. He lifted his head and looked to the man, then to the white-hot lake bed and then, squinting against the sun, to the hill behind his house. At its crest he could just make out the PVC pipes from last night, toppled and scorched. "You come out here to prospect?" he said. "'Cause this is BLM land on all four sides. You'd be digging for Uncle Sam."

"Prospect? Ha. No, sir. I'm no rock hound," said Castaneda. "I'm hunting chukar. Thought an old-timer like you might know the good spots." Castaneda nodded to his truck.

"Chukar." Harris stood upright and faced the man. He wiped sweat from his top lip and caught the acridity of nicotine on his fingers. "Don't know of no chukar around here." Because there weren't any chukar around here, not until White Pine County at least. Only thing you could hunt out here was rattlesnake.

"Well, shit," said Castaneda. He reached behind him and adjusted his belt. "Probably got the wrong gun for chukar anyway." He brought around a revolver, a .44 glinting in the summer sun. He held it limp in his palm, as if he only wanted to show it off. But Harris knew better than that. Standing there with a rock in his hand like a goddamn child, he at least knew better than that.

Just then, Milo began to snarl and bark. But she didn't bark at Castaneda, with the gun flat in his palm, looking earnestly to Harris. She was disoriented, maybe heat blind. The dog was barking at Harris.

Castaneda raised his voice above the dog. "I don't know what she told you," he said.

"Who?" said Harris.

Milo kept on.

"Don't make this hard," said Castaneda. "She's a good girl. She's just got an overactive imagination."

A sudden tinny blood taste came to Harris's mouth. "There's nobody else here."

"Oh?" said Castaneda, smiling now. "You lighting off fireworks all night by yourself then?" He began to laugh. This was where Magda got her laugh. "There's nowhere else for her to be, brother."

Harris took a step toward the man, the ore hot in his hand.

Castaneda nodded to the rock. "Don't."

"You son of—"

He raised the hand that held the gun. "You don't want to take that thought any farther." Harris stopped.

Castaneda tucked the gun into the waist of his Wranglers. He walked past Harris, stepping carefully over the piles of specimens where they'd been set in the dirt. An oily aftershave smell followed him. He went into the house. Minutes later—too fast—Castaneda emerged with Magda, his hand on the small of her back. Her face was limestone; it was granite. She did not look at Harris. Castaneda walked her around to the passenger side of the truck and opened the door in the manner of a perfect gentleman.

"Wait," she said before getting in. "I want to say good-bye." Her father nodded and took his hand from her. She walked over to Milo. The dog went quiet. Magda squatted and rustled both her hands behind Milo's limp ears. She put her mouth to the dog's muzzle and said something Harris could not hear.

"She wants to stay," Harris called in a strange-sounding voice.

Casteneda grinned and turned to Magda. "Is that so?"

Magda shook her head and looked to Harris pityingly, as though it was he who needed her.

Harris gripped the iron ore. Why not? he wanted to ask her. But he knew. What could this place give to anyone?

Magda returned to her father's truck. Castaneda took her hand and helped her in. Before he shut the door he smiled at his daughter and rubbed his hand along the back of her neck. It was brief—an instant—but Harris saw everything in the way the man touched her. His hand on her bare neck, the tips of his stout fingers along the black baby hairs at her nape, then under the collar of her shirt. His shirt. From where he stood, he saw all this and more.

The truck pulled away and began its descent to the bald floor of the valley. Milo resumed her barking. Harris told her to shut up, but she went on. Rhythmic, piercing, incessant. The old man had never heard anything so clearly. He felt a steady holy pressure building in him, like a vein of water running down his middle was freezing and would split his body in two. He lunged at the dog. He wanted ore to skull. He wanted his shoulder burning, his hand numb. He wanted the holes that had been her ear and eye growing wider, becoming one, bone crumbling in on itself like the walls of a canyon carved by a river. He wanted wanted wanted.

He took hold of the scruff of the dog's neck. He tried to pin her beneath his legs but she yelped and wormed free, and instead he fell back on his ass. He dropped the ore in the dirt. Milo scrambled behind the wheelbarrow where he'd been sorting. He reached up and grabbed the wheelbarrow's rusted lip and tried to pull himself up. The wheelbarrow tilted toward him, then toppled, sending Harris to the dirt again. Rocks rained down on him. A flare of pain went off in his knee and in the fingers of his left hand, where a slab of schorl crushed them.

He sat breathing hard, surrounded by heavy, worthless minerals. He took his wrecked fingers into his mouth. Then he fished his Zippo from his pocket and lit a cigarette. He breathed in. Out. The Ram shrank to the blinding white of the lake bed. He stayed there for some time, smoking among the hot alluvial debris, the silt and clay and rocky loam. He watched a fire ant stitch through the gravel and into the shadow of the overturned wheelbarrow; then he watched the truck. A pale cloud of dust behind it swelled, then settled, then disappeared. She was gone. And all the while Milo's unceasing yowl ricocheted through the valley, returning to him as the *boom* of the fireworks, the *levántate* Magda never whispered, the twin cackles of the Hastings brothers bounding over the cattle range, as every sound he'd ever heard.

THE ARCHIVIST

There was no salve for the space he left. If there had been—if science had developed an ointment for heartache or a pill for the lovelorn—I wouldn't have used it. I wanted pain. I wanted cataclysmic anguish. For that, our old ritual.

So every night I'd get home from my job as a clerk at the public library and draw a bath with water as hot as I could stand. On the kitchen chair beside the tub I'd put a cheap bottle of cab, a book, a pack of cigarettes, a joint and a sleeve of peanut butter cups I'd bought at the Winner's around the corner, where I bought the wine.

One night, especially plowed, I called my older sister, Carly. I told her Ezra and I were through. I said, "For real this time," which I said every time. She said she'd be right over. "Bring the baby," I said.

I waited for Carly in the bath, drinking wine from my blue-flecked enamel camping cup. Once, Ezra called the cup my cowboy mug, and with him gone I couldn't stop seeing it that way. I felt insufferably rustic whenever I drank from it, and yet I didn't stop drinking from it. That's what he did to me: permeated, saturated, submerged me in him. Now, I submerged myself. I surfaced, took a cigarette, and breathed him into my foolish hungry lungs.

I started smoking the night we met, when Ezra stood up from the bar where we'd been playing video poker, said, "I'm gonna go outside" and put two fingers to his lips, that smoker's sign language. It looked like he kissed them softly, the thick pads of his fingertips. I had a good man at home, waiting for me. I said, "Me too," followed him outside and smoked the first cigarette of my life. I was twenty-six. The street was dark except for a Winner's down the road, glowing like a beacon. Ezra leaned in and gave me a light. Then he pushed my hair back from my face. "I give this a week," he said. "You?" "Two," I said. "Tops." He smiled this absolutely lethal smile and we smoked silently against the quaking of the freeway and the darkened machinery of the recycling plant across the street. I asked my boyfriend to move out the next day. I knew then that I would follow Ezra anywhere he'd let me.

Carly let herself into the apartment and called for me. The baby squealed. Carly lost one of her fallopian tubes to an ectopic pregnancy when she was my age. Between that and her husband Alex's reversed vasectomy, my niece is a regular miracle. I love her more than a person ought to love one thing.

My sister came into the bathroom and said, "Oh, honey," her face creased with empathy. She set the Miracle on the floor beside the tub and surrounded her with pastel toys, which the baby ignored. The Miracle played exclusively with adult things. Keys. Eyeglasses. Cell phones. Just a year old and already she was a severe child.

Carly had lately taken to gathering the Miracle's feathery blond hair into a ponytail at the top of her head, a hairdo which resembled nothing more than the sprout of a cartoon turnip. The Miracle seemed not only aware of this resemblance but appropriately suspicious of it. She eyeballed me where I sat in the tub.

Carly discreetly removed the wine and pot from the chair. She left my cigarettes, the peanut butter cups, a *National Geographic* and the cowboy mug, which I discovered was inexplicably, disappointingly empty.

I listened to her in the kitchen, recorking the near-gone bottle and placing it on top of my refrigerator. "Red wine contains resveratrol and antioxidants," I called to her. "It's good for the heart."

Carly returned to the bathroom and sat on the closed lid of the toilet. She crossed her legs and unwrapped a peanut butter cup. She looked like our mother, sitting that way. She had our mother's legs, her long fingers. She touched her mouth the same way our mother did in pictures. Our mother was a beauty and an alcoholic. She died when I was ten and Carly was fifteen. She drove drunk into a power pole near Reno High at ten o'clock in the morning. For as long as I can remember, my sister has wanted to be the good mother we never had.

Carly folded the peanut butter cup in two and offered half to the Miracle. "Don't tell Daddy," she said.

"Thank you!" said the Miracle.

Carly said, "You're welcome!" Then, "I know you miss him, Nat. But you can't stay in the bath smoking pot for the rest of your life. You've got to keep moving. Get a hobby. They're starting a volunteer docent program at the museum. That would be *perfect* for you." She nibbled the edge of her peanut butter cup. Carly had never met Ezra.

"I'll think about it," I said.

"Do," she said. "Meet me for lunch. I'll introduce you to Liam." Her boss. Single, she'd mentioned more than once. She gave my foot a chipper little pat. She was happy to have a project.

Ezra and I lasted a year, barely. Every night, I would unlock my back door and get into the bath. I'd drink, read and wait for him. Some nights he never came. Those nights I would stay in the bath until the water got cold and there was no more hot water to warm it. On nights he did come—often from somewhere that left his pupils big and his hands trembling— he'd let himself in through the back door, come into the bathroom, touch the top of my head and sit on the lid of the toilet. I'd prop my foot on the faucet and he'd silently loop his index finger around my big toe. We'd read—me *National Geographic* and histories and remarkable true stories of people surviving plane crash, shipwreck, avalanche; him the local newspaper and slim volumes of plays. We'd talk and he'd roll us cigarettes. In flush times he would roll me joints too, with little strips of paper rolled up in the end so that I wouldn't burn my fingertips when I smoked them. Ezra was mostly into booze and coke. He didn't smoke pot unless he was already especially fucked up. This was also the only time he ever said he loved me.

Weeks passed, and I moved through the world perpetually bewildered, in the way of the shell-shocked and the heartbroken. Some days I did my best. Eventually I even met Carly for lunch, as promised. I waited for her in the gallery, where I was reminded why I disliked art museums in general and the Nevada Museum of Art in particular. The rooms were too well lit, and I didn't care for the way sound behaved in the place. There was a rooftop terrace where Carly hosted cocktail parties for members and prospective members. It was bloodless. My high school friends had their wedding receptions up there.

Car and I walked to a deli and ordered Reubens. At one point, and out of absolutely nowhere, she said, "Liam went to Yale."

"Cool," I said, through a mouthful of dressing-sogged rye. Carly looked at me for a moment, pained, then plucked a translucent shred of sauerkraut off my chin.

On the way back through the courtyard, we passed a

sculpture I'd never seen before. It seemed to be made from a hundred arcing pieces of soft gray driftwood, all delicately fitted together and balanced in the perfect form of a horse. It looked as though I could push it over. I loved this about it. "Touch it," said Carly. I did, and immediately realized that it wasn't made of wood, but of bronze patinaed to look like wood. The branches I'd thought were carefully interlocked were welded together. Just then, Carly called across the courtyard.

Liam was good-looking in a way that indeed suggested Connecticut. He was lean and jaunty, though he'd obviously made some effort to coax his hair into a state of semi-unruliness. Carly introduced us, then said, "Well," and retreated swiftly inside.

Liam smiled and removed his hands from his pockets as if just remembering some childhood reprimand about having them there. I struck the sculpture with the heel of my hand, and the blow made the hollow sound of a bottomless well.

"Carly says you have an art degree," Liam ventured.

"I thought this was wood."

"It was," he said, in a consoling tone that brought to my attention the fact that I had arrived at a state of needing consolation. He went on hurriedly. "Or, she molded the wood, anyway. Molded the wood and then burnt it out." He gestured sheepishly to a placard set into a boulder nearby, by way of citation perhaps.

"That's terrible," I said, suddenly feeling nauseous. "That's the worst thing I've ever heard." Liam started to speak again, nobly, but I interrupted him. "I'm sorry," I said. "I have to go."

Liam, maintaining his East Coast dignity, said only, "Right."

On the walk home, I stopped occasionally to brace myself against the bigtooth maples lining the street. I pressed my hands to my breasts where they'd begun to bloom up from my bra, and longed for a museum that didn't feel like a museum. I preferred the preserved homes of historic figures. I liked a quill ready to be dipped in a pot of ink, a bonnet tossed onto a rocker, firewood half stacked by a stove. A house waiting for people who would never come. This made sense to me.

Outside my front door sat a pair of tennis shoes, the heels trampled down, the canvas cracking in the sun. A plaque mounted on the brick above them might have read:

The End (1 of 3). The day was warm for fall. They had their feet in the Truckee River. They'd been drinking wine since lunch. She was drunk and he was getting there. She was telling him where the phrase *Indian summer* came from. He didn't believe her. They were laughing about this when all at once he stopped laughing and said, "A part of me wants this. More than anything." He was always saying this. She had long since begun to wonder how many parts he had. She knew she'd fallen for a puzzle of a man, all parts and pieces and fractions, but was only now seeing how few of those would ever be hers.

He took her hand. "I want you seventy percent of the time," he said. "No. Seventy-five."

Fucker, she thought, wanting badly to bite him in all sorts of places, all sorts of contexts. On the apple of his cheek. Through a cutlet of skin gathered from the back of his hand. There was nothing to say. In the silence it occurred to her that they were within walking distance of her apartment, and that they had been all day. She saw the route home the way a bird would.

He said, "I'm sorry. I hate that I said that."

"Then stop," she said.

"I can't."

She was brave from wine and unseasonable sunshine and the newfound closeness of home. She told him he was making things too hard on her. She told him she was afraid she'd let him do this forever. The saying of these things had been a long time coming—these and many others—and as she walked home, her feet riverwet inside these tennis shoes, she knew they meant the end of them.

A second placard, buffed shiny and mounted at chest height just inside the front door:

The End (2 of 3). Two days later a storm rolled in from the west and Ezra came, for the first time, to the front door. When she opened it he said, "Hey," and took her by the jaw and kissed her. She tried to find some sign in the way he worked his mouth against hers. But it was his same kiss—as brutal, as consuming. It did to her what it always had. He turned her around and pushed her up against the cool wall of this hallway. He put one hand in her hair roughly and kissed her neck, more teeth than tongue. He worked his other hand up then down her, shucking her clothes to the floor. The front door was still open, a wet autumn smell slipping inside. He pinned his knees into hers and spread her legs apart. She made uncontrollable gasping sounds, muffled by her mouth pressed to the plaster. He pushed harder against her and she tilted her hips into him. Then, as if he felt the fight go out of her, he turned her around so she faced him. He bent and kissed her once on the bridge of her nose. She managed to say, "We need to talk."

"Okay," he said. "Talk."

"Why are you here? What do you want?"

He smiled and kissed her fondly on the mouth and through the kiss he is to have said, "I want you to be quiet and let me fuck you."

And she was grateful, so she did. He slipped both his hands under her ass and lifted her, mounting her bare back against this very spot. Her legs bowed around him. She braced herself against his thick shoulders and he rocked into her. She let herself believe that this could be a beginning rather than an end. That this was them. Then she stopped thinking altogether. When he came he made the same quick half breaths he always did. He slackened and they slid slowly down the wall, their limbs loosely threaded together. They were unmoving and sweat-slick, his head resting on her chest. A car drove by, its tires sluicing cleanly through the rainwater. By then it felt natural not to say the thing that needed saying.

A third, positioned unobtrusively near the unmade bed:

The End (3 of 3). Afterward, he carried her to bed. Before they slept, she got up and nodded toward the fire escape. "I think I'll have a cigarette," she said. Without looking at her he said, "I quit, actually."

Just before dawn she woke to the sound of Ezra gathering his clothes from the hallway. Already she could feel two sore spots like crab apples above her ass where he'd worked her hips against the wall. (See placard two.)

She said nothing. Once he was dressed he sat on the edge of the bed beside her. "I know you're awake," he said. She did not move. He rubbed the soft place behind her ear with his thumb. "I love you," he said, and though she knew it was true she kept her eyes closed and said, "Don't say that." She did not want to allow that love could be so fearful and meager and misshapen. He left, and she did not try to stop him. She was through trying to stop him. She had been trying to stop him since the day they met.

That afternoon—after I'd abandoned poor Liam—Carly called me four times. I ignored her. I walked around my apartment, lightly touching the artifacts Ezra left behind in the year we were together. They were pathetic and few: a bag of white tea gone stale, a screwdriver we meant to use to fix a window screen but never did, some books, a toothbrush I bought him. I decided I would preserve these just as he'd left them, convert my apartment into the Museum of Love Lost. I envisioned other exhibits. An installation of all the clever, evasive text messages he ever sent me, a replica of the bar where we met, handmade dioramas of our finest outings. That night I woke to the sensation of the bedsheets against my nipples. In the dark I saw our happiest moments in miniature.

Here we are in my bedroom, just come home from a concert. We are made of clay and our limp limbs are clandestinely pinned in place with toothpicks. We've been to see a band whose music was frantic and heartsick and whose lead looked so much older than the last time either of us had seen them that we couldn't help but grow a little older ourselves as we listened.

Dawn is pressing lightly to the cellophane window beside the bed. My yarn hair is tangled, and if you look closely you can see a slight sweat sheen on us both. I am lying on my back on the handkerchief bedspread, wearing tall red heels that have been hurting my feet. They are Barbie shoes painted with careful strokes of ruby nail polish. Ezra sits at the foot of the bed with my foot in his lap. He is bent over, unclasping the tiny-toothed buckle at my ankle. When he is finished with this shoe he'll remove the other, then run a finger softly over the place where that strap cut into my ankle. His hands will cup the belly of my calf, make their way up underneath my dress. We'll make love. Afterward he'll say, I know I'm a pain in the ass. I'm sorry. I'll kiss his chest and say, Tell me you'll be true. I can't, he'll say. You know that. But in the diorama he hasn't said this yet. In the diorama we are frozen, his head bent, his sweet mouth gathered in concentration, his ossified clay fingers fumbling softly at my aluminum-foil buckle. I call it *Man Removes Shoe*.

In this one, we are papier-mâché in a restaurant alongside the Truckee. We sit at a dollhouse table on a Popsicle-stick patio stretching over a river of blue and green tissue paper, its crinkled rapids daubed white with foam. A shapely decanter of red wine stands in the center of the table, near empty. We have ordered a meal consisting entirely of appetizers. See the card-stock plates crowding the table. See the remnants of colored-pencil anchovies, prosciutto, bruschetta, oysters, soft white cheese coated with candied nuts, a gutted half round of once-warm bread. We smoke cigarettes rolled from wisps of cotton, and his fingers are sunk deep into my hair of soft felt. He is openmouthed, laughing that laugh of laughs. I am thinking, I would do anything to make you laugh. I call it *Us at Our Best*.

I hadn't talked to Ezra in six weeks, and I hadn't had my period in at least eight. I took a test, then another. I called Carly.

When I told her she said, "That's fantastic!" and meant it.

I said, "Go fuck yourself."

When Carly came over that night I was in the bathtub and had been for some time. She set the Miracle on the floor. The turnip sprout was ornamented with a blue velvet bow that perfectly matched her blue velvet dress.

I handed the Miracle the cardboard core of a toilet paper roll, which she accepted grudgingly and inserted into her mouth. "Is that her birthday outfit?" I asked, though I knew it was. I'd been at the party.

Carly said, "Have you told him yet?"

"Please don't start in on me."

"You need to."

"Why? I know exactly how it's going to go: 'We fucked up.' 'Oops. Here's four hundred dollars.'"

"He won't say that. He's a good person."

"No, he's not. And I know you know that." I reached for a peanut butter cup. "You should be ashamed of yourself, contributing to the romantic delusions of an unmarried woman with child."

She leaned down and placed her hand under the Miracle's chin. She said, "May I have that?" The baby allowed a wet shred of cardboard pulp to drop from her mouth to her mother's palm. Carly said, "Thank you," and the Miracle said, "Thank you!" Carly recrossed her legs and looked around.

"No wine tonight," she said. "No cigarettes. No pot. That's a good sign."

"It doesn't mean what you think."

"Tell him first, Nat. It's the right thing to do."

I sat up in the tub and extended my hand to my niece. I wanted her to grab hold of my index finger, wield for me some of that heartening babystrength. I wiggled my fingers at her. She regarded my hand and went on gnawing the tube, perturbed. The Miracle has dignity bordering on cruelty.

"I'm waiting," I said.

"For what?" asked Carly.

I eased back into the water. "I want there to be something else to say."

. . .

I used to tell Ezra that I knew no man's touch before his, that I was conjured up on this Earth for him, my virgin flesh materializing among the video poker machines in the back of that bar on Fourth in the same heavenly instant he walked through the door. We used to laugh about this. But before Ezra there was Sam. Poor, good Sam.

Sam and I once had a baby, technically. He wanted to have it and I didn't. Sam said he would support me, whatever I decided, which he did. Of course he did. This was maybe three months before I met Ezra and left Sam for him.

Sam sat in the waiting room for six hours. That's how long it takes, though the procedure itself lasts less than ten minutes. He and I arrived at the facility early in the morning, as we'd been instructed. The building was unmarked and located across from the Meadowood Mall, on the Sears side. We were buzzed in through two sets of bulletproof doors. In the waiting room Sam hugged me, then kissed me, then hugged me again. I went back and joined the other women.

All of them were white and teenagers or close to it, younger than me anyway, except one, who was black and considerably older, forty or forty-five. I was the last to arrive, and I'd passed all those teenage girls' fathers in the waiting room. There wasn't a mother in the whole place.

Except for when she was summoned by a nurse, the black woman talked on her cell phone ceaselessly. To a friend, I gathered. Not the father. She narrated everything we did. I hated her for this. I felt protective of the younger girls, perhaps, though I did nothing to act on this feeling. But her insipid narrating soothed me a little, too, because it had the effect of casting the facility in a less exceptional light, like the lobby of a bank or a chiropractor's office, not a place where one looked for some kind of meaning, which it was certainly not. I thought this was good for the younger girls to see.

The black woman told how one by one we all filled out a stack of paperwork and got blood tests and watched a video regarding our rights. She read aloud the Adrienne Rich quote on a poster in the room where we waited. She repeated the selection of pain medication offered to us on a tiered scale. For an extra hundred dollars we would be provided two substantial caplets of Vicodin. For a hundred and fifty we could be outfitted with a mask delivering a dose of nitrous oxide, which, we were told, smelled and tasted a little like bubble gum and would render us barely conscious during the procedure. These offerings, we were informed, could not be combined, but they were included in addition to a local anesthetic, which we would each receive at no extra cost, and which would be injected directly into the cervix immediately before the procedure. We were invited to consider these options in light of our individual needs and our budgets. Of course, if we wished, we were free to choose none at all. I chose none. I told myself it was because I was broke. At the time I mistook suffering for decency.

The black woman told whoever how one by one we all got Pap smears and pelvic exams. How the staff did an ultrasound on each of us, and asked if we wanted a copy of what we saw there. I said I did, mostly because the heavy woman operating the device seemed so pleased to be able to offer it. In the image there were white brackets around a dark space. That's all. Later, I put it in my glove box and did not look at it again. I never showed the image to Sam, though I knew what it would have meant to him. Being with Sam was like standing atop a small hill and seeing my whole fine life unfurled in front of me like prairie.

The procedure itself lasted under ten minutes, a fact that the nurses often reiterated and that proved technically accurate but did little to capture the character of those ten minutes. A nurse's aide held my hand. I envisioned Sam sitting out with the fathers. I wondered unkindly whether his presence deflated them. How, I wondered, did they reconcile the facility waiting room with a white, college-educated, clean-shaven twenty-six-year-old—the kind of man their now-wayward daughters would bring home one day, if they turned things around? Later, Sam told me he wouldn't have been in the waiting room then. He went for a walk, he said, though there was nowhere to walk really, so he just weaved up and down the rows of cars in the mall parking lot, waiting for me to call.

Afterward, they took us to a room and had us lie on cots. Some of the girls threw up there, including me. The aides gave us apple juice and two cookies for our blood sugar and a prescription for birth control so we wouldn't be repeat customers. I have told this story occasionally, to my sister and a few others. But Ezra was the only person who ever laughed at that last part. Another reason why I loved him, I suppose. Anyway, the whole experience was as awful as one would expect, and no more so. It was nothing I couldn't do again.

This was why my sister came every night, and why she brought the Miracle.

After she left with the Miracle in her birthday getup, Carly called. "Do me a favor," she said. "Promise you won't smoke or drink anymore."

"What for?"

"You never know," she said buoyantly.

"Actually, Car, the sad thing is how often you do know."

"Come on," she said. "For me."

"This is fucked up," I said; then I promised.

It should have been easy to quit; I'd only ever smoked with him, for him. It wasn't easy—I was anxious and found I didn't know what to do with my hands—but I did it. I stopped drinking, too, and took to having lemonade with my peanut butter cups. I read faster, and I became more disturbed by the things I read. Often, I had to stop. I'd set the book aside and look at my naked body. I imagined tumbling through plane crash, shipwreck, avalanche. I distended my stomach so it rose from the surface of the water. It was too early for that, of course. Those cells were barely the size of a cranberry, or so Carly told me. Sometimes I went underwater to see how long I could stay there. I opened my eyes, saw those brownblack wrappers moving above me like his boats, like insects alighted on the surface of the Truckee. I saw him there. I wished I didn't, but I did.

. . .

When Carly was pregnant with the Miracle she tried never to become upset or angry, always to be calm. That was why the Miracle turned out so even. But it seemed all I was was upset and angry. It is such a short distance from the heart to the womb. I could see foul chemicals injecting into Cranberry. What if the first feelings she ever felt were loss and fear and anger? It must sour a person profoundly to have these as first feelings. This is probably what happened to me.

The Museum of Love Lost could have a Mother Wing. Arranged in reverse chronological order, it might start with an archive of yellowing newspaper articles: *Fatal Accident Causes Major Power Outage*; *Thousands in Northwest Reno Without Electricity after Car Slams into Power Pole*. (Ezra, when I told him: "I remember that day. We got out of school early.") From there a visitor might move through a catalogue of all the matchbooks our mother gave Carly and me when she visited us at our grandmother's in Sun Valley. Carly kept hers in a mason jar on the dresser we shared—booklets from Sparky's, Bully's, Crosby's, little boxes from the Bonanza, the Horseshoe, the Polo Lounge. I burned my matches up as soon as our mother left, not because I wanted to destroy them, but because I couldn't resist the smell of them burning, or the satisfying snap of those chalky heads against that grainy strip.

There might be pungent tubes of the same variety of henna

our mother used to dye our brown hair red when we were girls, back when we still lived with her, because she wanted us to look more like her. Here is a photo of us sitting in the gravel driveway in front of our trailer, our hair swirled high on our heads with the rust-colored clay, letting, she said, the sun do its thing. We are maybe five and ten. I am wearing only white cotton under-pants.

The Mother Wing might end with a display of dried, pressed sprigs of sage and wild mint from the drainage ditch behind the trailer, which we used to pick by the armful and bring to our mother while she slept.

But most likely, the Mother Wing would be completely empty.

Carly came over the next night with the Miracle dressed in a fuzzy brown bear outfit. Small bear ears peeked up from the hood, and soft claw mittens from the arms, and a tail on the ass wiggled bearlike as she crawled.

"Why is she wearing that?" I asked.

"She likes it," Carly said. "Watch this." She asked the Miracle, "Who's a bear?"

The Miracle bared her newest teeth and dropped her mother's cell phone to display her claws. "Who's a bear?" Carly said again.

The Miracle squealed, snapped her teeth together and then roared a too-happy roar.

"That's adorable," I said, and it was.

Carly looked pleased. She said, "Maybe you should get out of the bath."

"Some days I thank God I can lock myself in my apartment and no one has to be around me," I said. "What if I always have those days? A baby is there. All the time." These things were just occurring to me.

"Have you thought any more about that docent program?" she said. "I could still get you an interview."

"I've already started," I said, waving her to my nightstand.

"What's all this?"

"Don't touch it."

She hovered over the things Ezra had emptied from his pockets our last night together. They were arranged on the nightstand just as he'd left them, waiting to be labeled and mounted on acid-free paper: a credit card receipt from a bar up the street. The chewed cap of a pen. Some change and a five-dollar bill creased in the middle like an accordion, which he used for a trick where he'd make it look like Abraham Lincoln was smiling or frowning, depending on how he held it. A near-empty sack of tobacco.

"What is it?" Carly called to me.

"Family heritage," I said. "In case Cranberry wants to know who her father was. There he is, girlie: generous tipper, oral fix-ater, Civil War buff, roller of exquisitely proportioned cigarettes."

Carly returned to the bathroom, ineffably bright-eyed. "Do you really think it's a girl?"

"God. I hope not."

Carly knelt on the floor beside the tub. She put her hand on my arm. "You don't have to do this alone," she said. "Alex and I could help you. Cranberry and the Miracle could be friends. Like us. It could be like when we were kids. Before things got bad."

I said, "Things were always bad."

"They weren't," said Carly. "You were too young. But they weren't."

"Why are you defending her?"

The Miracle screeched.

"I'm not." Carly stood and lifted her daughter, holding her like a shield. "It's just—do you have to be so hard on everyone?"

"I don't know. Probably."

The Miracle took her mother's earring into her mouth. Carly extracted it gingerly. "You make him sound like some sort of flimflam man."

"That's what he is, Car. A flimflam man."

"Come on—"

"No. That's exactly what he is. A flimflam man with a nice laugh. A cokehead flimflam man who left me with a nicotine addiction and some trash from his pockets. Tell me a baby's gonna change that."

The Miracle clapped her hands on the earring and said, "All right!"

"You're never going to feel ready for this, Nat. They make you ready."

"What if they don't? What if I have it and the only difference is I think, 'I'm going down and I'm taking this kid with me'?"

She winced. "It won't be like that."

I couldn't help myself. "It was like that for us."

After some time she said, "You're right."

I was thinking of our mother, but I was also thinking of Carly, of a time when I was at her house, just after the Miracle was born. In those early days their place throbbed with people. Alex's mother and father were visiting from Arizona, and Carly's girlfriends were constantly stopping by with dinners and hand-me-downs and complicated baby-soothing devices. I watched them the way a person watches a parade she's accidentally come upon.

Then, one afternoon, a strange quiet overtook me and I looked up from the sink where I was washing dishes. It was as though silence had swallowed the house and we were suspended in the dark warmth of its throat. Carly and I were alone with the baby. The Miracle was maybe four days old. Carly was feeding her in a rocking chair in the living room. When the baby fell asleep Carly motioned me to her. "Can you take her?" she whispered, nodding to the crib. I lifted the Miracle and laid her down the way I'd seen Alex do. When I came back Carly reached for my arm.

"I have to tell you something," she said. She looked like a badly weathered drawing of herself, exhausted. "I don't think I love the baby. I mean I do. But not the way Alex does."

I told her that was natural, that a lot of women feel that way at first. I was repeating some Oprah shit she'd told me months earlier. I said she was tired, that she should try to nap. She nodded emptily. "Of course you love her," I added as I walked her to her bed. She lay on top of the blankets.

As I closed the curtains she said, "I don't."

I said, "Shh," and went into the living room to fold laundry. The bedroom door was open and I could hear her breathing, her head softly shifting on the feather pillow. "I don't," she said over and over. "I don't." Then she fell asleep. We never talked about it again.

In this one Ezra and I are drinking coffee and sharing a miniature newspaper. We woke up with that loopy, underwater kind of hangover, the sort that pleasantly expands to consume an entire day. We walked to this shoe-box café, hand in hand. We are carved from wood blocks, and the midmorning sun glitters on our grooved faces. I've told him about that day, about how afraid Carly made me. How she was saying things our mother might have said. What I need to know, I've told him, is if that feeling ever left her. Because if it never left her, it would never leave me.

Ezra has leaned across the table and taken my face in his hands. "Hey," he's said. "Look at me. You're not her. You hear me? You're not anyone but you." I've pulled away from him. "You don't get it," I've said. "It's in me." He's hurt—see his eyes, his soft upturned hands—and I am surprised that I am capable of hurting him. "Christ," he is saying. "It's like I'm trying to dig you out when all you want is to be buried with her." I call it *The Truest Thing You Ever Said*.

When Carly arrived the next night, she came into the bathroom and closed the door behind her. The Miracle wore a pair of sparkly gold fairy wings and a headband with a giant sunflower mounted to one side. She held a pair of orange plastic nunchucks, the only toy I'd ever seen her interested in.

I was in the bath. "I thought she wasn't allowed to play at violence," I said.

"Guns mostly," said Carly. "We don't have a nunchuck policy." Then she said, "I have to tell you something."

"What?"

"I brought someone here. You should probably put some clothes on."

I rose out of the tub and wrapped myself in my bathrobe. Everything was worth it. Ezra would see how I'd kept our world as he'd left it, how I never stopped wanting him. I saw his fingers tracing over our old life. He'd take me in his arms and say what an idiot he'd been. He'd say, *I want this. One hundred percent. All the time.* Anything he said would have been enough. He could have said nothing.

Instead, bent over the artifacts on my nightstand was Sam.

The Miracle smacked her mother with her nunchucks and said, "All right!"

"Hey," Sam said. "How are you?"

I said, "Uh, okay."

He glanced at Carly. "I was thinking we could go for a walk," he said to me. He looked fitter, slimmer in the face. He wore a dark green sweater I didn't recognize. This baffled me, that he'd bought a sweater. I said, "I'll get dressed."

Out on the sidewalk, Sam said, "Which way?"

"Doesn't matter." We started out on our old route toward the river.

Neither of us spoke. My fingers were cold. I stuffed my hands into the pockets of my coat. "What's with the nunchucks?" I said.

"You never told me whether she had a boy or a girl."

We were quiet again, the only sounds our shoes on the sidewalk, and occasional cars driving by. "You could have gotten something neutral," I said.

He shrugged. I remembered that easy Sam shrug. "Those are cool, right?"

"Yeah. They're cool." We turned a corner and I pulled a dying leaf from a low-hanging branch. "What did she tell you?"

"Everything, I think."

I ripped segments off the leaf and let them fall papery to the ground. "Everything."

Sam nodded to the leaf. "Bigtooth maple."

"I know," I said. "I remember." I spliced the stem with my thumbnail and we went on quietly. Finally I said, "I'm not going to have it."

"She says you haven't made the appointment yet."

"I keep thinking things might change."

"And you haven't told him?"

"It's stupid. I know." We came upon the river. Midway across the bridge we stopped and leaned on the rail.

"She says you're saving his stuff."

"Not saving it." I let the last shred of the leaf flutter to the water. "I love him. I go to make the appointment and I can't.

I'm sitting there with the phone and my fucking calendar, you know? Like I'm having my teeth cleaned. It isn't the baby. Maybe it's just . . . I don't want us reduced to an appointment. We were more than that."

He sighed and dipped his head between his big hands.

"Sorry," I said, though I wasn't.

Sam rubbed his eyes with the heels of his palms. His face was red. "You never thought that about us?"

"That was different."

"Why?"

I turned back toward the water. He turned and faced the water, too. "I still think about it," he said. "Ours."

I felt ambushed, suddenly, though of course I had been all along. "I don't, Sam. Don't you get that? I don't think about it. I never have. I'm all fucked up. You never got that."

He laughed a laugh with an edge to it, a laugh I'd rarely heard from him and only toward the end. "I get that," he said. "Believe me. That's not why I came. I told Carly I'd talk to you." He looked up. "But I know you, Nat. I know what you're capable of. What you're not." His hands were trembling at the rail. "Look at you. You don't even want to be happy. We were good together. We were happy. Ours was the right one and you couldn't *stand* it. And now. This guy?"

"You don't even know him."

"I don't have to."

He was right and I should have told him as much. Instead I said, "We should get back."

He nodded once and turned. We walked back without

speaking, him always a few steps ahead of me. A couple times his back straightened and he inhaled sharply as if he wanted to say something. But he never did. In front of my apartment he said, "I'm going to catch a bus. Let your sister know, will you?"

I said, "Wait, Sam. Will you wait a second?" I brought my keys out of my pocket and unlocked my car.

It had been glossy when they printed it out but it had gone satin, somehow. The edges of the quarter sheet had curled in on themselves. He took it from my hand. "What's this?"

"They gave it to me." I pointed where the heavy woman had pointed, the white brackets, the dark space. "There," I said.

He opened his mouth a little. "You kept this?"

"Yeah," I said. It was true, though not in the way I let him believe.

He held it delicately, smoothing a curled corner with his thumb. He said nothing for a long time; then he ran his finger along the bottom edge. "What do these numbers mean?"

"I don't know," I said. "I didn't ask." He held it a while longer, closer to him. When he tried to give it back I gestured for him to keep it. It seemed he would, at first. But then, suddenly, he thrust it back at me and said, "What am I supposed to do with this?"

"I thought you'd want it."

He looked at it again, disgusted, as though he could see everything wrong with me in the image. "It's a piece of paper," he said finally. "It doesn't work like that."

"I thought—"

"Is that what this is about?" He laughed that hard-edged

laugh again. "It is. You're gonna have this baby as some kind of memento. The centerpiece to your little shrine up there? Jesus, Nat. You *are* fucked up."

"I love him."

He slipped the ultrasound into his coat pocket. "You don't love people," he said. "You love what they do to you."

When I went inside, Carly was at the window. She'd been watching us. "Jesus," I said. "What were you thinking?"

She put her finger to her lips and said, "Shh." She gestured to the bedroom.

"Fine," I said. I walked into the kitchen, retrieved a pack of cigarettes from on top of the fridge, and went out to the fire escape. My hands were shaking.

Carly followed me outside. "What are you doing? You promised."

I lit a cigarette and took a drag. "Why the fuck would you bring him here?"

"I was worried about you."

I exhaled. "The fuck you were. You're coming over here, dressing the Miracle like—"

"You promised," she said again.

"Get out."

"What?"

"Leave. Take her with you. Don't come back."

She began to cry. "Listen to yourself—"

"You listen. Do you know what you're saying? Have a *baby*? Look at me." I was shouting. "Look at my life. Why would you want anyone to have a life like ours?"

She wiped her eyes, sending out little sooty shooting stars of mascara. "You don't even sound like you."

"I don't sound like *you*," I said. I was crying now, too. A car alarm sounded somewhere. Beyond its wailing was downtown, the lights of the casinos crisp in the cold, the Truckee running through. Sam was on a bus, homebound. And beyond that, somewhere, was Ezra, his impossible laugh, his half breaths, his index finger looped around my big toe. Here was my sister, pulling me to her.

"I've got too much of her in me," I said. "I can feel it."

Carly took a deep breath of cold air. "Me, too," she said into my hair. She sounded surprised. "Me, too."

She held me that way for some time. When she let me go she touched the soft places under my eyes with the cuff of her sweater. She nodded to my cigarettes. "Give me one of those, would you?"

We leaned against the building and smoked in silence. Once, Carly turned and cupped her hands against my bedroom window. "Look at this," she said.

Inside, the Miracle was splayed out on my bed, asleep. Her wings and headband had been cast off, and the nunchucks Sam bought her were on the floor. She was sleepmoist, and the wild wispy hairs around her face curled in the dampness. We watched her stretch triumphantly, her brawny hands curled in fists.

THE DIGGINGS

for Captain John Sutter

There were stories in the territory, stories that could turn a sane man sour and a sour man worse. Three Frenchmen in Coloma dug up a stump to make way for a road and panned two thousand dollars in flakes from the hole. Above the Feather River a Michigander lawyer staked his mule for the night and when he pulled it in the morning a vein winked up at him. Down on the Tuolumne a Hoosier survived a gunfight and found his fortune in the hole the bullet drilled in the rock above his shoulder. In Rough and Ready a man called Bennager Raspberry, aiming to free a ramrod jammed in his musket, fired at random into the exposed roots of a manzanita bush. There he found five thousand dollars in gold, free and pure. Near Carson Creek a Massachusetts man died of isthmus sickness, and mourners shoveled up a seven-pound nugget while digging his grave.

In California gold was what God was in the rest of the country: everything, everywhere. My brother Errol told of a man on a stool beside him who bought a round with a pinch of dust. He told of a child dawdling in a gully who found a queerly colored rock and took it to his mother, who boiled it with lye in her teakettle for a day to be sure of its composition. He told of a drunkard Pike who'd found a lake whose shores sparkled with the stuff but could not, once sober, retrieve the memory of where it was. There were men drowning in color, men who could not walk into the woods to empty their bladders without shouting, *Eureka!*

And there were those who had nothing. There were those who worked like slaves every single day, those who had attended expensive lectures on geology and chemistry back home, those who had absorbed every metallurgy manual on the passage westward, put to memory every map of those sinister foothills, scrutinized every speck of filth the territory offered and in the end were rewarded without so much as a glinting in their pans.

And there was a third category of miner too, more wretched and volatile than the others: the luckless believer. Here was a forty-niner ever poised on the cusp of the having class, his strike a breath away in his mind. Belief was a dangerous sickness at the diggings—it made a man greedy, violent and insane. This fever burned hotter within my brother than in any other prospector among the placers. I know, because I lit him.

I. HO FOR CALIFORNIA!

My brother and I came to gold country from Ohio when Errol was twenty and I seventeen. Our father had gone to God in December of 1848, leaving us three hundred dollars each. I had not been especially interested in the activity out west—my eyes looked eastward, in fact, to Harvard Divinity. But my brother was married to the notion. He diverted the considerable energies he usually spent clouting me or bossing me around and put them toward convincing me to join him. I admit I rather enjoyed this process of conversion—it was maybe the first in all our life together that Errol had regarded me with greater interest than that due an old boot. His efforts having roused in me the spirit of adventure, I began to fancy us brother Argonauts, bold and divine.

We left our mother and sisters in Cincinnati in the early spring of 1849, and set out by way of the Ohio and Missouri rivers. In Independence we bought a small freight wagon and spent a week and what was left of our money readying it. We fit iron rims to the wheels, tightened the spokes, greased the axles, secured the bolts and reinforced the harnesses. We purchased new canvas from an outfitter, coated it with linseed oil and beeswax and stretched it across the new pine bows. My brother, despite his want of artistic aptitude, painted the canvas with a crude outline of Ohio and a script reading *Ho for California!*

In Independence we took up with a group of men who

called themselves the Missouri Overland Mutual Protection Association for California. Errol wrote what was by then surely his hundredth letter to Marjorie Elise Salter, whose family owned and operated Salter Soap & Lye. It was Marjorie for whom Errol was getting rich. That fall and through the winter Errol had developed the habit of slinking off to see her, leaving me to do his chores. I didn't think much of Miss Salter, I'll tell you now. I thought she waltzed rather better than I would want my wife to. But the once I alerted Errol to the infrequency with which Salter girls married into farming families such as ours, he rapped my collarbone with the iron side of a trowel, putting a permanent zag in it.

The day we left Cincinnati, Errol leaned from the steamer, tossed Marjorie a gold coin that had been our father's and shouted, "Where I am going there are plenty more!"

With the yobs and gamblers of the Missouri Company we followed the Platte, then the Sweetwater to South Pass, around the Great Salt Lake, then along the course of a river called the Humboldt, whose waters were putrid and whose poisonous grasses killed two of our party's oxen. At the place where that miserable river disappeared into the sand we found a boulder on which an earlier traveler had scraped some words with a nib of charcoal. It read: *Expect to find the worst desert you ever saw and then to find it worse than you expected. Take water. Take water. You cannot carry enough.*

And so we filled canteens, kegs, coffeepots, waterproof sacks and rubberized blankets. Errol removed his gum boots and filled them, then ordered me to do the same. Those we kept secret. We crossed the Hundred Mile Desert only at night, following in the moonlight a trail marked by discarded stoves and trunks and mining equipment and the stinking carcasses of mules and oxen.

II. ABANDONED AT CARSON SINK

At the westernmost edge of the Hundred Mile Desert our leaders unhitched the animals and led them ahead in search of a spring, to recuperate and reconnoiter. Errol and I were assigned, with some others, to stay behind and guard the wagons. The goldfields were close, we knew, and as one day passed and another and we were not retrieved, some of us began to suspect we had been deserted, left to die in that sink, thirsty and scalpless.

After three days without word a young man named Doble, of Shelby County, Indiana, proposed that we remainers set out for the diggings on our own. Errol and I were set to go when I experienced a troubling augury.

Since the time when I was very young I had experienced auguries, strange phenomena of the mind in which the visual composition of a scene before me summoned a vivid dream I had had of the same scenario. I was then able to recall the dream, including those depictions that had not yet happened in the waking world. They were a form of prophecy, though I experienced no tingling, weightlessness, chills, nor any other of the physical sensations associated with soothsaying. I felt only a sharpness between my eyes, which could usually be alleviated by removing my eyeglasses and pinching firmly the bridge of my nose.

My auguries came at random frequency, and were of random relevance. Sometimes they allowed me to see only the coming moment; other times I might distinguish the happenings of many months hence. Most events depicted therein were of little significance: our chickens would squabble over a scattering of corn; my youngest sister, Mary, would ruin a pair of our father's stockings while learning to stitch; winter would be cold. Until Carson Sink the most significant augury I had experienced occurred at the age of eleven, while I watched two men unload a freight wagon outside Edward Boynton's store. I saw that a keg of brandied peaches Boynton had received was tainted, and would make several people ill. I alerted Boynton of this and he—already suspecting this particular vendor of dishonesty—opened the keg, found the peaches were indeed spoiled, and lobbied a refund. I attempted to convey my condition, as I had come to consider it, to my parents, but Errol was the only who believed me. He was the only who ever believed me.

The visual arrangement which triggered the augury at Carson Sink was my brother's sack, partially filled, slumped to the right, and beyond it a bare craggy peak and the white sun, all in a line. Clear as a sketch I saw Errol and me following Doble and his company into the mountains. I saw the wagons down in the sink where we would leave them, circled like the spokes of a wheel. I saw three toes of my brother's bare right foot black with frostbite. I saw man consuming man in the snow.

"What's that?" Errol said, noticing my affliction. He took me by the arm away from the others. "What have you seen?"

"We cannot go with them." I recounted the augury. "We'll die," I finished.

Errol tore off a sliver of fingernail with his teeth and spit it to the ground. "We'll die if we stay," he said finally.

"Likely," I admitted.

"But you say we should stay."

"Yes." I had seen his dead body in those mountains as clearly as I saw his live one before me now.

"Damn you, Joshua. How do you expect we'll get rich without ever setting foot at those diggings?"

I looked at the range, which rose out of the ground as though she knew her peaks were the only thing standing between us and those goldfields. That was the main impression I had during our travels, that the ranges of the West had a way of making you feel watched. "I only know what I've seen," I said, fearing he would strike me.

Errol regarded Doble and the others, who were near ready to depart. He sighed. "Then we stay," he said. "For now." He ordered me to return our things to the wagon. Then he approached Doble and informed him of our intent to remain in the sink. "Storm coming," he said.

Doble looked to the sky, cloudless. "Boy, leave the weather to me."

"This is not the time to cross," said Errol.

Doble scoffed. "It's barely October."

Errol returned to our wagon.

I whispered that we ought not let them go.

"You're welcome to elaborate," he said, "and risk them shooting you to alleviate you of your madness. Kindly leave me out of it if you do."

We stayed. They went. I did not warn them. I was young and a coward, if you want to know the word. At the time I thought no fate worse than being considered a lunatic.

Errol and I watched from the valley as a tremendous storm took the range. It lasted three days, and the snow remained for ten more. Each night we built a fire and sat shuddering before it, the wagons round ours empty as fresh-built pine boxes. We did not speak of the storm nor the men up in it excepting the first day, when Errol said he would not care for a stroll in those hills right now, and I said I would not, either. That was, I think, his way of thanking me.

The report reached the diggings before we did. It went round and round and still goes round today: an expedition perished under a bad storm. The Missouri Overland Mutual Protection Association. Trapped in the mountains with nothing to eat but their own dead.

III. THE RESCUING SHE-ASS

We survived in the sink on quail which Errol shot and what scant rations the others could not carry. But both supplies and game swiftly dwindled. One night when I lay awake considering starvation and Indian ambush and cougar attack and worse, I saw shadows moving along our canvas. I remained in my ruck, petrified, not even reaching for the knife near my feet nor the musket near my sleeping brother's. The shadows grew monstrous in size until finally a dark shape loomed at the rear of the wagon. When the form emerged through the slit in the canvas, I nearly laughed aloud at my own cowardice.

It was the head of a burro. She stared at me, ears twitching, an almost intelligent expression on her long face. I donned my spectacles and climbed quietly from the wagon. I ran my hand along her coarse mane and dust rose from it. I did not recognize the animal. She likely belonged to another caravan and had been abandoned, like us.

In the dimness I saw that her back bore the black cross of Bethlehem. I traced my fingers along this coloring and felt beneath it each individual knob of her spine. I wished I had an apple to give her, or a pear. I was overcome then by the melancholy that had been accumulating in me since I left Ohio. I wrapped my arms around the beast's soft brown neck and wept. The jenny blinked her long-lashed glassy eye and began to walk. I, trail-weary and homesick and perhaps resigned to death, let her pull me along, stumbling and wetting her mange with my tears.

We walked together through sand and scrub and rock for I knew not how long. We crested a hill and then another. And then the old girl stopped. Before us, quaking in the moonlight, was the giant spherical head of a cottonwood. It was the first tree I had seen in seven hundred miles.

I ran down the hill to the tree, stumbling, and fell finally at its raised roots. Beside the cottonwood was a stream, icy and clear. I drank from it, drank and drank and drank. The water soon returned some of my faculties and I turned to account for the burro. She stood, miraculously, on the hill where I left her.

I retrieved her and we both drank. As the sun rose I rode the old girl back to the wagon, calling, *Hullo, hullo,* to Errol. The look on his face suggested he thought us a mirage, and indeed when I drew near he reached up and touched my jaw, lightly. The jenny and I led him to the cottonwood, a warm wind at our three faces. Errol took a bit of the stream in his hand. "It's meltwater," he said.

Errol wanted to set out that day but it was the Sabbath, and he surprised me by agreeing to observe it, which we had not done but once the entire journey. So Errol sat drinking beside the crick and I spoke a service, the first of my life. I knew then that the Word was my calling, but knew as well that it was too late to follow.

At dawn we loaded the jenny with our supplies and those which the others had not been able to carry. That same curiously warm chinook was with us as we followed the stream into the hills, where it branched from a mountain river throbbing with snowmelt. The river led us through the Sierra Nevada, and we spent some threatening cold days in those mountains, our burro growing so weak that we were forced to discard nearly all her load, save for the meagerest provisions and two books—the Bible and *The Odyssey*—which I insisted on keeping with me always.

Finally, she bore us to the diggings. I recall the moment we crested the last ridge on our journey. It was dusk, and lightning bugs blinked among the shrubs. I cleaned my spectacles and saw then that they were no insects but the fires of the goldfields, strung along the foothills below us. We howled in joy and exhaustion. I knelt, and asked Errol to do the same. I spoke a prayer of thanks to God and to the rescuing she-ass He'd sent us. Errol, blasphemer that he was, spoke a prayer of thanks to me.

IV. DECEPTION AT ANGEL'S CAMP

So it was that we arrived at the diggings penniless and without any equipment. Our first stop was the general store in Angel's Camp, which was at that time a log house rudely thrown together with mud. There, we had no choice but to sell our burro to the store's proprietor, a Swede who denied us a fair price, saying she was an Arkansas mule and not of the sturdier Mexican stock.

God had tested my brother with a wicked temper and a walloping hook. It was a test he often failed back home, bloodying Ohio noses and blacking Ohio eyes for no good reason I could see. I was worried he might put his pique to use here, where we had no one. I discreetly reminded by brother that we were not in the East anymore and that this man was likely the only merchant in the entire county. Inwardly, though, I envied the way my brother could make a man cower.

So, in the first of many injustices in the territory, we sold the jenny to outfit ourselves with a fraction of the very supplies we had dumped in the Sierra: an iron pan for the outrageous sum of sixteen dollars and a shovel at the ungodly price of twenty-nine. We also purchased two red shirts, two pairs of smart-looking tan pantaloons, a tent, a sack of flour, and a shank of dried pork.

Errol sent another letter to Marjorie, which contained many standard fabrications as to our good luck and our promising claim and the clement passage overland, which despite accounts to the contrary was entirely manageable for a lady. I scribbled a postcard to our mother, telling her only the truth: that we had arrived, and that we were alive. Outfitted, we hiked three miles to the American River and established our humble camp at a sandbar where the fat-pocketed Swede had told Errol there was gold for the picking.

I had envisioned the diggings a place of desolation and solitude—such was the portrayal in the literature on the subject—and so I was rather dismayed to find that the American had other forty-niners populating her banks. By their accents I made out Southerners and Yanks, Pikes, Limeys, Canadians and Keskydees. By sight I identified Mexicans, Negroes and Indians. A Pike who claimed he had been a riverboat captain in St. Louis informed me that the Negroes were former slaves—fugitives, though he didn't say the word. The Indians, he said, were current slaves.

Whether white or colored, every man wore the same red work shirts which Errol and I had so recently purchased, though most were by now a sort of purple with filth. Their pantaloons had gone a snuffy black. Some had added sashes about the collar for a touch of the dude, and most of these were all but shredded with wear.

The only deviants from this diggings uniform were two Chinamen who worked the claim adjacent to ours. I had never seen a Chinaman before and I fear I gazed quite rudely at them. The two—a father and his son, whose age I estimated to be around thirteen—wore billowing yellowish frocks gathered in a queer fashion. They panned not with iron but with the same type of pointed bowls of woven straw they wore as hats. Beneath those brims were their curious slit eyes and skin so hairless and smooth as to appear made of wax. But strangest of all were the snakelike black pigtails gathered from a snatch of hair at their napes and falling down their backs. The boy's descended past his shoulders impressively. But it was a sapling compared to his father's, which was so long that when he stooped at the river its tip dipped into the green water and swayed there as he panned.

We staked our ten-by-ten claim and worked it twelve hours a day for two days, Errol at the shovel and me at the pan, then, after Errol called me a duffer, another ten days with me at the shovel and Errol at the pan. Rumor had the territory brimming with gold so handy that men had gouged their wealth from the rock with a pocket blade or a spoon. In truth the work of extracting color was of the spirit-defeating sort, a labor which combined the various arts of canal digging, ditching, stone laying, plowing, haying and hoeing potatoes. The law required us to work our claim every single day, including the Sabbath, lest we lose our rights to it. Thus we toiled in the freezing river and under the burning rays of the sun from dawn to dark, day after miserable day. When finally we went to bed I could not sleep for the pain coursing along my back and between my shoulders.

Even Errol complained, his obstinate nature overridden by the numbness in his hands from rotating the pan all day. When I did sleep, I woke shivering and soaked in heavy dew. Soon I was rousing myself by scratching my body and scalp bloody where I'd been munched by fleas and lice, which the forty-niners called quicks and slows. Added to this misery was the constant terror of those dark mountains looming behind us, sheltering cougars and grizzly bears and other unknown beasts that I sometimes heard moving through the forest in the night.

During this period we dredged only meager flakes, not even an eighth of an ounce per day. These I stored in an empty mustard jar. On the thirteenth day my shovel hit foreign material, making an audible metallic *tink*. Errol and I both started. I reached into the hole with my hands to dig but Errol pushed me aside. He scratched at the hole zealously and finally pulled up an empty whiskey bottle, proof that our spot had already been excavated.

Errol swore and whipped the bottle into the river. He kicked our iron pan in after it. I plunged into the water to retrieve the costly tool. I returned ashore intending to scold my brother, but I was met by a look of such anger and shame that I could not speak.

"We've been had, Joshua," he said. "We've been taken on a damned ride."

He set out in the direction of Angel's Camp, cursing and swinging at every shrub and low-hanging branch along the way. I gathered our shovel and pan and followed him, wet to my waist, goldless California dust making mud on me.

At the Swede's, Errol directed me to follow him inside and not to speak. A hearty fear came over me, and I was glad we had no weapon between us. But my brother removed his hat and greeted the Swede cordially. "Say," Errol said, after trading some pleasantries, "we came up empty at that bar down the way."

"Eh?" said the slippery Swede from beneath his mightily waxed mustache.

Errol asked whether we might have better luck upriver or down, creekside or in the dry hills, in soil yellowish or redder, and the Swede dispensed advice freely.

"One more thing," Errol said to the Swede. "Has the coach been by? With the mail?"

The Swede laughed. "You'll know when it has, boy."

Outside, Errol was visibly glum. "It will come soon," I said.

"Have you *seen* it?" he asked excitedly.

"No," I admitted. "Only it's bound to."

Errol scowled. "Fetch our things and find me upriver."

"But he said downriver."

Errol took me by the shoulder. "Consider that man our compass, Joshua. He says downriver, we go up. He says hillside and we stay on the banks. Understand?"

V. LUMP FEVER

And so we moved upriver, and upriver farther three days after that. From there we were ever on the move. In years hence I have come to believe that the rotten Swede's deception combined with the maddening stories I have described infected Errol with a specific lunacy. Lump fever, it was called at the diggings. It left my brother perpetually convinced that gold was just a claim or two above our own, that the big strike was ever around the bend. He was mad with it.

What agitated him further were the Chinamen, who followed us whenever we moved. We would establish a new camp, and sure as the California sun they would relocate to our old claim. The Chinamen moved in the night, it seemed, for when we woke it was as though they had simply materialized at our abandoned claim. I thought them humorous, with their pointed hats and billowy frocks and pigtails. But they made Errol nasty with agitation. He would emerge from the tent each morning and immediately look downriver to where the tongs were already up and working the patch we'd left. "It's an ignorant strategy," he said often. Indeed, we never saw them pull anything of value from those worked holes.

Errol and I had panned flakes enough only to partially replenish our stock of meat and flour. The rest of what we needed we bought on credit. Each morning and night I fried a hunk of pork in the same skillet we used to pan the river. After, I mixed flour in the grease to make a gray, pork-flecked porridge. I was a lacking cook, I admit, but that pork would have bested the fairest housewife. Pickled, cured, or fried, the swine of California was the stinkingest salt junk ever brought around the Horn.

Errol sloughed off weight. One morning I watched him from behind as he rinsed his dish in the river. He had not yet donned his shirt and the way he was bent caused the bones of his hips to rise from his trousers in startling iliac arcs. He reminded me of a bloodhound we had once, with the same scooped-out space where meat ought to have been. This socket movement was hypnotic, so much so that I felt compelled to run my thumb along one of those bone ridges. When I touched my brother, he jumped.

"You've gone a beanpole," I stuttered.

He held the spoon he'd been washing at my eye level. The reflection was a skeletal version of myself, bug eyes and bony nose. I reached up and touched my whiskers, scraggly thin and clumped with filth. I was unsettled by my reflection and pushed the spoon away. I resolved to shave as soon as we could afford a whetting stone.

Throughout that day and others I considered that reflection. Its most unsettling aspect was not my thinness or my griminess, but my new resemblance to Errol. I'd somehow acquired his nose, his jawline, his seriousness about the eyes. He and I had never looked particularly similar before, but we did there, in the agony of starvation and ceaseless labor. The territory had twinned us.

VI. AUGURY AT AN AGREEABLE SLOUGH

Lump fever took us into November. We would shovel and pan, shovel and pan, shovel and pan. And without fail Errol would get to looking upriver, and we would have to pick up our stakes and start anew. At the rate we were moving, we would retrace our route eastward to Ohio by spring, a notion I would have found more than acceptable, were we not certain to die on the way.

Eventually we came to a sunny slough where the water was shallow and slightly warmer than we were accustomed to. We had barely begun our endeavor when, without a word to me, Errol began to pack our things.

I was crazy with fatigue, perhaps. Instead of packing I retrieved the mustard jar where I kept our flakes. On it I had pasted a strip of paper which I had marked from the bottom up with the names of foods available in camp: flour, salt pork, pork stew, pork and beans, roast beef and potatoes, plum duff, canned turkey with fixings and, at the very top, oysters with ale or porter. We had never eaten above pork and beans and I reminded him of it.

"Let's work this bar a while," I begged him. "A week, say."

Errol stood and looked to me. He made a sad clicking with his tongue. "This is not the place."

"We've been at it less than a day."

He resumed gathering our few things, including that evil keg of salt pork.

"Errol," I said.

"We haven't the time," he shouted. "Men are getting rich around us!"

"A cradle, then." I had read of men using rocking boxes during the rush down in Georgia.

Errol scoffed. "The Swede's asking a hundred dollars for one."

"We'll build our own. Work twenty times as much rock

through it." I held the mustard jar, shaking it like a babe's empty rattle. "This is the place."

Errol hovered over his ruck where he was rolling it. "You're certain?" I knew what he was asking by the way he asked it. He harbored such reverence for my visions that it changed the way he spoke. "You're *certain*?" he repeated.

What I was was homesick and hungry and bone tired. But my brother made no allowances for these. "I'm certain," I said.

Errol dropped his sack and clapped me on the back. "Ho, ho!"

A more decent man would have been troubled to see his own brother go giddy at such a lie. But my conscience was waylaid by his gratitude, which caused a sudden sting in my heart. I had long known my brother had brought me to California not for my strength or my intellect or even for my company. He had brought me so that my auguries could make him rich.

I'd never found the fact troubling; it was in keeping with the way he'd been to me as long as I'd been alive. But what comfort it would have been, I thought now, if but once on this long, torturous journey he had intimated that he wanted me along to help him, because we were brothers. Brotherhood had never been on his mind, and for the first time I hated that it wasn't. I hated that he considered me of use only when the visions overtook me. And in this thinking I saw his cure and mine: I would find our gold. I would tunnel my way to his affections. I would make him love me in the way of brothers.

I removed my spectacles, pinched the bridge of my nose and closed my eyes. "I have seen it," I said. "Oh, I have *seen* it."

VII. A CRADLE AND ITS TROUBLES

Back home we could have built a cradle in two hours for two dollars. But lumber was scarce and expensive, so we had no choice but to cut our own. From the Swede I procured a saw, a hammer and some nails, all on credit. Errol and I worked steadily at the cradle for three days, a lifetime in the gold hills. Once he took a step back to assess our work, the crude box set on rockers. "I must admit," he said, "I never imagined I would be caught a bachelor fashioning a cradle in the womanless wilds." I knew about the branch of juniper he'd notched, a notch for each of the thirty-six days since he'd dispatched his last pitiful letter to Marjorie. But he seemed in good spirits as we worked, and I softened toward him. He had a winning way about him when he chose.

With the cradle finally assembled, we saw that it would indeed move more rock, that neither of us had accounted for just how much rock it was capable of moving. The problem was that the cradle required constant rocking in order for the gold to be captured in the riffles while worthless sediment passed them by. For a day we tested different arrangements. First we had Errol rocking away while I attempted simultaneously to dig the pay dirt, scoop it into the hopper and pour river water over the sediment so that its finer particles might be strained through the canvas apron. Inevitably I would run out of either sediment or water and have to fetch some more, at which point the slurry would stop streaming and our momentum would be lost. The cradle, ingenious a device as it was, depended on a steadier rocking and pouring than we two alone could maintain.

Errol, seeing the imperfection of our new method, became frequently agitated, and would often curse me, take the shovel from my hand and push me to the handle. Attempting to man both the shovel and the bucket on his own, Errol would see quickly what I saw: our operation was a man short.

"This won't do," he said finally. "We're just rinsing the soil."

I nodded.

"We need more hands," he said.

I might have made that observation twelve long and fruit-less hours earlier, were I not sure he would smash up all our hard work in a fit. "What about the Chinamen?" I said.

Errol shook his head. "I won't split with them."

"And what's our choice? Split nothing fifty-fifty. Fifty-fifty salt pork and gruel? Fifty-fifty sleeping on the ground?" I cast my shovel to the ground. Now I was agitated, and from the corner of my eye I saw the elder Chinaman pause. "Do you know what we owe that Swede?"

Errol returned me the shovel. "You don't become a man of society by keeping quarters with Orientals."

VIII. THE FIRST COACH

When we rose in the morning the diggings were deserted. I trudged sleepily up and down the bank in my long johns. The place had gone a ghost town. Upriver each claim was abandoned, pans half sifted, the wooden handles of shovels jutting like masts from where their heads had been thrust into the soil. Downriver was the same, except for the Chinamen, who worked on, same as ever. I approached the father, aware that Errol was following.

"Where's everyone gone?" I said. I pointed to the manless claims. "Where are they?" The Chinaman began to speak in the tong language, which I had never heard. The sound was bizarre and impenetrable.

Errol interrupted him. "Has there been a strike?" he said loudly.

The Chinaman pressed his lips together, then began to speak again, slowly. And again, the language was entirely incomprehensible.

"A strike! A strike!" shouted Errol, hopping and flailing his arms in the general direction of the mountains. "Has there been a strike, you old fool?"

"No strike," came a clear, effeminate voice beyond the commotion. We turned to see the boy standing on the banks, holding his pan of woven straw. "He say, 'A coach. In the night.'"

We stared like idiots.

"Mail," the boy said.

Errol took off.

"Thank you," I said to the boy. "You know 'thank you'?"

"Yes," he said.

I dressed and followed Errol along the trail to Angel's Camp. Out front of the Swede's a monstrous crowd was gathered around a stagecoach. There were men in numbers I had never seen, hundreds of men not only from our fork of the American but from all of Calaveras County and Eldorado beyond. They were the roughest specimens I have ever seen, and nearly every one of them brandished a revolver or a musket.

The driver of the coach had climbed atop the cab and was arbitrating the rowdy crowd from that position. In his hands he clutched a distressingly small bundle of letters. Errol attempted to pry his way to the heart of the crowd. He pushed between men, struggling to get within shouting distance of the coach. Surely without thinking he shouldered past a ruffian at least half a rod tall with a beard grown down to his chest. The man—a Southerner—informed Errol that he had occupied that spot since before sunup and that he was unlikely to forfeit it to Errol or to anyone. For proof he showed Errol his Bowie knife.

It was then that we noticed that from the mob grew a tail of men. There were too many men to approach the coach at once, and we weaklings had been dispatched to wait in line. We followed this tail through town and out of it, finding its end finally in the woods, behind two Mexicans.

We stood in line for half a day. By the time we came back in view of the coach, emotions had reached the breaking point. Full-grown rough-and-tumbles shouted their names up to the driver and trembled while he searched his bunch. Men who had no letter waiting—and these were the majority—cursed their wives or friends or family for forgetting them. Some desperate fellows offered the coachman flakes in exchange for a missive, as if one might be conjured for the right price. But this was the one place in California where color held no sway.

Very occasionally I watched the coachman pluck a dirty, tattered envelope from his stack and hand it down. The coarse men nearest the coach took the letter as delicately as they might a baby and passed it among them until it reached its rightful owner. As the lucky man opened the letter the others moved away, as if to make room for his reading.

As we neared the coach we spotted the Southern ruffian sitting on a log, holding a letter gingerly between his massive hands. His beard was wet with tears. "Happy devil," Errol said.

By the time Errol and I approached, the deliveryman's bundle had become terribly thin.

"Boyle," Errol shouted, although it was not quite our turn. "Letter for Boyle?"

The coachman, who had by now taken a seat on the edge of the cab roof, searched his skinny bundle. It did not take long. "No letter," he said.

"You're sure?" said Errol. But the man had already solicited the next eager miner.

"Please, sir," I called out. "Check again. The name's Boyle. Errol. Or Joshua."

The coachman did check again, God bless him. "Apologies, my boy. Maybe next time."

I set out in the direction of the river. Errol did not follow me. When I turned, he was standing in the middle of Main Street, which at the time was nothing more than a dirt thoroughfare. His face was blank and he stared at the ground between us. His hands were upturned queerly, as though he carried a burden I could not see.

"Suppose I'll stay in town a bit," he said.

"And do what?" I said. But he was already shuffling toward the tavern.

"Forget her," I called. "She puts on airs."

He came at me swinging to heaven, and struck me once upside the head with a tight, demonic fist. I collapsed, hiding my head beneath my arms. I thought he would strike me again where I lay, but instead he said only, "Don't."

IX. BEASTS OF THE TERRITORY

I panned our claim halfheartedly and alone for what remained of that day, palming secretly the tender knob on my skull. By dusk Errol had not returned. I watched the sunset, gnawing on a rind of salt pork and listening to the heartsick yowls of drunken forty-niners. Errol was somewhere among them, I knew, blubbering about Marjorie. I cursed him. How my body complained, how my stomach wanted, how close we had both come to death how many times so he might win the good favor of a girl whose father owned a stinking soap factory!

I found his pitiful notching stick and snapped it, then snapped it again. I threw the pieces into the fire. One thing I learned from the diggings is that a love of destruction is in every man's heart, somewhere.

As darkness thickened, my thoughts went to my father. It had been nearly a year since his death and I had nothing of his to touch. I was in a wilderness where he had never set foot, where his spirit would not even know to look for me. I tried to remember everything I could about him. Anything. My freakish mind could conjure up sketches of the future but none of my father's features, not the smell or feel of him. I cried, a little.

I tried to go to bed early but the groans and rustlings of night turned sinister, if not in actuality then in my imagination. I became afraid. I rose and dressed and walked without thinking down the moist bank, to the Chinamen's camp.

The man and boy sat across their fire from each other as I approached, not speaking. Their hats were off and their heads—bald and yellow save for the thick tuft of bound hair at their napes—glowed in the firelight. There was something peaceful in their silence, and their fire was large and warm. The boy saw me first and startled. The man turned slowly, and I saw him reach for a switch at his side.

"I'm unarmed," I said, and raised my empty hands. They spoke in their language for a bit. It seemed they were trying to decipher why I'd come, or perhaps I ascribed those aims to them because I was wondering myself. Eventually the man gestured for me to sit between them.

"Cold out," I said, though it wasn't particularly. They said nothing. "Have you all been hearing those hollers?" I asked. Still, they said nothing. We watched the fire. After some time a pocket of sap popped loudly and I jumped like a Mexican bean. The elder man seemed to find this exceedingly funny. When he was through laughing, he said something to me in his language.

"He say you get a letter," said the boy.

"No," I said. "Not today."

He told his father.

"Sad," said the boy. He was only a child, I saw then, younger than I had originally estimated, but with a sharpness about the eyes that conveyed sure ripsniptiousness.

"Yes," I said.

A man yelped somewhere.

I felt the need to tell him that I didn't care for drink and the boy found this remarkable enough to relay to his father, who nodded what seemed like approval. We were quiet a little longer.

"Say," I said to the boy. "Can I ask you something?"

He nodded.

"Why have you both been following us the way you have? Why not find a claim of your own? Seems a fool's strategy to mine what's already been mined, if you will excuse my saying so."

The child conveyed my question to his father. They exchanged words for what seemed a good long time. I grew nervous and said, "Tell him never mind."

But the boy waved his thin hand in dismissal. Finally, he turned to me. "He say too many tongs killed that way."

"Which?"

"Like you say. Find own claim."

"I don't follow."

"He say *you* find lode, men happy." He pointed to me and then to the river. "*Tong* find lode men say 'steal.' They say 'hang.'"

The old man spoke again, and the boy's gaze went to the ground.

"What did he say?" I asked.

The boy looked at me. "He say to tell you my father hang that way."

"He's not your papa?" I said, gesturing to the Chinaman. "Your father, I mean."

"He *shu fu*," said the boy. "Uncle."

So we sat, two fatherless boys, two brotherless men. We watched the fire a little longer. I thought it was perhaps time for me to go, and that I should not have come at all.

Just then the elder Chinaman spoke to the boy. In turn the boy fetched a long wooden box from the tent and delivered it to his uncle. The box had been polished up nicely and gleamed in the firelight. The Chinaman removed the carved lid and lifted a long tubular object from the box. Initially I thought the apparatus was a flute or some similar musical instrument of the Orient. The stem of it seemed to be made of a lightwood and the lower portion had been adorned with a saddle of stamped brass. On this saddle was mounted a delicately grooved bulb made of earthenware, the top hemisphere of which the Chinaman presently removed.

From the wooden box he lifted what looked like a lady's perfume bottle and deposited some of its coalish black dust into the bulb's tiny compartment. At that point it occurred to me that the device was a type of smoking pipe.

The Chinaman reattached the bulb's lid, then bent and pulled a branch from the fire by its unburned end. The lit end of the stick flickered wickishly. He held the branch in one hand and the pipe in the other and tilted the pipe so the flame rippled around the bulb. He puffed there for some time before offering it to me.

My father had been a tobacco smoker. He especially liked his pipe late at night, on the back steps. In this way the Chinaman evoked some of the memories I had been longing for. I took the apparatus. The Chinaman held the stick to the bulb and said something.

"He say breathe," said the boy. He tapped his own breastbone. "Breathe here."

The apparatus was heavier than I had imagined, and had a fine, sturdy feel. I wiped the fluted end, put my lips to it and felt that the cylinder was made not of lightwood but of ivory. I puffed as the Chinaman had and he made sounds that I interpreted as encouragement. I took what felt like a chestful and immediately my lungs revolted, setting off a great avalanche of coughs. The Chinaman laughed at this, too.

I returned the pipe and I watched the old man at it. At this proximity I could see the many wrinkles like folds at his small eyes and around his mouth. He finished his puffing and smiled. His teeth were brown and soft with rot. I tried the pipe again, with more success. He took his pigtail in his hand and brushed its end on his own palm. The boy did the same. I had a good feeling from them.

"But how do you make a living, working tailings the way you do?" I said.

The nephew smiled a devious little smile. "I find smallest gold," he said. "Smallest and smallest. I see things white men do not."

I sat with them for some time, accepting and passing the ivory instrument and listening to the two talk. Sometimes, the boy would pause to translate some of their conversation for me:

"He say winter no trouble in Gum Shan."

"He say take much care with ball of mud."

"He say tong war coming."

I did not understand what the old man meant by these, but that didn't matter. I was very warm and now pleasantly drowsy, as though I had been submerged slowly into a hot bath. I removed my glasses and held them in my hand, content to watch the blur of the fire and listen. Their language seemed a beautiful thing, something I ought to have understood.

And then the elder Chinaman began to sing.

At first he sang so softly that I wasn't sure his song wasn't something I was imagining, a trick of the fire and the river. But then the boy joined in and they raised their voices together. They sounded like instruments, their voices. I thought nothing of Errol, except to note that I felt more at ease now than I had since setting foot aboard that steamer in Cincinnati. And though the two sang in their Orient language I knew by way of feeling that their song was about fleas and lice and vultures and blue jays and marmots and coons and cougars and grizzly bears, and through their soothing melody all these once frightful and malevolent creatures streamed into my heart as though it were Noah's, and nested there harmoniously.

X. AN OPHIR, AN EDEN

I was awoken by my own sickness. It was morning and though I had no recollection of returning to my camp nor of putting myself to bed, I lay with my torso in the tent, shirtless. I managed to rise and express my queasiness in a nearby manzanita bush. Only after I rose did I see Errol.

He lay faceup between the tent and the river, where he'd made a pillow of a stone. He was barefooted, bareheaded and bare-legged. His shirt was the only clothes upon his person. A pile of maple leaves had been assembled and arranged to conceal his parts. As I washed myself in the chilly river he woke, groaning.

Errol walked into the woods and emerged sometime later, dressed. "I've misplaced my long johns," he said.

"That is a shame," I said. "Because we've no means to replace them." I felt in no top shape myself but was not about to betray the fact to my brother. He came and looked at the salt pork I was fixing and groaned again. He smelled strongly of tanglelegs.

That morning we two worked at the cradle just as inefficiently as ever. The only difference was that Errol silently took up the harder work at the shovel. We did not speak. Near noon he paused in his ditching, nodded to my head and said, "See here, Joshua. I apologize for that. I do. Will you just speak to me again?"

"Will you consider taking them on?" My question surprised me.

"They're filthy," he said with a wave of his hand.

"We're filthy," I said. "We've got a city of slows on each our heads. You've got no long johns."

He spit.

"We need them, Errol. All the Negroes are free. All the Indians are owned. This is a new place, Errol. They work hard and they're honest. We are Argonauts. Christians. We needn't bring the prejudices of the East with us."

"Argonauts," Errol said. "You've got a good heart, brother."

"We won't have to pay them as we would a white."

Errol said nothing.

"They work like dogs. They've been pulling dust from our old holes."

This caught my brother's attention. "Have they?"

"The boy has a keen eye."

"And how did you come by all this? Been over there, have you?"

"No." It was easier to lie to him now, after the first. I was thrilled by how easy it was. "I've *seen* it."

Errol's face brightened. "You're sure about this?"

I ought to have hesitated from guilt. But it felt good to be heeded, and to be making decisions for once. "They're there, with us." I closed my eyes. "The boy pulls a nugget."

He deliberated a moment, then said, "They get fifteen

percent of our findings between them. They don't sleep in our camp. They don't socialize with us."

"Agreed." I was relieved, though by logic I shouldn't have been. All I'd done was recruit men enough to better sift through rock that could very well yield nothing. But perhaps I'd come to believe my lies, too. If nothing else, I believed that if only we could stay in one place long enough, California would offer herself to us. And I liked the Chinaman. I liked his boy.

"And they don't eat with us," Errol added. "I'll gut them if they try to eat with us."

"Agreed," I said. I did not ask who in the world would want to join us for our twice-daily pork sludge.

I brokered our new arrangement through the boy. They seemed at first not to understand the proposal, but then I took them over to where Errol stood at the cradle, shoveling a load of river rock into the hopper and then doing his best to pour water over the apron and rock the mud down the riffles at the same time. At such a pathetic sight, apparently, they immediately grasped the proposed cooperation. I was less confident in my ability to explain the proposed financial terms, but they seemed to accept the fifteen percent without comment. I wonder now if they believed they had no choice.

My brother remained silent until the conversation was over. Then he handed the Chinaman the shovel.

The arrangement worked well—the Chinaman on the shovel, me on the bucket, Errol on the rocker, and the boy at the sluice, to spot color. Errol grumbled that the boy was lollygagging there and ought to be hauling pay dirt. I reminded him of the boy's sharp eyes, to which he made a vulgar remark that I will not transcribe. I am sad to say that my brother routinely unleashed the heat of his character on our Chinamen during those days. He forbade them from speaking to each other in their language. He prohibited them from donning their straw hats and insisted their robes be cinched up tightly. It was not uncommon for foreigners or Negroes to be treated so cruelly, even in Ohio. But it seemed a particular injustice in the territory, because it was a place brand-new, like nothing we had ever seen, far from the achievements of civilization but also from its ugliness. California was an Ophir, not an Eden.

For two days a pair of old Pikes passing through camped near our claim. With them as audience, Errol strode over to the boy one afternoon and began tugging at his robes. "Where is it?" he shouted. He turned to me. "He's pocketed a nugget. I saw him. Hand it over, you devil."

The Chinaman stopped his shoveling. The boy, fairly shaken, denied taking anything.

"Turn out your pockets," demanded Errol.

"He has none," I said. It was the truth and Errol knew it was. Still, he pilfered the folds of the boy's robe saying, *Dirty thief, stinking tong.* The Chinaman moved cautiously closer to Errol and the boy.

Suddenly Errol whirled around, red faced, and pounced on the Chinaman. He drew his knife and took hold of the man's black pigtail.

I was quite frightened, and the boy was by now hysteric. But the Chinaman was still. Errol put the knife to the pigtail and spoke into the man's sun-scarred face. "Are you a citizen of California or not?" he asked.

"He can't understand you," I called, trying to remain calm. "Let him be."

Errol released the Chinaman as quickly as he'd grabbed him. He returned to the sluice as if it had all been a great tease, the Pikes up the bank snarling with laughter. But it was no tease. I had heard rumors out of Hangtown of three tongs hung by their pigtails from a tree, their throats slit.

XI. THE FORTUNE FORETOLD

Despite Errol's occasional volatility, the boy was soon pulling color from the sluice. It was chispa so small and aggregated that no white man would have ever dug it, and Errol said as much— but it was gold all the same. I directed the boy to deposit his findings in our mustard jar. In this way, little by little, day by day, we did accumulate some dust. Errol went to town whenever he had the chance, where he spent his share on card games and spirit. I spent my share on provisions. One Sabbath I had pork and beans. Another, while Errol was away, the Chinamen and I had secret roast beef and potatoes. That rump could have been the toughest, most befouled muscle ever served a man, but to my starved tongue it was gravy-slopped ambrosia.

Then, the day of the first frost, the boy approached Errol and without celebration presented him a grape-size yellow nugget, cool with river water.

My brother did not immediately take the nugget, as I'd always imagined he would. Instead, he leaped to embrace me, taking a long, affectionate look into my anomalous, all-seeing eyes.

After some celebration, Errol spirited the nugget into the tent, pounded it carefully to test for softness, distributed a petal of the malleable color to the Chinamen and a larger leaf to me. Pinching it, I was besieged by fantasies of sardines, tongue, turtle soup, lobster, cakes and pies by the cartful, a box of juicy golden peaches. Unsettling, how swiftly a tiny bead of element could enchant.

Errol instructed us all to continue. "More will come," he called out merrily, barely containing his urge to wink at me. And it seemed more would come, the day we found our nugget, the day my brother's infinite faith intersected with coincidence, the day of the first frost.

XII. WAR!

Two days later, Errol appeared by my side late one morning and said, "There's something I want you to see."

My brother fidgeted with his hands in his pockets excitedly as I followed him to Angel's Camp. "What is it?" I asked several times. His only reply was, "Something you'll have to see to believe." We passed the Swede's and continued down a small hill to where a glade flattened out. Many men were gathered there and my heart picked up some, with fantasies of a second mail coach or a bundle of letters lost and now found. But near the crowd Errol halted and tapped a poster nailed to the trunk of a pine:

WAR! WAR! WAR!

The celebrated Bull-killing Bear

GENERAL SCOTT

Will fight a Bull on Sunday the 15th at 12 p.m.
at Tuolumne Meadow.

The Bull will be perfectly wild, young,
of the Spanish breed
the best that can be found in the country.

The Bull's horns will be of their natural length
NOT Sawed or Filed

– ADMISSION IS $6 OR ONE-HALF OUNCE –

I had heard of Spaniards hosting contests of men versus bulls and the prospect of witnessing this even higher spectacle excited me. Errol and I hustled nearer the arena, which was composed of tiered seats enclosed by a wood slat fence. We could not see inside. Near the entrance two fiddlers played a lively tune, and a barker lured men by extolling the ferocity of the grizzly General Scott and the virility of the Mexican bull, whom he called Señor Cortés, much to the delight of the forty-niners.

But heavy as my pocket was, the entrance fee was prohibitive. As Errol continued to the arena I called after him, "That's a costly admission."

"I knew you would say that," he said. "Follow me, cheapskate."

I pursued him to the rear of the corral where a crab apple stood, its fruit already fallen and rotting in the grass. He climbed near to the top of the tree, then helped me up. From there we were afforded a splendid view of the arena.

"Look there," said Errol, pointing to the clearing at its center. "Your foe." There, tethered by a chain staked into the ground, was a massive grizzly bear. He scratched and scooped at the earth, his great scapulas moving like the machinery of a steam engine. He was carving a burrow for himself, it seemed. Even from our great distance we could see the thick neck shimmering, the monstrous hump at his back swaying, his knifelike claws making shreds of the meadow and the hard-packed soil. I both wished him to roar and feared that he would.

"Now that you've seen one you'll be less afraid," said Errol. I swelled with affection for him then, for I had not thought he'd noticed my fears. This was how I wanted us to be, always.

The barker was riling the crowd, playing on their terror. I

scanned the bronzed and bearded faces under hats of many hues, the gay Mexican blankets and the blue and red bonnets of the French. Among all those like mirages were Mexican women in frilly white frocks, puffing on their cigaritas. Until then I had ever conceived that my wife would be a Buckeye, or perhaps a New Englander. But from where I was perched in that crab apple tree it seemed impossible to choose a bony, board-shaped descendant of the Puritans over one of these rosy, full-formed, sprightly Spaniard women.

Errol said, uncannily, "I'll marry Marjorie in a meadow like this. Beneath a tree."

"I expect so," I managed.

"I'll marry her here; then I will build us a great big house on the same spot. Soon, Angel's Camp will be bigger than San Francisco. I'll have more land than Sutter. I'll buy the Swede's store out from under him. Mr. Salter will have to buy a parcel from me. No." Glee flickered across his face. "I'll *give* him one."

Errol's gaze cast out from the tree, across the corral and the meadow and beyond. "Marj and I will have sons enough to line the American River. You'll be there, too. An uncle."

It touched me to be included like this, in both the fight and the fantasy. "And Mother," I said.

"Yes, Mother, too. And Mary and Harriet and Faith and Louisa, too. Everyone."

Then we were quiet, because we knew it would not be everyone.

By now the action below was nearly afoot. The bear General

Scott had achieved a burrow several hands deep and presently he lumbered into it and lay there on his back, much in the manner of a happy baby. The crowd hated him for his merriment and screamed for the release of the bull. They stomped an infectious rhythm. Errol and I thumped the branches of our tree, too.

From the far end of the arena came a large, muscular bull, with horns like none I had ever seen. The crowd went mute.

"Here we go," whispered Errol.

"Are they going to unchain the bear?" I asked. Errol hushed me.

Initially, the bull seemed not even to notice the bear, so one of the vaqueros jabbed the bull in the rump with a prod, sending the beast galloping from the periphery. This was when he locked eyes on the bear. He stomped and snorted a bit, and then charged General Scott where he lay in his den. I gripped my limb as the bull struck the General in his flank, sending a frightful *thunk* through the meadowland. A cheer escaped from the crowd.

The bull retreated and immediately charged again. But this time the bear affixed his powerful jaws to the bull's nose. The bull let out an unsettling cry. But the General would not relent. He latched his forepaws around the bull's thick neck and held on. I whooped, and in so doing discovered my allegiance lay with the bear General Scott.

The bull attempted to free himself by pounding the General's chest with his mighty hooves. In response, the General dug his foreclaws into the meat of the bull's brawny shoulder. Blood spurted, and Errol and I both cheered. The animals separated. Where the bull's nose had been was now only a dark cavity from which dangled stringy bloodpulp. "My," I breathed.

Errol said, "Aren't you a delicate betty?"

The bull paused, then charged again, only to be locked by the General's devastating, traplike hug. The match went on like this, with the bull trying to hook the General and toss him out of his hole, the General gripping his antagonist and attempting to pull him down to where the bull might be ribboned. The crowd soon grew restless and booed the flagging bull. The impresario emerged, waving his hat, and announced that for two hundred dollars in gold he would release another bull. The hat was passed and the flakes raised. I heard some miners accuse the barker of saving his strongest bull to squeeze more color from them, and when the second bull was released I saw that it was likely true, for this bull stood half a rod taller than the first. His horns were twice as girthy and appeared to have been sharpened.

"Oh," said Errol, some trepidation in his voice.

With both bulls in the arena, General Scott was sorely tried. The first and smaller bull continued with his strategy of charging the grizzly and grappling with him, while the second bull attacked from the side. Soon the larger, nameless bull speared the General in his ribs and dragged him from his hole. The grizzly roared then, his long, blood-covered teeth gleaming in the November sun. It was a forlorn, haunting sound, not at all the monstrous bellow I had yearned for at the battle's onset.

Errol had gone quiet. His hand was drawn to his mouth, as was mine.

Exposed in the grassy open, the bear was a pincushion. Horns penetrated his abdomen, his ribs, his haunches and his back. One goring went into his throat and out the other side. Another stabbed his stomach and sliced up and out near the sternum, letting the bear's guts spill onto the grass. A hot fecal smell filled the air, causing the ladies to bring their kerchiefs to their mouths. There seemed no end to the blood that would spurt from this beast. Soon all the meadowland was wet with it.

The crowd had gone quiet and still, transfixed by the carnage. Finally the impresario directed his vaqueros to lasso the bulls and bring them in. He marched to the center of the arena, where General Scott lay grunting and gurgling in the mud made by his own innards, and declared the bulls the victors of the day. Without warning, he shot the General dead.

The mob slowly shuffled from the arena, no uproar or gaiety left in them. The fiddlers held their fiddle cases to their chests. Errol and I stayed unmoving at our branch perch for just a bit, the vinegar smell from the rotten apples rising all around us. When we finally climbed down, the descent reminded me of how high my spirits had been upon climbing into the tree, and how low they were now.

As we walked it began to rain and we went on, letting the rain get us. Somewhere, I thought, those señoritas are running with their lovely white dresses gathered in their hands.

After some time Errol said, "I believe that was a spectacle I would have rather prevented than witnessed."

"Me, too," I told him, and we went on in silence.

It had been easy to succumb to my own deceptions while eating plum duff and roast beef in the sunlight. But now they were suddenly undeniable. We were returning to a ten-by-ten plot of land which I had deceived my brother into believing held his fortune. All my brother had accumulated in California was a gambler's thirst and some salty talk. I was a liar, a manipulator and a freak.

I said, "You should marry her in a church."

"Don't you know?" Errol said. The rain had stopped now, leaving all the leaves and the soil wet and fragrant and colored vividly. "This is the greatest church there is."

XIII. ORACLE BONES

I had promised that more gold would come but more gold would not come, and after that mournful battle Errol was sick with expectation. He went to town whenever he had the chance, where he spent his share of element on card games and brandy and tarantula juice.

With him gone I spent more time with the Chinamen. The little one was an ace with a rock and it was one of my favorite pastimes to skip stones across the river with him. Sometimes we three whittled miniature boats to race on the water. The elder carved using a small blade with a milky jade handle the exact color of the river at dawn. His ships were the most graceful and well designed. Some of the happiest hours of my life were spent after a whiff or two off the Chinaman's ivory pipe, watching those moonlit vessels spear along the nighttime water and vanish into the darkness.

Some evenings the tongs took turns shaving each other's heads with the jade knife while I read aloud from the two volumes I had to my name. (The tongs preferred Odysseus to Christ.) One night the boy interrupted my reading to ask whether I might teach him. I was a frightful tutor, I fear, but his sharpness hid my inadequacies and soon he had memorized Homer's first song. *Muse! sing the Man by long experience tried, / Who, fertile in resources, wander'd wide.* He orated to his uncle, with the old one smiling dutifully, as though he understood every fine word.

One day the boy snared a deer, and that evening we sat smoking and pulling greasy venison from the spit. Full of roast meat and smoke, I found myself going on and on. I talked mostly of Errol, of the darkness I saw in him and the light I saw in him, too. Of my fear of what would become of him in the territory without me. Then, without thinking, I said to the boy, "I have peculiar vision, too. Like you at the sluice. I can see what's not yet happened. It's a condition I have. A deformity."

He translated this to his uncle, who paused at his venison shank, sifted another thatch of black powder into the bowl, and handed it to me. As I took it, he spoke through the boy.

He said, "There are many people see in all directions. At home, seers set bones in fire, read future in the cracks. These men are . . ." The boy searched for the appropriate word, settling finally for two. "A gift."

Something went through me then: a phantasm that warmed me, physically. The sensation of truly belonging in a place and a moment is a rare one. I have not felt it since.

The Chinaman had contentedly taken up his venison again. I must have gaped at it for some time, because the boy leaned toward me. "Wrong bone."

Errol never asked what I did when he was away, and I never told him. I grew more content, and he became more wretched. Often he would stay in some parlor or another until dawn, then walk the three miles back to the river and take up his post at the rocker, emitting a stench that could have felled a man at sixty rod. By now our silt had given way to orangey clay, then black rock. Each day Errol looked more deranged. This was the state of things when the second stagecoach came.

XIV. THE SECOND COACH

We heard the news from a man who hollered it across the diggings. Errol stopped his rocking, rinsed his soiled hands and face in the river, replaced his hat, and said, "I have a letter to retrieve." Then he set off without a word.

The tongs continued their digging and sifting. The old man was wary of large gatherings, and rightfully so. Forty-niners were a volatile bunch of drunkards and criminals, especially with their sentiments roused. And nothing so roused them as a mail coach.

I had to follow Errol. I had the sense that my brother stood at a crevasse, that the vellum keeping him on this side was as thin as a sheet of Marjorie Salter's stationery.

The stagecoach had stopped beneath the arms of a giant, leafless valley oak, and men were already gathered around it. Suddenly, I felt a pressing at my brow. The arrangement of the bare branches' veiny shadows along the side and top of the coach and the dusty pool of men's hats beneath it sent forth an augury. I saw from the beginning how the end would be. I saw Errol approach the coach, and saw him fail to receive the letter he so anxiously wanted. I pressed my hand to my forehead but took it away before my brother should notice.

The mind is a mine. So often we revisit its winding, unsound caverns when we ought to stay out.

At that moment I traveled down a long-forgotten tunnel of memory. At the end of the tunnel I found a cat. When I was nine or so, Errol twelve or thirteen, our mother let us feed a litter of barn cats. There was one for each of us children. Mine was white, with gray boots and gray, eyebrowlike markings. I called her Isabel, because I thought Isabel was the soundest name for a cat that ever there was. Errol called her Eyeballs, probably because she was a touch bulge-eyed. Each time I said *Isabel*—when I fed her or just when I went out to be with her—Errol would be right there, saying *Eyeballs, Eyeballs*. I can still hear him. And lo, the family started calling her Eyeballs, too. People took to Errol like that, even our own parents. He had a way of making you love him even while he was being cruel. I don't know why, but I think we could have been all right, Errol and I; I could have put up with his temper and his beating on me and the way he'd get quiet and mean at the smallest thing bothering him. I think I could have forgiven him all this, could have been on good terms with him come December of 1849, when we rounded the glade and saw the coach spidered with the shadows of oak limbs. I could have warned Errol of the heartbreak I saw at the coach, and maybe he would have been better able to accept it. Maybe not, but maybe so. Maybe we would not have been plunged down the dark path we were on. If only I had spoken up. If only he had let Isabel be Isabel.

And so I stood in line watching Errol worry the brim of his hat and squatting on occasion to sift some dirt through his fingers or toss pebbles. When at last we reached the coachman Errol nudged me to indicate that I should call our name, maybe out of secret superstition or because his voice had gone with nerves. I showed surprise at the gesture, though of course I had none.

"Boyle," I called. The coachman checked his bundle.

"Here," he said, passing down a lovely vanilla-colored envelope. I reached to receive it but Errol snatched it from the driver. His hands trembled as his large fingers carefully negotiated the letter from its paper case. He was smiling. It had been a long time since I had seen him smile. Then, nearly the instant he unfolded the paper, he dropped it to the ground, where our two pairs of boots faced each other. I retrieved the letter as Errol walked away from me. *My dear sons,* it began, as I knew it would.

From there I was back in the realm of the unafflicted, where we cannot know what will come next. I expected Errol to embark on another binge, and I braced myself for it. But he set out in the direction of the river instead and I followed, losing myself in reading our mother's letter as I went. I had never been so delighted to hear of my sisters' schoolwork or the comings and goings of livestock. I read and reread it all the way back to camp. December had crisped the air pleasantly, and the day was beautiful.

XV. THE DIGGING

That afternoon, Errol resumed his post at the rocker. His working did not soothe me. The Chinamen gave him a wide berth. Come sundown, the hour when we usually retired, Errol stayed at the rocker. I dismissed the tongs and stayed with him, clumsily shoveling and rinsing. I thought hard work might cleanse him of heartbreak and was happy to keep him in ore, if that would do it. But soon it grew so dark that there was no chance that Errol could determine the character of the sediment coming down the sluice. And anyway he was looking not at the sluice but at the stars.

Eventually I stabbed the shovel into the rock and said, "I think I'll heat some beans. Care for some?"

"No. I don't think so," said Errol, taking up the shovel. I fixed dinner and set some on his stump for him. As I ate I watched his futile efforts at the shovel, then the bucket, then the rocker, then the shovel again. He stayed at the shovel then, with his breath puffing into the cold like the stack of a steamboat. I went to bed with him still at it, figuring he would exhaust his frustrations and retire in his own time. I fell asleep to the skeletal scrape of iron against bedrock.

And in the morning I woke to it.

I emerged from our tent but Errol was nowhere in sight. I could hear his work but not see him. There was the cradle, unmanned. In the place where I had last seen him was a large mound of dirt. Beyond it, a pit. I approached. Down at the bottom of the pit was my brother, shoveling earth as steadily as he had been six hours before. The hole was likely five feet deep and vaguely rectangular. The shape of it alone frightened me, but I composed myself and adopted an air of nonchalance.

"Good morning, Errol," I called. "Would you care for some breakfast?" I peered again into the hole. The sun was not yet very high and so Errol was mostly in shadow. His head alone was illuminated, and it seemed to hover above the darkness of the pit, disembodied. His hat was gone. I later found it buried in the pile.

"I think I'll make some flapjacks," I repeated. "Would you care to take a break for some flapjacks, Errol?" His answer was a shovelful of dark sediment, flashing in the sunlight. It seemed there was nothing to do but what I'd always done. I fixed breakfast, and when I was through I tossed Errol a warm flapjack, only to have it ejected in yet another shovel load.

My brother remained in his mine all morning. The Chinamen arrived ready to work, but I dismissed them. I stood near the lip of the pit, saying his name again and again and again, until his name went meaningless as a tong word. He never acknowledged me, only dug.

I offered him water. He dug.

I read him our sweet mother's letter. He dug.

Noon came. The hole was not so deep that Errol could not climb out—not yet—but it was deep enough now that even when he stood straight, my brother's frame was completely subterranean. I might have lain on my stomach and reached down to touch the top of his head, but I did not. He dug. The ceaseless sound of his shovel on the rock penetrated my every thought.

I flattered him. He dug.

I taunted him. He dug.

I bribed him. He dug.

I told him we could go to San Francisco and nap in feather beds. He dug.

I told him, finally, that we could return to Marjorie. He dug.

By dusk the hole had gone narrower. It was now over seven feet deep. I sat near the lip, dejected and alone. I had no one but Errol here and I suddenly felt it was very important to touch him. I laid my belly against the cool earth, inched my way to the edge of the hole and extended my arm down into it. I called softly for Errol to pause in his task for just one minute, to reach up above his head and stretch his fingers toward mine. So I could test his temperature, I said. But he would not turn his face to me.

Night fell, and with it came fury. I cursed him. I stood on the edge of the hole and shouted at him. Men came down to have a look at the commotion, and I ran them off. I shrieked into the pit. I said things I had never said to anyone. Things I have not said since.

I must have slept that night, because I woke before light, shivering with frost, atop the mound he'd made. The scraping went on. The sides of the chasm sparkled with frost, too, and this brought me a strategy. I filled the bucket at the river, returned to the hole, and began trickling water down into it. "Errol," I called. "I think the river's coming in. Hear that? That's the river, old boy." He said nothing, but his scraping paused, I thought.

"Don't worry, Errol. I'll get you out." I tied one end of a rope to a tree. I refilled the bucket and poured it in. Then I flung the other end of the rope into the hole and called, "Grab hold, Errol! I'll pull you up!"

The digging persisted, but now there was a watery sound beneath the scrape of the shovel.

That night I sat jiggling the rope, touching the notch my brother had left in my collarbone, saying I was sorry and could he please please please please grab hold.

When morning came I gathered the heaviest rocks I could carry and assembled them in a pile near the lip. I was desperate. I intended to brain my brother, climb down the rope, tie it around him, climb up the rope and then pull him up. Giddy images of his wilted body dangling from the rope passed through my mind at the moment I noticed a strange sound. It was silence. The absence of shovel on bedrock.

I approached the hole, bracing myself for the sight of my brother's dead body at the bottom. Instead, he sat quite alive with his back against the earth wall, as if resting after a morning's work and not three feverish days spent burying himself alive. It was noon and the sun was beaming directly into the hole. I could see his scalp burned pink where his hair had gathered in clumps, and his blistered, bloody hands. He had removed his boots and one was half-submerged in the water I'd poured upon him. The rope was well above where he sat, curled like an animal in a waterlogged den.

Then he began to sing. It was the first I'd heard his voice since he declined the now-crusted beans still awaiting him on the stump. The song was a popular one, and he sang it with an unsettling bounce:

> Hangtown gals are plump and rosy,
> Hair in ringlets, fists of posy,
> Painted cheeks and jossy bonnets—
> Touch 'em and they'll sting like hornets!

"That's a fine tune," I said when he was done. I don't know why I said it, except that it was.

Errol looked up at me, finally, squinting against the light. His face had gone gaunt and grimed and socket-hollow. He did not look like himself. He said, "There's a good pile coming, Abigail."

That was our mother's name.

"I'm Joshua," I said. "Joshua. Your brother. Say Joshua."

"Sing me 'The Old Oaken Bucket.' You know that one, Abby?"

"Joshua!" I cried.

Errol reached his hand across the shaft and scraped some soil from the wall opposite him. He said, "There's a good pile coming, Abby girl."

I threw myself at the pile of rock and attempted to lift one. I intended to throw my boulders down upon him, smiting him as would the God of that hole. I did not care, at that moment, whether I stoned him to death or buried him alive. But the Lord had taken my strength. I only lay in the dirt and wept.

"Do you know 'The Old Oaken Bucket'?" whispered Errol.

"No," I said through my tears. "How does it go?" And then I passed into darkness.

XVI. A TROUT

A promise unkept will take a man's mind. It does not matter whether the promise is made by a woman or a territory or a future foretold. I know that now. But this was years ago, when I was young and felt the whole world of Errol's collapse was mine to bear. It is strange telling you this, because the boy I was feels so far away from the man I am now. I know I ought to consider that distance a blessing, given the darkness and the difficulty of the time I have described here. But it brings me no comfort to think how far I have traveled nor how much wiser I've become. Because though I was afraid and angry and lonesome much of the time, I was also closer to my own raw heart there in the territory than I have ever been since.

I woke at the Chinaman's camp. It was dusk. The boy sat near me with a tin cup. Behind him was his uncle, sitting on a stump near the fire, and behind him was the dusky blue Sacramento valley with fires and lanterns burning here and there.

"Where's Errol?" I said. "Where is my brother?"

The boy handed me the tin cup. "Where you think?" He frowned, as if disappointed in himself. "He is in the earth, still."

"Is he digging?"

The boy shook his head.

"Singing?"

"No."

I got up and walked upriver to the hole and looked inside. Errol sat in the muddy water with his legs folded to his chest, alive and shivering. He had removed his shirt and tied it about his head. I jiggled the rope and called to him, but he did not answer. He was apparently through digging, and his hole had not gained any more depth. Yet he felt farther from me than when last I saw him.

I returned to the Chinaman's camp and sat looking from the boy to his uncle. The old man was cleaning the blade of his jade-handled knife on his robe and chewing a stalk of grass. I wanted him to say something. I felt if he spoke he would have a way to end this thing. But he said nothing. And the yellow stalk of sweetgrass bounced in his mouth.

The Chinaman sheathed his knife and stowed it in the folds of his robe. Then he reached into a bucket beside him and brought up an enormous rainbow trout. It was dead, but freshly dead, shimmering still and with that gruesome pout that dead fish have. Fish were rare on our part of the river, so many were devoured by men upstream. It was a lovely creature, and I knew the tongs must have traveled a long way to catch it.

"For Mister Errol," said the boy.

Then, at the sound of the boy's voice and the gutted shimmer of the trout in the blue dusk, the providence of the thing burst upon my mind. I saw Errol climbing up out of his hole and sitting beside the Chinaman's fire, saw us four scooping soft, steaming handfuls of fish to our mouths. It was no augury, only the visions of my own hopeful heart.

The skin of the fish sizzled wonderfully, emitting a stirring aroma as we cooked it. Surely the meal would return Errol's mind and deliver him the strength and will to reach up and take hold of the rope. I watched it fry, feeling that the rest of my life was lodged in that trout.

With the cooked fish I approached the hole. It was dark now and the moon had risen. The night was clear and the gibbous moon so bright I expected to see its reflection dancing in the water pooled at the bottom of the pit. But there was only darkness. I called to Errol.

"I fixed you dinner," I said, holding the tasty rainbow over the hole. I could not see him but I heard the earth crumble a little as he shifted, heard some stones hitting the water. "Errol, will you come up and have some trout?"

He said nothing. No matter, I thought. I was convinced that all he needed was to see the thing, to lay his hand on its soft fish belly. He would eat it, head and all, and return to me. "Look out below," I said, and dropped the trout into the darkness.

I listened at the hole for some time and heard nothing. I returned to the Chinaman's camp to wait. The boy tossed pebbles into the river and we three sat listening to the sound of them dropping into the water. "He'll die down there," I said, for I had just realized it.

I spent that night in the China camp, stretched out on a flat sandy spot near the embers of the fire. Before sleep I resolved that at dawn I would descend into the hole, fight Errol into submission and bring him up. He would return to me.

No sooner had I fallen off than I was awoken by the mournful roars of a grizzly.

I sat up and saw the bear, standing on its hind legs, staggering toward me. It bellowed and I scrambled along the ground away from the beast. He came at me. I saw in my mind the purple innards of General Scott strung along Tuolumne Meadow and my bowels spasmed.

Through sheer dumb habit I brought my spectacles to my face, and with them saw that the grizzly was no grizzly. It was my brother, naked and covered head to foot with black mud. His arms were raised over his head. He carried something there, as though to an Old Testament altar. He came closer. Moonglow shone upon his lips, blistered and cracked and bloody and trembling. The nail of one of his big toes was missing.

He thrust the trout into my hands. He had not eaten a bite of it. He bellowed again, and this time I understood the word.

"Gold!" he said again, pointing to the fish.

Another man would have identified this as the raving of a lunatic. But I was dazed and accustomed to heeding my brother and did so now. I examined the mangled, mudded fish. I ran my hand along its sides and lifted its fins. Once I saw one I saw them all. Thousands of tiny gold flakes lodged amongst its scales.

The Chinaman and his boy emerged from their tent. The Chinaman was bare-chested, the first I had ever seen him so. Errol pointed a filthy, trembling finger to where he stood.

"You!" he bellowed. Errol charged at the Chinaman, toppling him to the ground. The boy shouted. Up came the sounds of fist on flesh. When the men rose, Errol had the Chinaman by his throat. The Chinaman's eye was cut. He scratched frantically at Errol's hands where they held him.

"You had it all," Errol said.

The Chinaman stomped and kicked at Errol but Errol did not flinch. I stood in horror with the trout in my hands as Errol dragged the Chinaman to the river. The two descended into the slow, dark water. The Chinaman flailed wildly now, sputtering. Errol lifted the Chinaman slightly and then plunged him under the water.

I dropped the trout and ran into the river. Water filled my long johns and pulled at them. A shape flashed at my side and then past. It was the boy, plunging toward the place where his uncle was being drowned.

I did not see it immediately, only saw the boy launch himself at Errol and cling to his backside. Errol screamed and released the Chinaman and the Chinaman surfaced, gasping for air. Errol flung the boy off him. It was then that I saw the jade-handled knife still in the boy's hand where he'd been tossed, and that Errol had a long gash across his bare haunch. Errol twisted to examine the wound and as he did so it opened and out rolled a rivulet of black blood.

The Chinaman and his nephew stood on the bank, checking each other for wounds. The boy was trembling. I approached them. They watched me a moment, then fled.

Errol looked from the gash to me. He motioned for me to come to him, but I could not. "You see," he said, serenely. "It's so clear. They had it all along."

I fled. I could not endure the fact of his believing, believing, believing beyond the rotten end. That's all I can say about it.

XVII. EPILOGUE

When I finally came upon San Francisco Bay, it was so dense with abandoned vessels that their masts made a leafless forest atop the water. I found work as a torch boy for the Knicker-bocker Fire Engine Company, and with them I fought the Christmas Eve fire of 1849 and the Saint Valentine's blaze. When finally I had earned enough money I bought passage aboard a thousand-ton sidewheeler called *Apollo*, where I was the only human cargo among sacks and sacks of gold bullion. Eventually, I disembarked in Boston Harbor. I intended to return to Ohio from there, but it was many years before I was able to meet my mother, the woman whose son I had abandoned in the wilderness. I went to church, and to school. By the time I had the courage to see her I was a grown man.

While in San Francisco, I read in the *California Star* that in Angel's Camp two tongs, father and son, had been captured by a mob of citizens and tried for the crime of robbery and attempted murder. They were hanged, said the report, though I knew that would be their fate the night I sat hiding in the woods above Sacramento, listening to nocturnal beasts moving through the scrub, when the snow ring around the gibbous moon triggered my final augury. As to last words, the *Star* reported that the tong boy recited a passage of Homer.

In the years following the rush, it became fashionable for Easterners to decorate their parlors with gilt-framed daguerreotypes of forty-niners. In these years I've seen many such portraits of Argonauts posed proudly with pan or pick or troy scale, their whiskers cut back in a semblance of civility. Each time I encounter one I hope to see my brother in it, although I know it is unlikely he ever had himself pictured off. And it is a false art, I realize. Most of the men used props on loan from the portraitist. Some were models sitting before drop cloths in New York City. But a great deal of what I like about those faddish daguerreotypes is that they show no trace of the darkness I remember of the diggings, none of the loneliness or the madness or the hunger. Even the pistols in the men's belts seem tucked there in jest. I'd very much like to see my brother there someday, in his red miner's shirt with his hat tipped back, a fresh sash at his collar, brandishing a fine new pickax and a lump. I'd like to see him poised at the center of a gleaming gilded frame, as if color was every bit as bountiful as we'd been told. I'd like to see him posed with his endless belief and at last surrounded by bright soft gold. And maybe if I saw him there I might see the Argonaut believer within myself, too, for we looked so similar in the territory.

What I now know of Errol I know from a postcard he sent our mother twenty-five years ago, which was postmarked Virginia City, N.T., and said only that the lode had a hold of him.

VIRGINIA CITY

We were at a house party last night, Danny, Jules, and me, leaning over a low, sticky coffee table playing Texas Hold 'Em like always, when Danny mentioned that his parents got married in secret up in Virginia City, in the back room of some casino, to escape the Jehovah's Witnesses. He'd never told me this in all the years we've been friends. Jules got stuck on it, saying over and over again, "What? That's so fucking crazy!"

Danny leaned back and got all quiet and smug the way he does when he knows he has something you want. "You can still see the room."

And Jules said, "You guys, we have to see this place. This *means* something. Iris?"

And I was drunk or high or both by then, so I said, "Yeah, sure. We'll drive up there."

I meant it then but didn't this morning, when I woke up to the underwater thuds of a fist pounding on the window of the only bedroom I've ever had. I cracked my blinds to see Jules straddling a furrow of my mom's failed vegetable garden, her fingers folded into metal horns, yelling, "Virginia City! Fuck, yeah!" Danny stood behind her bleary-eyed, holding a Mountain Dew. When Jules gets stuck on something she doesn't let it go. I used to love that about her.

I drive—I always drive. Jules and Danny sip road beers, him in the front seat of my car, her in the back. Danny turns the music down and asks Jules what's become of Drew.

I have to strain to pull a memory of Drew—the scene trash Jules went home with last night—to this side of my hangover. Jules mashed into the couch with a skinny boy in tight pants, hibiscus flowers and sparrows and bug-eyed koi creeping up his forearms. Or later, her arm looped through mine, nodding indiscreetly to where the guy stood by the door with his coat on, drinking a tallboy, waiting. Jules yelling over the music to Danny, saying she didn't need a ride home. Drew is a ghost. A placeholder in a parade. Like all of Jules's boys, Drew is real only to Danny.

"Working," Jules says. "He's in that band, the Satellites. You know them." She gestures with her Coors Light, part of a twelve-pack she stole from the party. "We saw them at XOXO. They opened for that emcee from Sacramento. They're like indie slash electro slash power pop."

"Keep that can down," I say.

"Which one?" asks Danny. "What does he play?"

"I don't know. Synth? I think there was a keyboard in his room."

"If I get a ticket you guys are paying it."

"Synth," says Danny. "You sure? Where does he work?"

He's trying to make her admit something. He should know better. Jules has never been ashamed of sleeping around. That would defeat the purpose. She shrugs and sips her beer, looking out her window at the gnarled piñon pines clinging to the mountainside, or Reno down beyond the guardrail, shrinking away from us.

Danny takes a drink. "You don't even know where he works?"

She smirks at me in the rearview mirror. "I didn't have a chance to ask."

"How was it?" Danny's only ever been with one girl. He's twenty-four years old and still fascinated by the fact that people sometimes fuck people with whom they aren't in love. This is what he likes to hear—the anonymity, the baseness, how a person can do what Jules does. A good friend, she is always willing to oblige.

"Not bad," she says. "Oral, oral, missionary, doggie-style, money shot. Nothing flashy."

Poor Danny. He lives with his parents and Jules is the kind of girl who makes sure every man she meets falls in love with her, in case he comes in handy later. She tilts her beer on end, finishing it. Danny does the same.

"Keep that shit down," I say. Then, because I sound, just for a moment, like the me I was before Jules, I say, "The Satellites are basically a sloppy Joy Division cover band."

She shrugs and looks out the window. "They are what they are."

I met Jules in our capstone seminar the fall before we graduated. She was a BFA student, a painter. Even though the seminar is basic humanities, you're supposed to take it within your college. The nursing seminar was full and I didn't want to wait for the next semester, so I'd begged my adviser to let me into another section. It wasn't until I got into the art auditorium that I realized how much I hated the other girls in nursing, their white shoes, the face-framing layers in their hair, their gel pens and highlighted, color-coded note cards.

On the first day of class, Jules called to me from the aisle of the auditorium like she knew me. I remember her ugly brown boots unlaced and splattered with paint, her short, bleached-out hair. It wasn't just that I didn't know her; I didn't know anyone like her. She made her way over and sat beside me and gave me a flyer for a show downtown where her friend was deejaying.

"I thought you might be into this," she said. "Last time he was in town he absolutely killed." I didn't know it then, but I'd been sitting in lecture halls for three years, staring straight ahead, rounding out the bell curve, waiting for someone like her.

She sat beside me whenever she came to class. I missed her when she didn't, and she often didn't. She invited me to more shows and gallery openings, showed me the flyers she'd redesigned herself because the bourgies at the gallery had used some bullshit motel art on theirs. I always went. One day she came into class and convinced me to leave with her before our professor arrived. We took the Spirit bus downtown to the Eldorado and spent the afternoon drinking gimlets and playing the penny slots. She taught me how to smoke. It was the best day I'd ever had.

Jules liked that I was a local. I made her feel authentic, which is especially important to Californians. Soon she was taking me along with her to after-parties and all-night diners with whichever guy had orbited into her life. Nick who worked at Sundance Books, Brady from the co-op, her Life Drawing TA, Corbett, a visiting "electronic installation artist" from Ireland, with his insufferable chronic irony. They asked me stupid questions, like did I come here when I was a kid, and did I know the Heimlich, and what would I do if they started choking. One time I said, "Nothing," and Jules laughed like a dream I had of her once where she laughed so long and hard that her laugh lifted us both above the city and over the mountains, hand in hand, flying.

That was three years ago. Later, Jules got drunk and told me that she'd only called out to me that first day because she'd thought I was some girl from her sculpture class.

In the car we pass billboards advertising casinos and tourist attractions. One says *The World-Famous Suicide Table* and another says *Virginia City: A Town of Relics and Memories and Ghosts of the Past* and another says *Bonanza or Bust*. Danny says,

"That's it. The Bonanza." He looks so pleased with himself that I wonder if he's making this whole thing up.

We crest the hill and see Virginia City below us, the little strip of Main Street restored to look like the Old West boomtown this once was, the sharp white spire of Saint Mary's of the Mountains on one edge of town, the iron-gated cemetery creeping up the bald man-made hills of rock on the other. We've been here before, the three of us. But every time I see this view I'm struck by how the buildings huddle together on the hillside, how a small town's like a big family.

We park on the street and stand around the back of the car with the trunk open while we each down a beer. Jules finishes hers first and belches. We toss the empties into the trunk. Jules takes three unopened silver cans from the twelve-pack and puts them in her purse. She puts the last three in mine. "I'm hungry," she says.

We cross the street and walk for a while. Danny says he likes the hollow sound of our steps on the wood-plank walkway. He's said this before.

Jules squeals and points and takes pictures of everything like a tourist: a man leading a fat brown horse down a gravel side street, two local women dressed as Old West whores in dyed ostrich-feather hats and corsets, the rotating stainless-steel arms of a machine pulling purple taffy in the window of a candy store. She stands for an absurd amount of time at the plaque about Mark Twain, running her fingers over his little bronze mustache. She pretends not to notice when Danny takes a picture of her there. It's exhausting.

Danny points to the old-looking hanging sign for the Bucket of Blood Saloon, a sign we've seen half a dozen times though we've never gone inside. "How about that?" he says.

"That's fucking awesome," says Jules. Everything is fucking awesome. Inside, the place is painted all red and has red velvet drapes too big for their windows. Chandeliers dangle from the ceiling, and large oil paintings with ornate gold frames hang on the walls. As far as I can tell, we're the only patrons not wearing cowboy hats. Jules nods to some old men at a nearby table. "Howdy," she says. Fucking howdy.

Jules flirts with the bartender, an old guy with the silly striped apron of a nineteenth-century barkeep hanging from his neck. His name tag is handwritten and says Bernie. Jules asks him to fix her his favorite drink and he brings over a Bloody Mary, pungent with extra horseradish. He shrugs shyly and says, "That's how I like 'em."

"That's how I like 'em, too," she says.

Danny and I taste her Bloody Mary and order two for ourselves. We all order bacon cheeseburgers, which Jules says is lame of us but Danny says is actually super interesting because by having the same meal in the same place we'll be closing the gaps between us and come closer to fully understanding each other's experience. These bacon cheeseburgers, he says, have the opportunity to be transcendent.

Jules rocks forward on her stool. "It's hard to picture your parents eloping." It is. Danny's mom, Lucy, is the head pediatric nurse at Saint Mary's, and his dad, Dick, is a high school principal. They play Boggle and tennis together. Every Saturday morning Lucy organizes the recycling while Dick washes the car.

Our food comes, the meat slippery in the buns. "Tell us what happened," I say.

"Yeah," says Jules, her mouth full of burger.

"What do you want to know?" says Danny, chewing on the celery stalk from his drink, loving the attention. "When my mom was eighteen she was engaged to this guy Wally, who worked in a tire factory off Wells. He was a Jehovah's Witness, like my mom's whole family. Wally's dad was an elder in their church and everyone wanted them to get married. And they were going to, too, but my mom met my dad at school and called it off."

Jules says, "Fucking awesome," and Danny's happy to make her happy. I've seen her with so many men but none of them have ever looked at her the way Danny does.

He goes on. "But this guy Wally took it pretty bad. They found him butt naked in the Truckee. In March. And I guess he was saying some crazy shit. I don't know. They should have checked him into a mental institution. I mean, he was *eighteen*. But his dad, the elder, decided that Wally's breakdown was actually God talking through his son. At one point the whole congregation was at Wally's bed, praying, talking about 'the one hundred and forty-four thousand' and 'the Lord's Evening Meal.' All that shit."

The bartender comes over and Danny orders another round of Bloody Marys and two fingers of bourbon for himself. Jules says, "Thanks a million, Bernie. You're a doll."

"Anyway, the elder went and talked to my grandma and grandpa about how God had revealed His Great Will and how my mom marrying my dad—a Catholic, of all things—was not, you know, in the divine plan. And the fucked-up part is that they believed him. They told my mom she couldn't see my dad anymore. Then the three of them—my mom's parents and Wally's dad—sat my dad down and said he'd better stay away from my mom, or else. Fucking *or else*. They thought this kid Wally was some kind of prophet."

"Which makes your dad what?" says Jules. "The Antichrist?" This is funny, Dick the Antichrist, soaping down the minivan in his too-tight running shorts and tennis shoes from Kmart.

"Dude, but check it," says Danny, slapping the bar, eating it up. "My dad didn't care, right? He wanted to get married anyway. But my mom believed that shit, I think. Even though she agreed to marry my dad, she wouldn't do it in Reno. She said they had to come up here so no one would know. So it could stay secret."

"Is that what she said?" I want to know. We're done eating, just picking at Jules's fries. Why hasn't Danny told me this before?

He shakes his head. "My dad told me. My mom doesn't talk about it."

Our check comes. Bernie the barkeep says our drinks are on the house. Thanks a million, Bernie.

Outside, the boardwalk and the street are crowded. We've

just missed a mock gunfight, and the smell of fired blanks still hangs in the air. People are milling around, dazed from the excitement of vigilante justice. Jules and Danny walk ahead of me, weaving through the crowd. We stop to watch two horses pull a covered wagon down Main Street, an old man holding the reins loosely, two sheepish-looking bandits in the back. The horses' hooves make a satisfying *clop-clop* on the asphalt. I pull my thin jacket closed. It's cold up here and it's only September.

Outside the Silver Queen, a sign promises the actual Silver Queen. We've all seen her before, but Jules wants to go. Danny shrugs and says, "Since we're here." I'm just glad to get away from the crowd. We walk through the narrow, dim casino to a mural of a woman, at least fifteen feet tall. She's sort of Frida Kahlo–looking, only white. Her gown is made out of hundreds of the shiniest pure silver dollars you'll ever see. Rows of them ring her neck and wrists, and stack to make a crown nestled in her brown updo. Jules hands us beers from her purse and takes one for herself. The beer is warm, and something about that warmth feels good.

Jules reads the plaque and tells us the silver is from the first strike of the Comstock Lode, which we already know. The silver dollars glint like the scales of a fish. I want to touch them, but the whole thing's been covered with Plexiglas to keep people from prying the coins from the wall with their fingers. Who would do something like that? We would.

Jules gives me her camera and poses in front of the mural with her hands on her hips, just like the queen herself. Danny joins her. I set my beer on a stool in front of a slot machine and watch them through the camera's viewer. They grin, posing with their Silver Bullets in front of the Silver Queen, their arms around each other.

These are my friends. These are the funny, ironic things we do so we can be the kind of funny, ironic people who do them.

I stand way back with the camera, boozy and flushed, listening to the clicks of its machinery and the prerecorded metallic *ping, ping* of phantom coins emptied from the slot machines. Danny and Jules shift through the poses of old friends, figments of the way we were. I take another step back, trying to get the whole thing in frame.

J ules and I were friends for a while before I introduced her to Danny. Danny and I had been friends forever, since we were kids. He used to joke that my new friend Jules was imaginary or—hilarious—my secret lover. I didn't keep them apart on purpose; it seemed then that there was simply no opportunity for us all to get together. But now I know that somewhere in me I never wanted them to meet. I thought that if they had each other they wouldn't need me. I didn't want to be left behind.

But we three hit it off. On weekends we bought astronaut ice cream at the planetarium and lay in the grass with our heads resting on each other's stomachs. We drank from Jules's flask and felt the chalky sweetness of dehydrated ice cream dissolve on our tongues. Summers we went up to the lake. We swam fifty yards out to the broad flat boulders off Chimney Beach and felt the coarse glacier granite against our bare feet. We jumped into the warm green water, one by one by one. Sometimes Jules and I took off our tops. She flung hers aside and I kept mine balled in my hand. Danny pretended not to notice, or not to care. The three of us lay there on the rocks, letting the sun touch us dry.

Nights we went to little clubs—XOXO, the Green Room, Imperial, the Hideout. We danced together in the pulsing colored lights, shoulder to shoulder, a perfect triangle. We spilled out onto the street or into the alleys for a cigarette or a joint or a bump or just some air. When it was cold, I watched the steam rise from our sweat-soaked bodies, from Jules's bare arms and shoulders, from the wet slope of Danny's neck. We walked home together, crunching frost beneath our feet or listening to the early morning songs of birds.

Then, the beginning of our dissolving. Danny and I met up with Jules at a house party last Halloween. By the time we got there she was already wasted. She'd dressed as a robot and her cardboard body was crushed; most of the knobs and gauges that we'd pulled from the busted washing machine in the alley behind her studio and the gas stove in her apartment had been knocked off. She'd developed runs in her shimmery tights and her greasy silver face paint was smeared in places. The day before, Jules had convinced Danny to be Peter Pan. He had a green paper hat with a red feather, and a plastic dagger she'd lifted from a window display at Walgreens. I wasn't dressed as anything, and all night people kept asking me, "What are you supposed to be?"

Toward the end of the night I found Danny and Jules in the empty kitchen, talking. I sat at the table with them and we had a round of shots from shot glasses shaped like skulls, which Jules later slipped into her purse. Danny and Jules talked about music and art and women Danny knew the year he lived in Berlin. That's what he called them, women. I knew I shouldn't, but I hated hearing him say things to her that he'd never said to me. I hated how she listened.

That night Jules went home with one of the sweet-smelling coffee boys from Café Bibo. Afterward, we got free fair-trade lattes for a few Sunday afternoons in a row. But after Jules left, Danny curled up on the rank-ass couch out on these kids' porch with a bottle of green apple vodka that wasn't his, saying, "Man, there's just, fucking, there's never any time."

When I walked Danny down the hill to his apartment he was incoherent and stumbling, almost crushing me with his weight. The sun was coming up. I helped him inside and went to get him a glass of tap water and a slice of white bread. That's all he had. When I came back he'd passed out in his costume. He'd lost his hat. Before I left I took a wet paper towel and in the half-light wiped silver face paint from his neck and hands and mouth. I've been waiting for them to leave me behind ever since.

I can see why Danny's mom thought even God wouldn't be able to see her in this little chapel. It's a secret place, situated in the far back corner of the smoky mirrored labyrinth of the Bonanza. Danny holds the heavy door open for us. I smell him as I walk inside. He looks beautiful in here, in this light.

The chapel is more cave than church. The walls are made of big cold hunks of stone, and the ceiling is so low that I can reach up and touch it. There's an organ in the corner, two displays of yellowed silk flowers at the altar with milky white candles sticking out of them. There are maybe twenty khaki-colored metal folding chairs, separated by a bolt of threadbare red carpet. A dusty wooden crucifix hangs on the wall. The place probably hasn't changed in thirty years.

I sit in the front row and try to imagine Lucy and Dick at the altar. They were younger then than we are now. Did Lucy think, as she said her vows, of her old beau Wally, strapped to a bed in his father's house?

Danny fiddles on the organ. He hardly plays anymore, and his fingers are clumsy. Plus, he says, half the keys don't work. Jules plucks a spray of fake flowers from its Styrofoam holder and takes it to the back of the room. She motions to him. Danny does his best at "Here Comes the Bride," though some of the notes are dead. Jules begins a slow, stumbling walk down the aisle.

Danny motions me to the altar. This is a nowhere place, the stone walls too thick for jilted seers, the door too heavy for cuckold ghosts. I stand and fold my hands, solemn as a groom. I sway ever so slightly, awaiting my bride.

Jules arrives and Danny joins us. We three stand quiet for a moment at the altar where his parents were joined, at the place that made all this possible. Jules drops the bouquet on the floor behind her. She takes my hands in hers.

We are quiet; then Danny says, "Jules, do you take Iris to be your lawfully wedded wife, to have and to hold, as long as you both shall live?"

"I do," she whispers.

"And Iris, do you take Jules for better and for worse, in sickness and in health, until death do you part?"

"I do."

Jules squeezes my hands.

Danny sweeps his arms into the air triumphantly. He says, "You may kiss the bride." The air is gone from the room.

Jules pulls me to her, firmly. She kisses me. Her breath is hot and her lips are keen. Her tongue moves over the front of my teeth like the ocean might, or like someone beckoning, saying, *Come here.*

I kiss her back and we are weightless with the warmth of the mouth, floating in the taste of bloody meat and horseradish. My hands holding her hips lightly, her fingers pressing on the back of my neck, her bottom lip held ever so softly between my teeth. This means something, I think. It has to. She pulls away.

"Dudes," Danny says, "that was fucking beautiful."

A laugh spreads across Jules's big bright face, ravenous the way a wildfire is. "I know, right?"

I laugh too. These are my friends. These are the funny, empty things we do so we can be the kind of funny, empty people who do them.

. . .

At the Bonanza's glassy bar we switch to whiskey and video poker. We hit the buttons as slow as possible, like Jules taught us, trying to stretch our money long enough to get a few free drinks, long enough to make it worth our while. Willie Nelson is on the jukebox, a muted soccer game on TV. We pluck olives and cherries and slices of lemon and lime out of their plastic bins when the bartender isn't looking. The front doors are propped open, and outside the wind is picking up. "It's because you grew up in Reno," Jules says, answering a question I don't remember asking. "You don't know how great this town is."

There are plenty of good reasons to find yourself in Virginia City. The first time we came, we came because Jules wanted to stand in the spot where Mark Twain stood. She wanted to see what Mark Twain saw. Danny and I watched her. She stood on that plank walkway, quiet and reverent, looking out over the foothills, searching for something. I'd never seen her like that, before or since. There was none of that reverence in the chapel and it seems now that there should have been. Yes, today is a day for reverence, for some goddamn sincerity of emotion. I'm drunk. When did today become that day?

Jules comes close to a flush, and calls us over for luck. We each put a finger on the red plastic *draw* button. This is our ritual. How many times have we layered our three hands atop the last card, stacked our fists like totems on the lever of a slot machine, laid our hopeful fingertips on one last deal?

Danny says, *Wait*. He pops a maraschino cherry into his

mouth, then one into Jules's. Her teeth glow pink with cherry brine. Poor sweet Danny. We can't help who we love.

The wind blows a swarm of golden mesquite leaves inside. Jules says, "One. Two. Three."

The queen we needed winks up at us. The payout is close to four hundred dollars.

Jules and Danny scream and throw their arms around each other. They slap the bar. They say, *Fuck, yeah*. They say, *You like that?* I'm feeling severe. Danny stands on his stool and fishes the last olive from the bin. He is less and less himself these days. He holds the olive in front of Jules, the juice dribbling down his wrist. She reaches for it gleefully but he pulls it away and slips it into his mouth.

"We should cash out," I say.

Danny only smiles, revealing the little plug of olive pinched between his teeth. Jules laughs that helium laugh of hers and takes Danny's face in her hands. She presses her mouth to his. I watch. I expect their kiss to be urgent and ambitious but they're unhurried, dreamy. She moans gently as he arches her back against the bar. He slips one hand under her shirt and holds his whiskey in his other, like he's been doing this his whole fucking life. Afterward, he's slack-jawed and electric eyed and Jules munches happily on whatever is left of their olive. "We should cash out," I say again.

Jules mumbles, "Yeah," and at the same time Danny says, "Fuck that," and taps *deal* again.

"What are you doing?" I say.

He laughs and says, "Having fun."

"No." I grab his wrist. "Cash out."

Jules says, "Hey, hey."

"Get off me," says Danny. A bit of whiskey slops onto his shirt. He pries my hand from his arm. "This isn't about you."

"It doesn't mean anything," I say. "You. Me. Nothing she does means anything. Tell him, Jules."

The machine blinks below us. Jules looks at me pityingly. The little mesquite leaves are whirling in the doorway like insects hungry for light. Suddenly there is that sincerity I thought I'd never see again; there is a glimpse of that foothill searching. "Don't do this," she says softly. A tiny golden leaf flutters and lands on her cheek.

"Do what you want," I say. "You don't mean anything to me." I walk outside, wishing it were true.

It seems impossible that it's still daylight but here is the sun, reaching behind my eyes, stinging the place where cords meet brain, where meaning is made out of light and the absence of light. I need to sober up.

Last year, the day after Halloween, we came to Virginia City. Danny wanted to go to church. "It's Sunday," was all he said. Jules and I teased him about this, because Sunday didn't mean a damn thing to us. But we went, telling ourselves we were going for the same reason we did anything back then, for the fuck of it. We walked along the gravel road to Saint Mary's, bumping into each other, trying to kick the same rock out in front of us, pretending nothing had happened, that nothing would ever happen.

Inside, the church was eerie quiet and smelled like melted wax. Danny put a dollar in the box and crossed himself. He showed us where to kneel and how to touch the soft tip of our longest fingers to our heads and hearts and shoulders. The sun came through the stained glass and it was warm and so beautiful. In the light Mary was weeping in yellows and blues and Jesus was weeping in reds and one guy was holding a big key and another half a loaf of bread and another a lamb. I didn't know what that meant and still don't. I wish I were Catholic. I remember kneeling, thinking, *More of this.* That's all. That's what I prayed for then: divine preservation of something I would never understand, the safeguarding of something I'd already lost.

I have to drive us home. I'm sick of Reno, sick of going to the same bars and seeing the same bands. I'm sick of eating the same two-dollar slices of pizza and buying the same sworn-off cigarettes from the same glass-faced machines. Sober up.

I can't get us back, I know, but I wanted to have lost something that meant. Danny and Jules come outside as if summoned, blinking and bewildered. Jules says, "Iris." It's like I've never heard her say my name before. How tender it sounds coming from her. How pitiful.

I say, "I need to walk." We stagger through Virginia City, against the wind. The commotion in town has subsided. It's cold.

There's a fence around the cemetery. We climb it. Danny trips and stumbles in the dirt. He takes Jules's hand and helps her over. The graves here are old; lots of them are babies' graves. I'm sorry for everything, even the things that had nothing to do with me. Especially those. We weave up the hill through the headstones, calling out deaths to each other like we're trying to find our way in a storm.

"Consumption."

"Scarlet fever."

"Flu."

"Pneumonia."

"Consumption."

"Whooping cough."

"Childbed."

"Consumption."

"Cholera."

"Drowned."

"Consumption."

There are plenty of good reasons to find yourself in Virginia City, if you need one. It used to be people came for the silver, but the silver's long gone. In summer we come for the swap meet, for the camel races, for the cheap DVDs and the overweight belly dancers and the figures etched in crystals by lasers. For the gray-haired Indian who wears a feather headdress and who for a dollar will let you take a picture with the old fucked-up-looking panther he keeps chained to the back of his truck. There are plenty of good reasons to find yourself in Virginia City, but there's only one reason. We came to time-travel.

From the top of the hill we can see the whole town and the valley and the debris hills beyond. I love that. Danny sits on a thick square headstone, his legs swinging softly in the dusk.

Jules sits beside him. She puts her head on his shoulder like he's always been there. Like the three of us have always been right here. I feel the last three beers resting like silver nuggets in the bottom of my purse. Below us glow the blue-orange flames in the lamps along Main Street. We drink and watch the sun dissolve into the Sierras, and for a small sparkling moment, we are who we once were.

GRACELAND

for Delilah

All the great land mammals are dying. There were once birds the size of sheep. Pinnipeds used to be huge; walruses had tusks six feet long. Jackrabbits had feet like two-by-fours. Armadillos were as big as minivans. Now, they are all dying off. African elephants are going thirsty, having to dig wells in the dirt with their trunks to find water. Bengal tigers are shot and skinned. Polar bears are drowning. Imagine! The world's largest carnivorous land mammal drowning, an entire species drowned to extinction. You know what'll be the largest land carnivore after we've shot all the tigers and drowned all the polar bears? The grizzly bear. Which is to say, some mornings I wake up before the alarm goes off and just lie there and think how I'm not sure I want to live in a world where the largest carnivorous land mammal is the goddamn grizzly bear. Peter tells me I have a sweet misunderstanding of the theory of natural selection. But then, he has also said that he finds my cartoon science very sexy.

My sister, Gwen, says it's not so bad, living in a world where the largest land mammal is the grizzly bear. Largest *carnivorous* land mammal, I say. Okay, she says. Our mother killed herself six months ago, and Gwen thinks I should start letting myself be comforted by the natural world. She says when I feel anxious I should ride my bicycle down to Ocean Beach and stand on the ruins of the Sutro Baths and look out at the water and imagine the dark silhouettes of blue and gray whales moving like submarines through the sea. She says I should be more like Peter, on his little research vessel out on the bay, dipping his measurement tools into the water, listening. She says if I let myself, I'll be comforted by my smallness. But then, she has always been braver than I.

I don't tell Gwen that I have tried this. When I got back from Las Vegas, from scattering our mom's ashes on the red sandstone foothills of Mount Charleston, Peter took me to the San Francisco Zoo. I saw the western lowland gorillas and the giant anteater. I cried and cried on a bench outside the Asian white rhino exhibit after seeing the marks in the enclosure where the rhino had worn his horn down to a stump, scraping it against concrete sculpted to look like mud. It was foggy at the zoo, and Peter sat silent beside me while I cried, his large hand on the small of my back, light as the fog mist on my skin. People walking by probably thought he'd broken my heart, when it is likely the other way around. We sat like that for a long time before he said, What's wrong?

Just the same old thing, I said.

And he said finally, Ecosystems are complex things, Catie.

I have tried taking comfort in my smallness. I went whale watching off the coast of Oregon three times that month and never saw more than the drops of saltwater spray on my slicker from what they later told me was an adolescent hump-back breaching about seventy-five yards off the opposite side of the boat. I don't tell my sister any of this. I don't tell her that I can't go to the Sutro Baths anymore because I can't stop think-ing of the drowned boy and his drowned stepfather, whom I read about in the paper. The boy was walking along the rocks and slipped in. He kept his head above water, calling to his parents. His stepfather went in after him and both were dragged out to sea. They never found their bodies. The article didn't mention it but there must have been a wife, a mother standing on the shore, watching her whole life slip toward the horizon. I don't tell my sister that I can't look out at the sea without imagining it filled with the waterlogged corpses of boys and polar bears.

I have seen old photos of the Sutro Baths from before it burned in 1966. It looks like it was a wonderful place, a giant glass-and-iron dome housing seven indoor swimming pools— six saltwater and one fresh—right at the edge of the sea. I even have a replica postcard on my refrigerator with a wide-hipped girl in a swim cap wading in the water and waving to the camera. It reads, *I met her at the Sutro Baths. I said, "You swim like a duck." She said, "O! You're making a game of me!"*

The photographs show great tall slides shooting swimmers out into the water, young men standing on one another's shoulders, diving from the tiers above, piling as many people on the giant slides as can fit. But the beach has changed since those photos; the sea level seems higher, the beach narrower. If you go to the ruins now and envision, as I have, the great dome of glass and iron rising from the cement foundations of the seven pools, all that's left, you can easily imagine the entire structure slipping into the sea.

I fear someday soon people will be the largest animals on the planet. Imagine living without the African elephant or the humpback to remind us of our scale, our relative size. What a place this would be without anything of such great weight and girth. When I explain this to him, Peter touches my hair lightly and says, You know what, little one? As a species we are getting larger. But we still seem so small.

My sister, for instance, is very small, like me. When new people stand close to me for the first time they often say, Oh, Catie, I didn't realize you were so *small*. Sometimes they rest their elbows on my shoulder, or my head. I find this extremely obnoxious. But Gwen is smaller still; the crown of her head could nestle in my armpit. I admit that I sometimes rest my elbow on her shoulder, especially when we have not seen each other for a long time. One of the things I liked immediately about Peter was that he never leaned on me as though I were a walking stick.

Last November, my sister married a very tall, very wonderful man named Jacob, who I suspect never treats her like a walking stick. They have a big apartment in the Sunset District with a garage and a little rooftop garden. These things are not easy to come by. For example, I have a crumbling studio above a taqueria in the Mission. There are brown water stains dotting the ceiling, and both of my windows open to the view of my neighbor's windows, so close I can lean out and press my fingertips to the sills.

When I first moved in, about two years ago, when Peter and I had just started dating, we painted my apartment together. Now, that memory baffles me. Or rather what baffles me is who we were then, the way we stood in the aisle at the hardware store, side by side, our fingers moving delicately over color samples. As though the perfect shade of pumpkin-colored paint would make the hot water run longer, the thick smell of carne and cilantro lighter, the neighborhood better. As though it would do anything for anyone.

Jacob, my brother-in-law, is six-four. He has long ropy limbs and can pick Gwen up like the elephants in *Dumbo* pick up poles with their trunks when they are assembling the circus tent. Do you remember that scene from *Dumbo*? Well, Jacob can hug Gwen like that and he often does. My heart is warmed by tall, ropy Jacob. I beamed at their wedding. Jacob and Gwen are having their first baby soon, and I hope Jacob's tall genes do not go to waste. I hope they average each other out, at the very least.

On our second whale-watching trip Peter and I sat on a narrow wooden bench inside the boat, wet and cold. Peter worked half-heartedly at a crossword puzzle. I asked him to do a Punnett square to see if Jacob and Gwen will average each other out at the very least.

He said, Catie, Punnett squares are not tarot cards. It is when he says things like this that I am reminded that Peter once knew me better than anyone in the world, very briefly, and that one day he could again.

Though they haven't been told the sex of the baby, I have a feeling that Gwen will have a daughter and that she will be beautiful. She will be tall and thin and lithe like Jacob, with Gwen's great big brown eyes. They will average each other out and I will be grateful.

In the third grade I won a spelling bee with the word *grateful*. When she was alive, my mom often told the story of how she felt when I won. She told it as this funny anecdote about how she and the other parents would let out a little cheer each time their child passed a round, and how each round there were fewer and fewer cheers, and how gradually, as I advanced, she became alienated from every other parent in the gymnasium. I cannot remember her even being there.

When I returned from Vegas, the bar where I work gave me time off, paid. Though I wanted to work, needed the tips, I took the time. Peter said we could do whatever I wanted, but the only thing I could think of was to go to the zoo, which we did. After that I wasted my days. Slept in. Watched *Law & Order* marathons and *Dumbo*. Napped. Waited for Peter to get off work. When he came home we ordered vegan Chinese, and on one of these nights I asked Peter to take me out on the bay in his research vessel, though I knew this was not allowed.

I said, I need to see the dark silhouettes of blue and gray whales moving like submarines through the sea.

He said only, Oh, little one, which is what he always says these days.

Instead, Peter took some personal days and we left that weekend for the Oregon coast, our first whale-watching trip. It was the second trip to Oregon on which I felt the saltwater spray of the adolescent humpback and on which Peter refused to make me a Punnett square. For the third trip I borrowed Peter's car and went alone, though he said, I can get the time off, and meant it. I have not made things easy for him.

I saw no whales in the Oregon sea. I missed my sister. I hadn't seen Gwen since we got back from Vegas, two months before, and I was sick over it. And yet as I drove toward the city I didn't want to go home, didn't want to see her. I took my time unpacking, folding clean clothes neatly. I didn't call Peter to say I was back, that I was okay. I slowly rode my bike out to Gwen's apartment.

I buzzed and buzzed. There was no answer. From the street I saw that the apartment was lit, though the shades were drawn. I could see Gwen's silhouette moving from the living room to the kitchen and back, so I used my key and let myself in. Inside the apartment, I came down the hallway and found Gwen wiping the kitchen counter with a sponge. *Graceland* blared from an old CD player on the counter.

Oh, she said, startled. She turned the music down. I must not have heard you buzz.

This was her way of saying, I hope you aren't abusing your key.

After a bit she nodded to the CD player. Mom used to play this, she said.

I remember, I said. All the time.

Gwen isn't a music lover. She probably hasn't listened to anything besides NPR since her senior year of high school. Once, we rented a car and drove to Santa Cruz and I made her listen to Common and she complained the whole way there. And here she was with Paul Simon. I thought, if you were a musical hermit and your older sister had been recommending you new bands and burning you CDs since you were in the sixth grade, why would you suddenly, after all these years, run out and pick up Paul Simon? Which is to say, of all things to listen to she picks that?

But I didn't say anything and she went on wiping the counter, standing on her tiptoes to reach the center of the wide island. I picked up a tangerine from the fruit bowl and started peeling it with my thumbnail. I watched how she turned her body to avoid pressing her large belly against the edge of the counter.

I often think about my unborn future beautiful niece. I have plans to buy her nongendered, nonbranded toys: books where the girl characters are smart and adventurous and independent, chemistry sets, plastic models of all the great land mammals, extinct and not. I will read her Rudyard Kipling and show her *Dumbo*. I hope being a beauty will not be as lonely as they say it is. I am not sure our family can handle much more loneliness.

Finally I asked Gwen, Can we turn this down?

I moved away from Vegas when I was eighteen, so I've been flying there for nearly ten years. In these years I have formulated a theory that all flights into Las Vegas are purposely orchestrated to be as festively stupid as they are to make the idea of traveling to the city for any other reason than to gamble seem hopelessly, painfully bleak. Gwen's and my flight was no exception. As the plane ascended, the flight attendants flung packets of peanuts down the aisle, gravity pulling them toward the tail, and a voice over the intercom urged us to grab them as they slid past.

It said: Ladies and gentlemen, you'll find your return flight to San Francisco to be a bit more crowded. The voice said this though the flight was full.

It said: Weight restrictions on this Boeing 757 allow more passengers on return flights from Las Vegas, as their pocketbooks are significantly lighter. And the passengers chuckled and munched their peanuts and they were happy happy happy. And I'll tell you I envied them. Because this was the voice's way of saying, We're going to drop you off in this city and it will take you by your ankles, turn you upside down and shake everything from you. And this was something my sister and I had to learn for ourselves.

As we taxied at McCarran International, the voice came over the PA again. Pick up as many peanut wrappers from the floor and seats around you as you can, it said. They will bring you luck!

The woman in the aisle seat next to us leaned forward against her seat belt, reaching eagerly for a wrapper. Without taking her eyes from the woman, Gwen said, Do you ever dream about Mom?

No, I said. Not really. Not any more than I dream about anyone else.

The last time I rode from the Mission up the hill to Sunset— to Gwen's—I rode with bags strapped to my back. Because her place has a washer and dryer and mine doesn't, I often abuse my key privileges to do laundry while she and Jacob are at work. That day, I put my things in the washer and went upstairs to wait for the cycle to finish.

The apartment was different, filled with new things. New posters on the walls, framed. New books on the shelves, new CDs near the computer, new magazines on the coffee table. Georgia O'Keeffe. Tony Hillerman. *Our Bodies, Ourselves*. James Taylor. *The Utne Reader*. The Indigo Girls. *Annuals, Perennials and Bulbs*. Albert Einstein's *Ideas and Opinions*. *Baez Sings Dylan*. *Cadillac Desert*. The "Heart of Gold" single.

All our mother's things. But not hers exactly, new things, uncracked book spines, unfolded pages, CDs instead of tapes. No water damage, no dust, no coffee rings, no scribblings in the margins. Things from the house where we grew up, but not from the house where we grew up. Things from Barnes & Noble and the Best Buy on Geary. It was disorienting, gave me the feeling you get when you wake up from a nap and the sky isn't black or blue but hazy gray, and you can't tell whether it's five a.m. or five p.m., can't tell how long you've been asleep. I got dizzy. I went to the bathroom, thought I might throw up but didn't. I knelt at the toilet for I don't know how long, staring at a copy of *Reader's Digest* on the tank.

I rode home hard and fast, without my things but still weighed down. At my apartment the warm scent of taco meat and raw onion was heavy in the air. I wanted to call Peter, or rather I wanted to want to call him, to tell him what happened and what it meant, to let him back into me and never shut him out again. But instead I turned on *Dumbo*, letting the light from the TV wash over me.

I cannot watch *Dumbo* without crying. It's that scene with the mother, or more specifically, the way the tears literally roll down baby Dumbo's cheeks when they lock her up, and the way she stretches her trunk out through the iron bars and cradles Dumbo, rocks him to sleep. If I could have called Peter, this is what I would have said: If you were the Stork and you were delivering little baby Dumbo and you had to maneuver his bundle between iron bars to lower him down to his mother, wouldn't you think twice about delivering him in the first place? Which is to say, how could the Stork bring a large-eared, sensitive and easily frightened baby elephant into this world?

When Peter came over that night, I was nearly asleep on the couch, the blue glow from the TV the only light on in the room. He sat on the edge of the couch and stroked my hair.

Have you eaten today? he said.

Tell me again, I said. About Sutro.

He sighed. Okay, little one. The currents in the bay have not significantly changed in the forty-one years since the baths burned. The beach is as sound to hold that structure as it was in 1966.

But, I said, keeping my eyes closed, you do concede that one can easily *imagine* it slipping into the sea.

Well, one can easily *imagine* anything, he said, as if that were a good thing.

Not that we'd rebuild them anyway, I said. They'd just be swallowed by the rising sea level.

Oh, yes! said Peter, kissing my head. The oceans will rise and we'll all swim to work! I'll pick you up for lunch and say, You swim like a duck.

He said this in an old-timey voice that very nearly made me smile.

O, I said. You're making a game of me.

After Peter and I have sex there is some smallness in me that wants to turn to him and ask, In your professional estimation as a scientist, how long can a relationship be sustained on pity and anthropomorphism and a postcard on the fridge?

But there is such bigness in him that he would say, As long as it takes.

Were they rebuilt, the Sutro Baths would not actually slip into the sea; I know this. Peter is doing research for PG&E about wave farms, which are basically underwater wind farms where the ocean's currents generate electricity by turning a turbine, the same way wind does, only more consistently. This is not a joke. PG&E already has twenty-one underwater windmills along the floor of the San Francisco Bay for the project's pilot. Peter is the biologist they've hired to track the project's effects on local marine life. Talk about being part of the problem. If you ask me, he is the biologist they pay to say the project has no effect on local marine life. To that he says, Can't you let even one thing be simple and good?

I'd like to tell Gwen or Jacob or Peter even that our mother's things look absurd here, in this foggy damp peninsula, so far from the desert. They're out of context. The type on the magazines looks too dark, the album art too small, everything untouched by the sun. These things can't survive here. The moisture from the sea will mold the prints, rot every page of those books.

I haven't been to see Gwen in eight weeks. I left my wet clothes stuck to the walls of her washing machine. She has not called me in nearly as long and I have not called her. The last time we spoke she said, I've started reading *Cadillac Desert*.

And I said, What is *wrong* with you? When what I meant to say was, Are you okay?

Jacob will do something. He will put an end to this. He

will come home and find his apartment filled to capacity with replicas from our mother's life and he will take Gwen by the hand and say, You have got to stop this. She will cry. But he will wrap his trunklike arms around her and hold her until she stops.

These days more and more I think I should not expose my beautiful unborn niece to *Dumbo*. Suppose she is struck by the cruelty of those lady elephants, the ones that taunt Jumbo Junior. Suppose she wants to know whether there really are adults so mean and selfish as those lady elephants. Suppose she asks, Well, Auntie, are there?

Then I would have to say, Yes and no. There are adults in this world capable of a viciousness you would not believe. There are adults in this world who will never think of anyone except themselves. Your grandmother, for example. Yes, in this world there are adults with cold, hard hearts, little niece, but there are no more elephants.

Jacob will do nothing. He's visited our mother's house only twice. He doesn't know about *Baez Sings Dylan*. He doesn't know what it means for Gwen to hang O'Keeffe's *Black Iris* right beside *Oriental Poppies* above the sofa. He doesn't know what it means that she listens to *Graceland* while she works.

This is what it means:

It is late spring in Las Vegas. Or it is midwinter or early autumn or the peak of summer's heaviest heat. Gwen and I walk home from the bus stop or our friend's parents drop us off, or our boyfriends do, driving recklessly, or we pull our own cars into the driveway. We are four or fourteen or twenty-four. We can hear music coming over the fence from the backyard. *Graceland*.

Our mother stoops in the garden, prodding at the dirt, pulling weeds. She darts from hose to shovel to fertilizer, never doing much with any of them. We know some things, and no matter how old we are it feels like we've known them our entire lives: She will be out in the garden until after the sun goes down and we've made ourselves dinner and stayed up to watch *Unsolved Mysteries* and put ourselves to bed. She will flip the tape over every time it clicks.

When she finally goes to bed she will stay there for a long, long time, whether the next day is stinging hot or beautiful or a workday or a birthday. If we ask, and Gwen does more than I, Mom will say it is Joan Baez that's made her cry, how she tries so hard to understand Dylan, or the cities in *Cadillac Desert* sapping all the moisture from the ground, or small, sweet Paul Simon convinced he's found redemption. She has these reasons, and though we know them to be inadequate, we believe her. *I've reason to believe we all will be received in Graceland.* The truth is our mother stays in bed for reasons we won't begin to understand until we are older, until a hole is opened in us that can't be filled. Which is to say, until now.

I am the only one who knows what it means, this compiling. I am the only one in Gwen's life who can see what she's doing. We have no one else—our father is long dead; he died when Gwen was a baby, like Jumbo Senior. We are alone and I cannot believe how long it's taken me to realize this. I am the only one who can say, This has got to stop. You have to quit this and go back to normal and have a baby, a daughter, a beautiful daughter who won't have to worry about her mother, who will be loved and never alone.

I do dream about our mother. Always in these dreams her death is a big misunderstanding. In these dreams she has won a stay at the Sands and simply forgot to call; she has been laughing and whirling around the roulette tables, and she comes back to her house on Stanford Lane wearing a plastic visor and a new bright white T-shirt. *I Got Lucky at the Sands!* And she's brought us prime rib from the buffet, wrapped in tinfoil, and her plants are wilted and their soil is bone dry but none of them are dead.

Always in these dreams we have a great laugh about this misunderstanding and I am never mad that my mother didn't call, just grateful that she is alive and that the confusion is cleared up. And then, when I wake, all that grace is gone.

But—and this is what I would have told Gwen when she asked me on that airplane, were I not a coward—in these dreams our mother looks and smells and sounds and feels just like she did, in a way I can't re-create when I am awake. Which is to say, in my dreams she is alive in a way I cannot remember her ever being. And these dreams are a blessing, or as close to a blessing as it gets anymore. And for that at least, I am grateful. G-R-A-T-E-F-U-L. Grateful.

Gwen wasn't a cowardly kid, just very small. She used to say everything twice, once aloud and then a second time, whispered it quietly to herself. She did this with everything she ever said. Said she was recording it in her mental journal. Even then you could tell that though she was born later, she was much older than me.

This morning, I woke before my alarm went off and I lay there thinking about the grizzly, how before the city there used to be grizzlies on this peninsula. How Peter told me that on our first date. About what other magic he could give me if I let him. I took a long ride around the city, trying to imagine grizzly bears loafing through eucalyptus groves. I rode to the Sutro Baths.

They've put signs up at the baths. They say, SWIM AT YOUR OWN RISK or CAUTION: STRONG CURRENTS or some other euphemism for LOOK OUT! A BOY AND HIS STEPFATHER WERE DRAGGED OUT TO SEA HERE AND THEIR BODIES WERE NEVER FOUND (WE SUSPECT SHARKS) AND IT COULD HAPPEN TO YOU; IT COULD HAPPEN TO ANY OF US. The signs have a picture, an illustration of a stick swimmer being swept out by a squiggly current, his stick arm in the air. I think they should put these signs up everywhere, not just at the beaches but throughout the entire city, call this what it is.

I rode hard from the Mission through Castro up to Golden Gate, then back down Lincoln to Baker Beach, through the Presidio to the wharf and back. Pumping up hills, hurtling down them. I wanted to get away from here, and for a moment I thought I felt my feet pushing me far from here to Canada, following the humpback's route. Putting distance between me and her. But that's all wrong. This city is a peninsula, seven miles by seven miles, and I just ricocheted from one edge to the other. I was never more than seven miles from anything.

I rode to Gwen's. She wasn't in the apartment. But then, I hadn't expected her to be. I kept climbing the stairs past her floor, and here I am. I step out onto the roof. Great deep planters line the roof deck full of ice plant and bird-of-paradise. I don't want her to be up here, but she is. She sits on a deck chair with her short legs stretched out in front of her, big tortoiseshell sunglasses over her eyes, her hands on her stomach.

And there's a thousand things I want to tell her—about the Sutro boy and the whales I never saw, about Peter's turbines turning and turning down in the bay without ever rousing anything, about all the great land mammals—and I want to say them all so bad I could say them twice, once to her and once to me, two thousand ways total to say, I know you're slipping out to sea; please don't go. Don't leave me on land by myself.

Instead I say, Have you watched *Dumbo* lately?

Gwen looks up to me, lifts her sunglasses from her eyes. And right away I can tell she's been crying. No, she says.

I was thinking, I say. If we call Dumbo Dumbo, aren't we, you know . . .

A part of the problem? she says.

And maybe it's that her stomach has gotten so big in the months since I last saw her, or that I can see the ocean from up here, but she just looks so *small*. She looks like she did when we were kids. She looks like a child.

Yeah, I say. We ought to call him Jumbo. Jumbo Junior.

Okay, she says, Jumbo Junior. And then, so brave for someone so small, she says, Catie, are you okay?

I watch the sun dipping down into the water. From here I can make out the dark shapes of whales like submarines down in the sea, hear their songs. They sing James Taylor; they sing Paul Simon. I see the drowned boy on his stepfather's shoulders in 1951, wading in the freshwater pool at the Sutro Baths, his wide-hipped mother waving from the tiers above. I see tall Jacob spinning the roulette table at the Sands. I see Peter out on the savanna with the African white rhino, rubbing ointment on its stump, encouraging the horn to grow back. O! You swim like a duck, he says. I see Jumbo Junior and my beautiful long-legged unborn niece swayed to sleep by his mother's great gray trunk.

Acknowledgments

Thank you:

Christopher Coake, my mentor, pep talker, and friend. This book exists in large part because you took me aside and said it could.

Nicole Aragi, for your vision and your vigor.

John Freeman, my fairy godfather, for picking up what I was putting down.

The MFA program at Ohio State University and my extraordinary teachers there: Michelle "Do Better" Herman, Erin "The Good Is the Enemy of the Great" McGraw and Lee K. "Let Us Not Get in the Habit of Excusing Poorly Executed Art" Abbott. Thanks also to Henri Cole, Kathy Fagan, Andrew Hudgins and Lee Martin for your wisdom and support, and to Kelli Fickle, for looking after everyone.

ACKNOWLEDGMENTS

My top-notch professors at the University of Nevada, Reno, especially Michael Branch, David Fenimore, Justin Gifford, Gailmarie Pahmier, Hugh Shapiro and Elizabeth Swingrover.

Percival Everett, Sue Miller, Padgett Powell and Christine Schutt for advice and encouragement.

My editors, Rebecca Saletan and Ellah Allfrey, for believing in this book, and for making it better. Jynne Martin for all the sage and all the good vibes that came along with it. Elaine Trevorrow and Yuka Igarashi, wondrous helpers. Christie Hauser, the Sir David Attenborough of publishing.

The magazine editors who first put these stories out into the world: Aaron Burch and Elizabeth Ellen, John Irwin, Kathryn Harrison and Robert Arnold, Patrick Ryan, James Thomas and D. Seth Horton, Scott Dickensheets, Hannah Tinti and Maribeth Batcha, Lorin Stein and David Wallace-Wells, Caleb Cage, Jill Patterson and Jonathan Bohr Heinen, Conor Broughan and Jessica Jacobs, Susan Burmeister-Brown and Linda Swanson-Davies.

The Ohio State University Presidential Fellowship and the Sewanee Writers' Conference, for financial support. My exceptional colleagues at the Sewanee Young Writers' Conference and Bucknell University. *The Journal.* My students. Peter Harrison, ever-hospitable dreamer. Kirsten Chen and Lumans. Every single person at Riverhead.

Reno, especially Nicole and Justice Mañha, Seth Lagana, Mallory Moore, Andrei, Jonathan Purtill, Jeff Griffin, Curtis

Bradley Vickers and Jessica Seidl, Ben Rogers, Sundance Books, the Boyntons, the Laxalts and the Urzas.

Pahrump, especially Jesse Ray and the Tungs: Ryan, Jason, TJ and Jan.

Columbus, especially the Go Big Tuesdays: Alex Streiff, Bill Riley, Clayton Adam Clark and the Hammer. Special thanks to my friend G. Robert Urza, Nevada royalty, for taking it out and chopping it up, and for always talking me down. Isaac Anderson, Kim Brauer, Michael Brennan, Catie Crabtree, Brad Freeman (who supplied the best line in this book), Ben and Lily Glass, Holly Goddard-Jones, Donald Ray Pollock, Samara Rafert and Pablo Tanguay. And the best damn band in the land: Cami Freeman, Gina Ventre, David Macey, Dr. Jess Love, Andrew Brogdon, Maria Caruso, K. C. Wolfe, Christina LaRose, Elizabeth Ansfield, Jenny McKeel, Ken Nichols and the Albers: Mike, Julie, Natalie and Willy.

Beth and Annie, my dearest friends. Tri-tri's forever.

My family, who never made art less than essential: Aaron, Aunt Mo and Uncle Jack. Ron Daniels and the whole Daniels clan. For all their insanity and all their love, the Watkinses: Al and Vaye, Uncle John, Auntie Jane, Aunt Lynn and Uncle Chris, Ben, Shannon, Lea, Luke, Eli, Jos, Paulie, Zanna, Char, Kai and Una.

Mary Lou Orlando-Frehler, toughest lady in the West, for the thrift stores, Zion, the doilies crocheted with obscenities, Caesar's Palace, the cowboy boots, the turquoise and sterling silver, long johns, ponchos, Willie Nelson, Wet 'n' Wild, the hats and hats and hats for winter. For everything.

ACKNOWLEDGMENTS

Nic Baker and the tender, spazzy, virtuoso bean, Delilah Claire.

Derek Palacio. Thank you for having me. Thank you for being.

My sisters, Lise and Gaylynn, whose love goes everywhere with me. This book is you.

Claire Vaye Watkins is the author of *Battleborn*, winner of the Story Prize, the Rosenthal Family Foundation Award from the American Academy of Arts and Letters, and a Silver Pen Award from the Nevada Writers Hall of Fame. *Battleborn* was named a Best Book of 2012 by the *San Francisco Chronicle*, *Boston Globe*, *Time Out New York*, and *Flavorwire*, and a Best Short Story Collection by NPR.org. In 2012, the National Book Foundation named Claire one of the 5 Best Writers Under 35. Her stories and essays have appeared in *Granta*, *One Story*, *The Paris Review*, *Ploughshares*, *Glimmer Train*, *Best of the West 2011*, *Best of the Southwest 2013*, and elsewhere. A graduate of the University of Nevada Reno and the Ohio State University, Claire has received fellowships from the Writers' Conferences at Sewanee and Bread Loaf. An assistant professor at Bucknell University, Claire is also the codirector, with Derek Palacio, of the Mojave School, a free creative writing workshop for teenagers in rural Nevada.